By SARIA BRYANT

ELEMENTAL THRONES
Shadow's Wound
Wild's Scar

TOUCH OF LEATHER
If You Let Me

UNDERWORLD MAGES
Mage's Marines

Published by DREAMSPINNER PRESS
www.dreamspinnerpress.com

WILD'S SCAR

SARIA BRYANT

Published by
DREAMSPINNER PRESS

8219 Woodville Hwy #1245
Woodville, FL 32362 USA
www.dreamspinnerpress.com

Wild's Scar
© 2025 Saria Bryant

Cover Art
© 2025 Andrei Bat
https://99designs.com/profiles/bandrei
Cover content is for illustrative purposes only and any person depicted on the cover is a model.

Trade Paperback ISBN: 9781641088435
Digital ISBN: 9781641088428
Trade Paperback published October 2025
v. 1.0

To Tana, my cat of nearly twenty-one years, who was lost in the middle
of writing this—the silence is too loud without you.

CHAPTER 1

Fucking Fate bonds.

He was too old to deal with one appearing on him.

Vesryn was over six hundred years old, and he'd served the royal family for more than five of those centuries. He'd taken countless lovers through the years and had even bedded Prince Callith—now King Callith—on numerous occasions, but he'd never found someone he wanted to share the rest of his life with.

Vesryn was content with his role in the kingdom, and he was thankful his only duty was to protect Synne. If he had the weight of the kingdom on his shoulders, they'd likely all be dead from a civil war.

He couldn't help flexing his fingers, staring at the shimmering red thread that stretched up to a higher floor. He couldn't feel it, but his finger insisted there was a hint of a tingling sensation, as if it were on the verge of falling asleep.

"Vesryn?"

He glanced at Synne, returning her raised eyebrow with one of his own. "Yes, Princess?" He restrained a smile when she wrinkled her nose at him.

"Are you ill?"

He couldn't quite fight back his scowl. "No," he said, but her brow twitched higher in a familiar expression of disbelief.

"You should get some rest."

Vesryn started to say he was fine, but the threat of a pang beneath his ribs stayed his tongue. He was well accustomed to the discomfort that came with lying, but it was still never pleasant. The worse the lie, the deeper and sharper the ache. Truth be told, he did need rest. He hadn't been sleeping well, kept awake at night by the thread on his finger. Since Synne could be far more stubborn than her older brother when she chose, he swept a low bow and stepped back.

"As you wish." He turned and motioned for two other guards to move in and take his place. Then he headed out of the throne room and stopped by Duaia's office, surprised to find her at her desk for once.

He rapped his knuckles against the door to get her attention before stepping inside. "Can you assign someone to Synne for a few days?"

Duaia eyed him in surprise, sitting back and tucking stray wisps of bright red hair behind her ear. "Shouldn't be a problem. Elwin has been asking for something other than prison duty."

Elwin was a good choice. He was levelheaded and had the quick reflexes innate to all feline beastkin, and he was part of Callith's kingsguard. With the king currently out of the city, the kingsguard were spread out to help with the patrols and city guard.

Vesryn nodded his thanks and stepped back, escaping before she could try to pry and stubbornly ignoring the twinge of guilt. He might be centuries older than Duaia, but as the only sorceress on this side of the Wound, he knew better than to catch her attention. She could be as ruthless as Synne when it came to protecting her own, even if it meant berating someone until they wept.

With the sudden lack of immediate responsibility, exhaustion pressed in on him. He intended to go to his room, shower, and try to sleep. Instead, he found himself following the Fate string and stopped outside the closed door of the fae's room.

This was a terrible idea. What could Fate possibly want with Vesryn, an elf with a fractured magical core? He had no talent for the sun magic most elves were gifted with. The only magic he had ever been able to control was fire, but he couldn't even start a fire with condensed sunlight. No, the fire had to already exist; then he could call on the flames and manipulate them. And only natural flames answered to him. He'd been of no help at all when the Black Sun set fires to their granary and the library and the temple, the alchemical-borne flames tearing through everything far quicker than a natural fire.

He may have been one of the most skilled with a blade, but he paled against the warriors who'd been lost in the war. Surely there were others who could offer more.

He lowered his hand and turned away.

If he was to speak to the fae for the first time, he'd need honey.

Chapter 2

Flesh was a prison.

The sense of time he'd lost during the three centuries when his essence was trapped in the ley lines returned to suffocate him now.

Every moment was filled with the swirl of air in his lungs, the pulse of blood in his veins, the rough clothes chafing his skin, the sharp bite of itches in his wings. Even the blissful taste of honey bordered on too sweet, the thick substance lingering on the back of his tongue long after he'd eaten it.

The only relief was the slow, steady pulse of the ylren tree around him. It was old, far older than him, the deep, lingering pool of fae magic in its roots a balm against his senses. The sweetness of its blossoms was as nostalgic as it was a painful reminder of everything lost because of him. Because of one moment of weakness.

He didn't have the excuse of youthful folly either. He'd known the risks, knew humans were rarely trustworthy, even before they stole the throne. Even when they'd had only the ability to work basic magics, they were disturbingly greedy for more.

Not that fae were better, but at least with fae, it was expected that the glint of silver was a dagger and not a coin or trinket. Fae were masters at twisting words and meanings, but the human ability to lie was as fascinating as it was dangerous, especially when they could lie even to themselves.

As much as he might want to stay here, he didn't belong. Elves may be descended from the first fae to tame this realm, but they weren't his people. He had no people in this realm, and after what he'd wrought here, he may well be executed if he tried to cross into the fae realm.

Except he had to restore the balance first.

Already the ley lines were in flux without him restraining the wild magic. With the last piece of the throne completely destroyed, the thin connection holding the balance of elements in check, the connection that Draekor had manipulated and violated, was broken. Wild magic would overcome the other elements, return them to chaos, and tear this realm apart, reducing it to the land ravaged by violent storms and noxious air it had been before his ancestors tamed it. Before the Second Daughter of the Queen of the Wild Court stepped through the veil and separated the threads of magic into their elements, grounding them in their respective Thrones—Light, Frost, Sea, Nature, Air, and Wild.

Humans called it Shadow when they stole his family's throne, but his people called it Wild. The shadows might have been part of that, but he'd ensured the humans never learned to tap into the creation magics, or the ability to reshape the realm. To call on the earth to form mountains or valleys, or for the skies to flood the land, or the deep, hot pools of liquid rock to burst free of the confines of the earth, or to ask the seasons to change before their time.

Shadows were the weakest essence of wild magic. A cloak or a shroud, or the ability to step across a great distance. Even still, the humans had turned them into a formidable weapon, and they would have discovered their ability to harness all the Wilds if he hadn't stopped them. But even that came with a price, and he saw the consequences of his choice every time he looked past the city walls and into the Wound—the barren, magic-void, lifeless wasteland that had ripped across the center of the continent when Sorren sacrificed him.

If there was to be any hope of healing the land, the Wild Throne had to be restored and placed on the largest ley line of the realm, but he had no idea how to do that. There had only ever been one Wild Throne created, long before his birth, and the humans had tainted it, filled it with shadows, before the Sun King destroyed the last piece of it.

He brushed his fingers against the delicate petals of a ylren blossom before turning and sitting on the window seat. This was his mistake, his responsibility. He was fae, a descendant of Lilithani, Queen of the Wild Court. He was—

He was....

What was his name?

He could remember everything that Draekor had done to him, everything Draekor's ancestors had forced him to do, but everything before he gave his name to a human was a blur, and even his name wouldn't reveal itself.

Truth be told, that was a relief. He couldn't be trusted with it. If he didn't know his own name, he couldn't make the same mistake again, and Fate, whoever the Fate was now, seemed intent he do exactly that.

He glanced at the Fate bond wrapped around his little finger, absently rubbing his thumb against the faint shimmer of magic and wondering if it would vanish if he cut off his finger. If it would linger there, as if attached to a phantom limb, or if it would simply attach to the next finger.

Fate usually didn't meddle in the affairs of fae, but he supposed he deserved this. Maybe it was punishment. If not for being naive enough to give his name to a human and allowing himself to be enslaved by them, then perhaps for staining his hands with the blood of his family. Or maybe because he'd placed that fake Fate bond on Haru and Sorren that ensured the end of Draekor's bloodline.

He knew what Fate wanted. Or thought he knew.

With the backlash of his resurrection, the veil he'd sealed Ages ago had blown wide open. He could feel some of the tears from here, open wounds where the magic of the fae realm was already seeping back into this one. While that meant restoring life to the ylren trees, it also meant the creatures there could once again roam this one. After so long existing with their absence, this realm was not prepared for that.

The light knock at the door drew his attention from the glimmer of red around his finger. He looked up as the door opened, expecting the usual servant with food and a bit of honey. Instead, it was an elf.

A surprisingly attractive elf, and the elf he was Fate bound to.

He stilled, cursing his wings when they shifted, the faint rustle of feathers loud in the silence.

The elf set a tray of food and a jar of honey down with a bow of his head before stepping back. When the elf opened his mouth after a long moment of silence, he expected a plea for a chance to spend time together, to talk or walk or fuck. Instead, the elf said, "I'm sorry—"

"Leave." The word was out of his mouth before he understood what the elf said, but that didn't matter. He had no interest in getting to know anyone, elf or otherwise. Even if he remembered, he certainly never intended to grant his name to another soul of this realm, so the Fate bond between them could never amount to anything more than an unfulfilled promise.

The elf flinched as if struck, but he didn't protest. Merely dipped into a polite bow and backed out of the room.

He waited several long moments to ensure no one else entered before standing from his perch in the window. He surveyed the tray, recognizing most of the fresh fruits as ones originating from the fae realm. The news that some of this city's crops had changed in the days before Draekor's attempted coup wasn't surprising; he'd been losing his grasp on his own essence at that point, and his fae magic had seeped out where it could.

He picked up one of the red fruits with soft skin and bit into it, his teeth easily ripping through the flesh. He'd forgotten what eating was like, but he was sure it had never been so tedious before. After three hundred years stuck as an entity of magic while the raw power of the ley lines slowly burned and ripped his essence to pieces, he'd forgotten most everything of having a corporeal form.

He licked a trickle of sweet juice from his wrist, savoring the subtle flavors as he methodically ate through the food provided, saving the small jar of honey for last. He dipped his finger into the golden substance and licked it clean, then vanished the jar from this plane into his hollow with the others. His personal holding space was empty aside from the jars of honey and some scattered seeds from the fruits he'd eaten.

He wasn't sure how long he would stay here, but he intended to have a sizable collection of honey to sustain him when he left.

For now, he needed a name.

Aster was a whisper in the back of his mind, but that name wasn't his. Aster had died long before he took possession of the human's body, his essence swallowed by the fragment of Draekor that had survived in his descendant's bloodline.

He'd underestimated Draekor's will to survive when he'd orchestrated Sorren's death; he hadn't thought to eliminate distant relatives as well. But there'd be no more coming back now; he'd made sure to destroy the last of Draekor's essence when he took this body for his own.

He moved to the large balcony and hopped onto the railing, gripping it with his talons before crouching and staring out over the city, wings spread to keep his balance.

The stench of iron and silver from the large building across the river left an acrid burn in his nose, though the people here would likely need it for protection soon enough. The bustle of the people below was a distant chorus of voices, merchants shouting and children laughing. The scent of fresh baked bread and cut herbs and roasting meat drifted on the air.

He was intimately familiar with the heartbeat of this city, but it was different seeing it from above.

He tipped his head back, closing his eyes and letting the sun warm his face. He wanted to take to the skies, but he doubted his wings or magic were strong enough yet to carry him. If he tried now, he'd surely plummet to the ground, and while it might not kill him, it would be painful.

He opened his eyes, staring at the clouds and breathing in the hint of rain. The promise of life.

He might be fae, one with the curse of the raven wings, but he doubted he would live an immortal life.

That would be a suitable name.

Fey. Fated to die.

CHAPTER 3

Vesryn stalked to his rooms, muttering soft curses under his breath the entire way. He'd known nothing would come of speaking with the fae. He had no desire to leave his home, and a fae would have no reason to stay. The chance of there being a second crisis to keep them both in the city so soon after the first was too much to hope for.

No, whatever Fate was scheming, it would surely take him far away from here.

Fate bonded to a *fae*.

What few myths and stories they had always painted the fae as solitary or cruel or mysterious creatures. They had powerful magic, allowing them to control others simply by knowing their name. And they were more likely to stab someone than to help. Why would Fate create a bond between anyone and a fae?

He barely refrained from slamming his door shut before tossing his sword onto his sofa. He jerked his tunic off and paced the length of the room, stuffing the tunic into a ball before throwing it into a corner. He was more irritated than he should have been. It should have been a relief to know the fae also had no interest in the bond between them. It *was* a relief. Except that did nothing to remove the Fate string binding them.

Even if they both refused it, Fate wouldn't let them go.

He braced his arms against the wall, hanging his head between them and breathing.

What in darkness was he supposed to do? He never asked for this. He was comfortable with his life here.

He ignored the pang in his chest as he pushed away from the wall and stripped off the rest of his clothes on the way to the shower. Maybe it would have been easier to ignore the bond if the fae had been hideous, but even Rashi's descriptions paled against the brief glimpse Vesryn had gotten. Vibrant violet eyes and short hair the color of a sunset spilling over the Wound. Large black wings long enough to brush the floor. None of their legends mentioned fae having wings, and Vesryn wondered if they were rare or special.

The fae was certainly one of the strangest creatures Vesryn had ever seen, but he could understand Rashi's fascination. At least until the fae spoke.

He may have been used to Synne dismissing him as overbearing, but the fae didn't even know him. It shouldn't irritate him, but it did.

He blew out a harsh breath and finished his shower. It was far too early to sleep, but he collapsed onto his bed anyway and tried to ignore the pit forming in his stomach. He was tempted to seek out Julius, but he hated the thought of bothering the Seer when he usually had far more important things to deal with. Though with Callith out of immediate reach, maybe Julius was finally getting some well-deserved rest.

Rolling over, he smashed his face into his pillow to muffle his groan.

After several long minutes, he gave up trying to suffocate himself to sleep and rolled out of bed. He refused to dwell on something that he had no power to change, at least not without consequences worse than leaving his home. *Except*, came a whisper at the back of his mind, *had this ever* truly *felt like home?*

He ignored that thought and pulled on a pair of trousers, a loose cotton shirt, and his boots. He combed his hair and tied it into a short tail at the back of his neck. Then he snatched his sword on his way out of the room.

When he reached the stables, he grabbed one of the horses. If he couldn't sleep, he would do the next best thing: go to the barracks and earn some coin.

The ride through the city was peaceful enough. No ominous markings of Black Suns smeared with blood, no fires, not even the yowling of cats fighting in an alley. The crash of waves against the shore reached him before he saw the barracks, the familiar sound soothing some of the restlessness crawling through his veins.

He breathed in the stronger tang of sea air as he dismounted, resisting the urge to peel his boots off and wiggle his toes in the sand. He handed the horse off to a page and headed inside instead.

It was still early enough the main floor was almost empty, but he spotted Zaos' familiar dark hair in the corner, his feet stretched out along the bench seat with a book and a bottle of good liquor.

Zaos would make a far better and safer distraction than gambling, so Vesryn made his way over. "What is it this time, a steamy romance?"

he asked, sliding into the opposite seat with a forced grin. Perhaps if he feigned normalcy, he could ignore the anger and helplessness trying to eat him from the inside out.

Zaos pointed an accusing finger at him without looking up. "I know you read the one with the siren and the wolf beastkin."

Vesryn shrugged and didn't try to deny it. Zaos knew him far too well for him to even try. They were the same age and had grown up together, though where Vesryn lacked any true magical capacity, Zaos was one of the few remaining battlemages who had survived the war. His skill and power were rivaled only by Duaia, and Vesryn wouldn't want to bet against either of them in a true fight.

He reached for the bottle, shocked to see it was ylren blossom wine. Considering the last couple of weeks were the first time the trees had blossomed in three Ages, the bottle was priceless. Then again, Zaos was pragmatic in the extreme. Now that the ylren trees were blooming again, there would be more wine on the market soon.

"How much did you sell a taste to the winemakers for?"

"What do you take me for?"

Vesryn raised an eyebrow and didn't waste his breath answering.

Zaos finally looked up from his page with narrowed eyes before smirking. "A bottle from the first two batches."

"Only two?"

"From each winemaker."

Almost a dozen bottles, then. Vesryn shook his head with a soft laugh and picked up Zaos' glass, tilting it in question. When Zaos flicked his fingers, he took a sip, closing his eyes with a soft hum. The subtle floral sweetness tasted like spring lightning storms and sunshine-soaked honey. He couldn't help but think a fae would like it. He took a bigger sip, and when he opened his eyes, he found Zaos watching him with a concerned smile.

"There a reason you're drinking while the sun is still high?"

Vesryn caught a drop of wine on the glass with his lip. Zaos knew him too well to believe a half truth, but he hadn't told anyone of his Fate string. He knew Haru had seen it when he'd confirmed all the threads that had connected Callith's inner circle had vanished, but as far as he knew, the dragon hadn't spoken a word of it either.

He swallowed the last bit of wine in the glass before setting it down. "I have a Fate string."

Zaos' raised eyebrows were the only indication of his surprise. "When did that happen?"

Vesryn slumped in his seat. "The same time the fae appeared."

Zaos dropped his feet to the floor as he sat up with a hissed curse. He pushed his book to the side of the table. The cover was a dark crimson with strange symbols like the Magic Speakers of Ages past preferred to use. Not a steamy romance, then.

When he dragged his gaze back to Zaos, he saw all the fears he refused to acknowledge reflected back at him. Thankfully, Zaos didn't speak any of them aloud. Instead, he stoppered the bottle and slid out of his seat.

"I think we need something stronger."

Vesryn wasn't about to argue that. He slid across the bench until he could stretch his legs out on it, letting his head thunk against the wall as he dragged his tongue across the lingering taste of wine on his lower lip.

As Duaia's second in command, Zaos could have had a room in the palace, but he chose to live here since he usually handled scheduling the rotations of patrols and gate duties, while Duaia focused on keeping the palace secure. It meant dealing with the crowds of younger guards whenever Vesryn sought Zaos out, but it also meant that Zaos tended to have a nice stash of alcohol when he confiscated it to keep people from teetering over the line from drunk to belligerent.

He reached for the book and tugged it closer, tracing his finger over the gold symbols before flipping it open, already knowing what he was likely to find. A few times a century, Zaos got it into his head that he could find a cure for the fissures in Vesryn's core, if he only looked hard enough. Vesryn wasn't the only elf unable to use magic well, but it wasn't common enough to dedicate resources to. Not when those resources were needed to ensure their survival.

Vesryn kept telling him not to worry about it. He was in his sixth century now. He wasn't sure what he'd even do with magic at this point, and he knew better than to admit it aloud, but his core couldn't be fixed with a simple spell. Other elves with weak or damaged cores could still access their sun magic, enough for simple warming or light spells, but Vesryn was the only elf he knew of who couldn't even sense the sun's blessing.

Zaos would go mad without a problem to solve, though, so Vesryn never offered more than token protest when he came back around to researching again.

He flipped through the pages, not even pretending to understand the diagrams, but they held his attention until Zaos returned and set a large bottle on the table. The color and label gave him pause. The bottle was solid black to block any light from damaging its contents, with a design of seaweed wrapped around it.

"Siren brew?" They were notorious for fermenting seaweed into a liquor strong enough to put a dwarf on their ass. Vesryn had tried it once. He didn't remember a single thing from that night.

Zaos shrugged and set a second glass on the table before settling across from him. "Seemed appropriate," he said, pulling the cork out and pouring a generous amount into both glasses. The liquid was a deep, dark green that bubbled. He put the cork back into place, then lifted his glass with a wink. "May the sunrise have mercy on our eyes."

Vesryn snorted softly before echoing the plea.

The first sip was like swallowing seawater. He choked on it, pinching his nose, though it did nothing for the burn making his eyes sting. Then the taste cleared into an almost pleasant earthy flavor. "Fuck," he hissed, turning a blurry glare on Zaos when he laughed. "I prefer the wine."

Zaos snickered. "I don't want to deal with you when you're wine drunk."

He felt his lips twist into a pout. "Why not?"

"You get handsy."

"I do not," he protested, rubbing at the burn in his chest. He wasn't nearly as bad as Aelin when he got drunk. Callith's cousin flirted with anyone and everyone when sober, but once he was drunk, he did his best to get into everyone's pants.

Zaos gave him a knowing look over his glass before taking another sip. Somehow, he didn't even flinch.

Not to be outdone, Vesryn tossed back the rest of his own and closed his throat until the threat of a coughing fit passed. He stared at his glass as Zaos refilled it. "Oh, we're getting *drunk*," he said. At least he'd already told Duaia not to expect him for a few days.

"Seems like the best idea." Zaos cleared his throat and sat back in his seat, cradling his glass and absently rubbing his thumb against his little finger. "Have you talked to your new bonded?"

Vesryn sneered and took a large swallow. "I spoke two words before he told me to leave."

"Did you take honey?"

He turned his sneer on Zaos. "Of course I took honey." He rubbed the tip of his tongue against the tingling left by the bubbles on the roof of his mouth before taking another sip. The liquor wasn't too bad after the first taste.

"What's he look like?"

Vesryn slumped into his seat with an involuntary, wistful sigh, clutching his full glass in both hands as he recalled the fae. Tall and lithe, with warm sable skin. Short summer-sunset hair. Ears a bit longer than an elf's. Violet eyes and large black raven wings, with the taloned feet to match.

He blinked when he found Zaos smirking at him. "What?"

"Tall, dark, and beautiful. Sounds like your type."

Vesryn scowled. "You wish you were beautiful," he muttered, ignoring Zaos' laughter as he stared at the bubbles forming seafoam at the top of his glass. "If you compare me to Alais—"

"Alais, the great hero of the Third Age. Slayer of a manticore. Tamer of a hippogriff. Friend of the pixies. Brought to her knees by the sorceress Hycis, who said she smelled worse than a drunken dwarf fresh from being shat out of a girallon's ass."

Vesryn groaned and drained more liquor. "Please spare me," he begged, though he knew Zaos was only getting started; ancient history was one of his favorite topics. Vesryn was routinely subjected to long tales, most about battlemages or epic battles of Ages past or magic theory on how the Thrones kept their realm viable for life.

Undeterred, Zaos continued with how Hycis refused to acknowledge their Fate bond. She repeatedly told Alais that she'd let fame and glory go to her head and refused to speak with her until she learned to put down her sword.

"And where did that get her?" Vesryn demanded. When Zaos didn't answer, he pointed at the two Zaoses across from him. "They were ambushed. Alais didn't have her sword in reach, and Hycis was taken by surprise and nearly killed."

"Nearly," Zaos said, but Vesryn continued as if he hadn't spoken.

"Hycis called down lightning and fire and destroyed their attackers, but not before Alais lost her hand. If Alais had had her sword, she wouldn't have been injured."

"Maybe," Zaos conceded. "Are you saying you wouldn't give up your sword?"

Vesryn took another sip, hardly tasting anything beyond a hint of seaweed. "Why should I give up my sword? I'm a guard of the heir." Even if he became a guard of the fae, he'd need a sword; it wasn't like he could protect anyone with magic. His fists and feet would work in a pinch, but he preferred to have a blade of some kind.

Zaos propped his cheek on his fist, swirling the liquor in his glass. "Well, then you'll just have to ask him what it would take to speak to you."

Vesryn blinked at Zaos. Then blinked quickly a few more times until the three of him returned to one with blurry edges. "That won't work," he said, reaching for the bottle when Zaos laughed.

"Why won't it?"

"Because he won't *talk to me*." How was he supposed to talk to someone who refused to be in the same room with him for more than a few moments?

He hissed as he spilled bubbling green liquid over his fingers, but at least his glass was full again. "I don't need to talk to him anyway," he muttered.

"Ah, here we go," Zaos said and drained his own glass. "Don't tell me you're going to refuse the bond."

"I didn't ask for it! I don't want it!" Especially not now, when the Fate bonds of everyone else had vanished. If he'd ever needed proof that Fate cared only for the outcome and that they were all disposable in Her eyes, the Fate bonds disappearing after Aster was defeated was proof enough.

Fate and mate bonds were rare enough that he never resented how many had existed within Callith's inner circle. If anyone needed help from higher powers, it was the royal family. Vesryn had sworn his loyalty to the Sun Throne a few years after he came of age and never regretted it.

But he did resent the Fate bond now wrapped around his finger. If he was going to leave this city, it should be his choice. Except he'd grown complacent. With the Wound threatening their borders, there'd been no chance to or point in venturing past the city walls, but that couldn't be used as an excuse now.

"Ves, you know fighting the bond won't change anything."

Vesryn glared balefully at the mess of bottles and battlemages in front of him. "Fate can go fuck Herself."

All four Zaoses chuckled, lifting their glasses in agreement. "She won't, though. You'll be the one fucked."

"Fuck you."

"Tsk. What would your bonded say?"

"Fuck the fae too," Vesryn snarled, draining his glass again before slamming it on the table. He reached for a bottle, but there were too many of them, and all of them passed through his fingers.

"I think you've had enough," Zaos said, plucking Vesryn's glass out of his hand.

"No."

"You never could hold your liquor."

Vesryn growled and slapped at Zaos' hand, trying to get the glass back, but he hit the table instead. "I wanted the wine."

"You can have the wine later."

That sounded like a trap; Zaos was never that nice, not even to Vesryn. "Really?"

"Sure. As soon as you go talk to your fae. You can save it to share once you've consummated your bond."

Vesryn snarled and pushed himself upright, grabbing the underside of the table as the room tilted dangerously. "Hope you get dry itch in your asshole."

"I love you too," Zaos replied dryly. "Won't be long before you're murmuring such sweet nothings to your fae."

Vesryn scoffed and finally managed to get to his feet, only for the liquor to truly sink its teeth in like the sirens who made it. One step later, everything went black.

VESRYN WOKE in a strange bed, his head pounding, his eyes burning, and his mouth feeling like an alley cat dragged a rotting rat carcass into it while he slept.

He rolled over with a groan, his stomach twisting in warning. His hand hit the edge of a bucket, and he promptly snatched it closer, right before his stomach emptied itself.

"Ah, the stench of our youth," Zaos said, far too brightly.

Vesryn groaned and blindly gave him a rude gesture before flopping onto the bed again. He cracked his eyes open when something cold pressed against his cheek. He took the vial of blue liquid and drank it with a grimace. "What happened?" he croaked.

"Before or after you stripped and started dancing naked on the tables?"

Vesryn squinted a glare at Zaos. "That didn't happen."

Zaos grinned. "You'll never know."

"I despise you."

"I don't believe you." Zaos settled on the other side of the bed despite looking like he'd been up for hours already. He at least had the decency to keep his mouth shut for a long moment, until the potion had enough time to ease the nausea and headache. "So what is your plan?" he finally asked.

Vesryn groaned. "I don't know."

"Do you want my advice?"

"Not if it's to talk to the fae."

Zaos snorted and rolled over to face him, dark hair spilling into his eyes. "Don't fight the bond."

Vesryn already knew that wasn't a choice. He liked his limbs exactly where they were. "You know I won't," he muttered, hating the thread of resentment already forming in his chest. Why Fate thought She had the right to manipulate people like pieces in a game— What good had She ever brought that wouldn't have been resolved anyway?

The entire mess with Justice and Aster only started because Haru and Rashi ended up in prison, because they'd been following their Fate strings across the Wound. He had to believe Callith and Julius would have found a way to fix things without destroying part of the city.

Zaos flicked his nose, snapping Vesryn out of his spiraling thoughts. "You'll come back," he said with conviction.

Vesryn swallowed hard and couldn't risk agreeing. He wouldn't be able to bear the pain if it was a lie. "I want to," he whispered instead.

Zaos nodded and clasped Vesryn's wrist with a firm squeeze before getting up. "What are your plans for today?"

With another groan, he pulled a pillow over his head. "Staying here." Zaos laughed and yanked the blankets off, but Vesryn didn't move. If he didn't leave the bed or the barracks, he wouldn't have to deal with the bond or the fae.

"Come on. Let's go for a ride. You haven't seen the Wound since the king left, have you?"

Vesryn made a face and tugged the pillow aside enough to look at Zaos. "What happened to the Wound?"

Zaos grinned and tossed a clean shirt at him. "You'll see."

Vesryn rolled his eyes, but he pushed himself up. If something was changing in the Wound, he may as well prepare himself for it now.

GREEN.

That was the only thing that came to mind when they rode past the city gates. What had once been a dreary gray, barren, crumbling, magic-void wasteland was green again. Wild grasses and flowers and a few young saplings stretched out in front of him.

When Callith, Haru, and Rashi first tested combining their magics outside the gates, a small patch of grass and flowers sprouted in a circle around them. Instead of crumbling to dust as usual, the plants thrived. Now they were spreading.

The wasteland of the Wound was still visible a stone's throw away, but it no longer pressed against the city gates as it tried to claim the only remaining healthy land between it and the sea. Not even a week since the king left and the patch had spread several times over.

"Amazing, isn't it? Never thought I'd actually live to see this. Afamrail is already drafting where to plant new crops."

Vesryn slanted a disbelieving look at Zaos. "You thought this would last several Ages?"

Zaos shrugged. "It was only a matter of time before the Wound seeped past the walls and destroyed our crops. We've barely had enough to sustain the city the last few years, especially with the rate the humans reproduce. I wasn't sure we'd even survive another hundred."

"That's a depressing thought."

"You're the hopeful one."

Vesryn glanced at the red string on his finger and wondered how hopeful he could possibly be now.

Zaos elbowed him. "Stop looking like the Wound is about to swallow you." He winced when Vesryn gave him a bland look at how close to the truth that might be. "I need to get to my post at the docks. Take the wine. Share it with your fae."

He snorted softly. If honey wasn't enough, he doubted the wine would be. But he would save it as Zaos suggested, even if he never got to drink it.

By the time he returned to the palace, ate, and showered, it was early in the evening. He sank onto the edge of his bed and eyed the wine on his dresser. He wasn't tired, but he was too restless to settle with a book.

The glimmer of the Fate string caught his eye, and he scowled. Nothing good could come of it, but they would have to come to an understanding sooner or later.

With a groan, he pushed to his feet and grabbed his sword as he strode out of the room, settling it on his hip as he walked. When he reached the fae's room, he knocked and reached for the handle, but he stopped before opening the door.

The fae had been here long enough to have gotten his bearings by now. Surely he could open the door himself.

He released the handle and waited, though he wasn't surprised when there was no movement on the other side of the door. He knocked again, and then again several moments later. Finally, he heard a shuffle nearing the door before it cracked open and a vibrant violet eye appeared.

He swallowed hard, sure if he said anything the fae would slam the door in his face. He raised his left hand so the string was in their line of sight. He didn't miss the flicker of a scowl before the fae focused on him again.

"Please," Vesryn said softly.

The fae narrowed his eyes and closed the door, but almost immediately flung it open again.

Vesryn blinked at the fae stalking away from him and took a hesitant step inside before nudging the door closed. He watched as the fae sat in the window and drew a leg up, his focus on the brilliant pale gold sunset. The light seemed to make the fae's hair glow, brightening the copper and deep reds.

He cleared his throat and pulled his attention away from the fae's hair. "I don't like this any more than you do," he said, letting out a soft breath of relief when the fae didn't tell him to leave. "But we are bonded for a reason."

"Because Fate thinks They have a right to intervene," the fae said with a sneer.

At least they had that in common, but the wording gave him pause. "They," Vesryn repeated with a frown. "Not She?"

The fae flicked his fingers in a clear dismissive gesture. "I don't know who the Fate is now, and I don't care. They had no right to put this string on me."

Vesryn stared for a long moment before deciding Fate's changing identity was the least of his concerns. "Do you know of a way to remove it?"

The wings rustled, and the fae flexed his fingers before turning his head, focusing an annoyed gaze on Vesryn. "No. You can leave now."

He bit back a soft snarl of frustration. "Tell me what I have to do for you to speak with me."

The fae lifted his chin. "Give me your true name."

Vesryn had faced down assassins, Synne's temper, and Callith's grief after losing first his mother and then his father, but none of that compared to the lance of fear at the thought of giving a fae his name. No physical pain or punishment or fear of death could compare to the possibility of losing himself. Fae may have faded from the realm like all the creatures that once haunted the night, but the legends and tales of caution were still very much alive.

The fae could control Vesryn with his name. Order him to kill or destroy his home or betray the Throne. He wanted to believe Fate would never tie him to someone who would do such a thing, but the fae had given no indication whether he could be trusted. He had no way to know. Not unless Julius was willing to speak with him.

Surely the Seer could tell him that much.

He inclined his head and stepped back before turning for the door. This late, he suspected even Julius would have retired for the night, and he was loath to bother him, especially for a personal matter that posed no immediate threat.

Tomorrow, if he hadn't come to a decision, he'd go visit the Seer.

CHAPTER 4

FEY TURNED his attention back to the sunset as soon as the elf left. He didn't expect the elf to give him a true name, Fate string or not, but it didn't matter. His wings grew stronger by the day, and he knew he would have to leave soon. He wasn't sure how much the elves would be willing to give him, or if they would even spare a weapon, but he didn't need much. A handful of seeds and he could grow food along the way, even if he didn't find a water source.

A few days. Maybe a week. That was all he could allow himself. The longer the tears were left open, the bigger they'd become. Unlike the established pathways he'd sealed before he'd been forced to relinquish the Wild Throne to the humans, the tears had no set boundaries to keep them contained. The influx of magic might be needed to restore the Wound, but the creatures he would rather not have to deal with; most were as dangerous as the Summer Court fae, though not nearly as ruthless. He would certainly need a weapon, but he hadn't held one in so long, he hardly remembered which one he preferred. His talons had usually been enough to deter humans and fae alike.

That was a problem to be solved later. His bigger concern now was the Fate string.

As the sun slipped below the horizon, the sunstones in the room and across the city flickered to life. His attention settled on the red glimmer around his finger. He knew its magic well enough to mimic it, to place a fake one when he'd had access to the raw energy of the ley lines. The magic itself was fae in nature, which meant breaking it by force would require a heavy price.

As if sensing his intentions, the string tightened and he felt a sharp pressure, as if it were a tangible string cutting into his flesh.

He bared his teeth with a hiss. "Release me," he snarled. "I refuse to be at the mercy of another again."

The string tightened further as if threatening to cut his finger off.

"Do it if I don't need a finger. I don't care about your plans. You have no authority over the Wild Court."

The string released as if sighing, but it didn't fade. If anything, it seemed to glow brighter.

"Fucking fae," he snarled, shoving away from the window and into the bedroom to throw himself across the bed. He shoved his hand under a pillow to hide the string. He would find a way to get rid of it eventually. Tomorrow, he needed to venture out of this room.

In the morning, a knock came as he was finishing breakfast. He expected it to be the elf with sea-kissed golden hair again, but when he opened the door, it was a young elf with a delicate sunstone circlet, a crescent moon of mythril resting in the center of her forehead.

She smiled and held out her hand, palm up. "Sun's warmth upon you. I am Calaesynne Ratearynn, heir to the Sun Throne," she said, ignoring the hiss of the guard behind her.

Fey couldn't help the shocked rustle of his wings as he stared at her; even the king hadn't given him a true name. He felt the hum of magic around her name, loud and pure after so long denied even hearing a nickname among his human captors. She was either incredibly foolish or brave, but he didn't care which.

He placed his palm lightly against hers. "Wilds keep you, Calaesynne. Call me Fey."

"Fey," she repeated, lifting briefly onto her toes. "Please come with me. You need supplies, yes?"

He inclined his head and dropped his hand. When she turned, he fell into step behind her.

She turned with a frown and a tilt of her head. "Walk beside me?"

Fey silently cursed his wings when they threatened to snap open. He remembered well his lessons on remaining unobtrusive and silent. A pretty, broken creature at the Shadow King's mercy. Stepping out of place was never pleasant, but he was no longer a slave. Hadn't been for three hundred years, but the ley lines had been their own unique form of torment.

With a quick breath, he stepped beside her and kept pace when she resumed walking.

Her smile was almost blinding, and he could feel her excitement, almost as tangible as the fox's had been. "I have so many questions, but our stories say fae rarely give answers about themselves."

He watched her from the corner of his eye, waiting for the questions, until he realized she expected a response first. That was far more consideration than he was accustomed to, and he cursed himself for falling into ingrained habits. "I will answer one question."

She made a sound like a cutoff squeal. "I'll think of which I want to ask. For now, Juls—our Seer—suggested you might find a weapon to your liking in the Vault. If you let me know what else you need, I can see what we can spare."

"Seeds," he said. When she tilted her head in question, he added, "From fruits or vegetables. Any of the fruits from the plants that changed should be fine."

They reached a large, ornate door and Calaesynne pressed magic into it. The door slid open, revealing a narrow, spiraling staircase. Sunstones flickered to life on the wall as they started down the stairs.

"Is that all you need?" she asked. "No clothes or shoes? Do you wear shoes? I'm sure we could have some made for you."

"No," he said, amusement a strange sensation in his chest. He'd forgotten what it felt like. "I used to wrap my legs with leather."

"Oh," she said, sounding intrigued. "I'm sure that won't be a problem to find."

When they reached the bottom of the stairs, they came to a small alcove with a door the color of autumn leaves, the dawntree wood emitting a soft glow. The phases of the moon were etched in an arch across the top, and Calaesynne whispered in ancient Elvish as she pressed magic into the sun motif in the center. The door swung open without sound and with a whoosh of stale air.

The moment Fey stepped inside, he knew this was more of a tomb than a vault. He felt the echoes of magic from countless creatures. He knew this place well, though it was different seeing it from inside rather than as a magical essence. He absently wondered if he was about to meet his own end here, but the Fate string was enough to assure him he wouldn't die so easily.

Calaesynne motioned him farther into the depths of the Vault. "Most of the weapons are kept back here."

He tensed as he saw pieces of creatures displayed on pedestals. Sphinx paws. A girallon skull sitting atop its white hide. A selkie skin. Two large wings behind spelled glass, their delicate gossamer membranes glowing with a bright green and silver that felt similar to the ley lines.

He looked away as they neared the weapons and felt fae magic reaching out to him. He straightened and scanned the swords and bows, ignoring them as he followed the pull deeper, until he reached a long spear.

It glowed with a faint red aura. The end was a sharp, straight blade in the center, with two curved blades on either side like wings. Below the blades was a band of sharp spikes. The shaft was ylren wood with the grip wrapped in leather. Spells for true aim were woven into each blade and spike, faded with time, but a touch of fae magic would bring them back to full power.

Beside the spear was a sword, the blade dull and chipped, faded to the color of ash, but the fine stone in the pommel was still bright and glinted with what felt like a powerful restoration spell. A strange spell for a sword, but the fae who originally tamed this realm were all a little mad, and both weapons felt at least that old.

"These do not belong to you," he said, picking up both sword and spear. He turned, tilting his head as the feline guard moved to put himself between him and the princess. With a twist of magic, he opened up access to his hollow and slipped both weapons inside. He glanced around the Vault again, but he sensed no other fae magic.

He started back the way they'd come, wanting away from the evidence of so much slaughter. When they reached the top of the narrow staircase, he turned to Calaesynne. "The Seer you mentioned. I would like to speak with him."

"Of course." Once the entrance was sealed again, she led him to another floor of the palace, this one busier. Nobles and servants alike walked across the open floor, with guards standing at the entrances of hallways and what looked like the throne room.

She headed down one of the hallways and knocked on a door before poking her head in. "Fey would like to speak to you." A moment later, she straightened and pushed the door open, motioning Fey inside with a smile. "Fey, this is our Seer, Juls."

An elf with deep autumn gold hair stepped around from behind a large desk. "It's Julius," he said, offering his hand palm up as the princess had done.

Fey rested his own on top, feeling the same hum of truth in his name. "Call me Fey," he said, studying the Seer. Julius' eyes were pale, as if someone had dropped milk into what was once likely a striking green. That was all the warning he needed; the more powerful the Seer, or the more chaotic the immediate future, the greater the toll on their bodies and health. "Seers who herald the new Ages tend to lose their minds," he said quietly.

Julius grimaced. "I'm aware."

He nodded and stepped back. He knew better than to ask for any details; mixing fae and prophecies was usually a bloody event. He wasn't sure what he actually expected from meeting the Seer. Perhaps he only wanted to see the lingering connection between fae and elves. Sight was a rare gift, even among the fae. The first Seer was the First Fate Herself, though the ability to create or manipulate Fate strings was something only the one holding the title of Fate could master. The only reason Fey had managed to put a false Fate string on Haru and Sorren was due to the massive power of the ley lines.

Julius' Sight was proof that fae magic was still strong in this realm, even if the elves had bound their magic to Light and the Sun instead of the Wilds.

"Is there anything else I need for my journey?" he finally asked.

Julius' lips twisted as if he'd bit into something unpleasant. "You'll have everything you need," he replied after a moment, a tiny tremor of power in his words, and Fey could only hope they held true.

He turned for the door, but Julius spoke again before he could reach it. "Speaking as an elf and a friend, and not a Seer, please don't hurt him by fighting the bond."

Fey paused, staring at the door rather than turning back to face the Seer. Even he knew the legends of those who tried to deny Fate. Disaster and tragedy. Consequences often far worse than whatever outcome Fate had set them to prevent. In the earlier Ages, Fate strings had been far more common. Necessary tools to shape this realm into someplace comfortable rather than simply habitable.

And yet, those times were long past.

He glanced at the string on his finger with a silent snarl. He wouldn't make that promise. He couldn't. Even before he'd made the mistake of giving his name to a human, he would never make that kind of promise, but he didn't need to. The elf that Fate had offensively tied him to wouldn't be leaving here with him. Especially if that elf gave him a true name.

He tugged the door open and stepped out, only to find a sorceress waiting for him. His eyes flicked to the tiny black horns partially obscured by wild red hair.

She smiled and offered her palm. "I am Duaia. Sun's light upon you."

"Call me Fey," he said, resting his palm on hers.

"Synne said you vanished some weapons into a personal holding space. Will you show me?"

He tilted his head, but it was a simple enough request. He activated the magic and pulled the sword free. He didn't understand why she looked so shocked. It was a basic ability that most anyone with magic discovered as a child when trying to hide things from their parents or siblings.

"By the Wound," she breathed, her shock only growing when she reached for the magic herself and opened her own hollow. "Why has that never worked before?"

His wings rustled as he realized why she was so surprised. Most basic spells weren't tied to the elements; they drew raw energy from the ley lines. From wild magic. When he'd sealed the shadows, he'd initially sealed all wild magic in the area. That was part of why the Wound had never recovered. But those first years or decades, all magical creatures here would have been cut off from the Wilds that allowed them to create hollows or properly renew their thresholds.

Only in the last few decades, when his control began slipping, would they have regained easy access to those magics.

He pushed aside the guilt and returned the sword to his hollow. "Any of your lost magic should be returned to you now."

Duaia looked up in confusion before she paled, her eyes widening. "You restrained all that magic. And the shadows?"

"Shadows are only a small part of wild magic."

"Wild.... Of course," she murmured. "Humans changed the name." She turned as if in a hurry to share her discovery, but she turned back. "Tha—" she started, before catching herself. "Your guidance is appreciated," she said instead. "May you stay in the Sun's sight."

"Wilds keep you," he replied, his lips twitching. Amusement fluttered in his chest again as he watched her hurry away. He should have been offended, being thanked, but being enslaved by humans for so long had skewed his reactions to everything, even a near miss of misplaced gratitude. Could he even truly consider himself fae anymore?

He'd stolen a human body and remade it for his own. Even his own magic felt off, but maybe that was simply because he was no longer being slowly destroyed by the ley lines.

He spotted Calaesynne speaking with some nobles at the end of the hallway, but she turned and motioned him closer with a smile. By the time he reached her, the nobles had stepped away. "Would you like me to take you to the clothier?"

The thought of venturing into the city where there were sure to be more humans than the few he'd already seen filled him with dread. He wasn't sure he wouldn't try to kill any who stepped too close to him, and he couldn't risk ending up in the prison or the vault tomb as another trophy. "No."

She accepted that with a nod. "Is there anything else you'd like to see? You are free to roam."

He would have been fine with returning to his room, but fresh air might do him some good. "I'll find the gardens."

Her smile widened. "They're beautiful right now. The rains and the shift in magic gave them one last bloom before winter." She motioned to another guard, an elf with unusually dark hair. "Please accept a guard. If anyone bothers you, Zaos is very skilled at chasing them away."

Zaos glanced at her with clear exasperation before offering a polite bow to Fey. "The quickest way to the gardens is this way."

Fey inclined his head to Calaesynne before following the guard down the stairs and out a side passage into late morning sunlight. The scents of dozens of different flowers reached him as he moved down the path leading to the gardens he'd seen from his window. A few tall trees were scattered throughout, dwarfed by the ylren tree, but no less impressive with the gentle glow of dawn emanating from them. Leaves of deep crimson and gold littered the path, their veins faintly glowing like the trees themselves.

He picked up a leaf as he walked deeper, letting his fingertips brush against the various plants. Lavender, thistle, sweet berries. It wasn't until he reached a small batch of crimson foxglove that he realized what was missing in his magic. He could feel the depth and breadth of the gardens, but he couldn't touch them. He should have been able to coax them into blooming more, or sprouting from the fallen seeds half buried in the earth. Before he'd been sacrificed to the ley lines, foxgloves used to bloom in his footsteps. Even coaxing a single, transient flower into existence should have been as easy as breathing.

He crouched in front of some delicate flowers and rested his arms across his knees, but no matter how he pushed or pulled or how deep he reached into the limitless magic around them, nothing happened.

A Wild Court fae without the ability to urge a flower to bloom wasn't a Wild fae at all. Not daring to reach for any of the other wild magic, he tilted his head instead, glancing at the elf hovering nearby. He didn't sense hostility exactly, but Zaos kept frowning at him. He caught the elf's eye the next time he looked over and held it, raising an eyebrow.

Zaos narrowed his eyes before sweeping a quick look around them, then took a few steps closer. "What are your intentions with the Fate bond?" he demanded quietly.

Fey pushed to his feet. "It doesn't concern you."

The elf's glower was impressive. "It does when you're bonded to my friend."

Fey tilted his head as he studied Zaos, noting the hand clenched around the hilt of his sword and the flux of restrained magic. "Friend or lover?"

The glower deepened. "Friend," Zaos snapped.

He held out his left hand, the Fate string reaching towards the sea in the distance. "Do you know a way to remove it?"

Zaos flinched as his scowl melted into a look of horror. "No," he all but shouted. "The only way to sever a Fate bond is through death," he said tightly. "Surely you know that."

"Yes." He also suspected that if Zaos killed him, there was a chance the Fate string would transfer the bond to the elf in his stead. Zaos was powerful. Fey could sense the deep well of magic in him, but he doubted Zaos would be able to seal the tears or prevent creatures from the fae realm from coming through. "Are you going to try to kill me?"

The elf's expression shifted into something wary, as if he couldn't decide if he should flee or not. That was a look Fey was more accustomed to. Even when he'd been enslaved by humans, as the only fae left in the realm, he was as frightening as he was intriguing.

"No," Zaos finally said. "And I hope you won't fight the bond."

Fey looked away. He wouldn't make promises, even if he could keep them. He had no intention of hindering himself in such a way ever again. "I'm done here," he said. Before the elf could press further, he turned and headed back into the palace.

He found the way back to his room easily enough, and it was even easier to ignore the glare focused on the back of his head until he shut the door behind him. Once he was alone again, he let out a deep breath, then drew out the spear as he moved to the center of the room to test its weight and balance. When he swung it, magic suddenly activated and ripped the spear from his grip.

It flew across the room, the blades sinking into the back of a chair, piercing all the way through the thick wood and splintering through the other side. The band of spikes flared with another spell, expanding through the veins and whorls in the wood, others lancing through the joins of the seat and legs. In the time it took Fey to blink, the entire chair was reduced to a mess of shattered wood. The only piece somewhat still intact was the back of the seat where the blades had embedded themselves.

He eyed it with a touch of dismay before retrieving it. He expected some kind of resistance, but the spikes retracted when he gave it a tug. Once he'd picked the pieces of ruined wood from between the spikes, he tucked it away again to worry about later. It was far too powerful to be using without a proper target.

He opened the balcony doors and stepped outside. The subtle scent of ylren blossoms filled the breeze. When he tipped his head back, he spotted the nearest one with pale pink petals above his head. He frowned at the lack of magical aura around it. The ylren trees were sacred because the flowers were a direct link to the health of the ley lines. Only the flowers that drew enough raw magic from the ley lines would glow, and only those seeds were viable.

As he looked over all the blossoms he could see, not a single one glowed. That may not have worried him too much, considering he'd disrupted the magic in the area for three hundred years, but he needed viable seeds. The ylren trees of this realm were the only things that could quickly seal the tears. If he'd had the Wild Throne to draw from, he could have tried sealing them like when he'd closed the veil, but with the throne destroyed, he couldn't hope to channel enough power.

And until he could restore the throne, humans would retain access to the shadows. Or until magic became unbalanced and began ripping this realm apart.

As soon as he could trust his wings to carry him, he would have to scour the trees for viable seeds. If there were none, Fate would have to do more than put a string on his finger.

CHAPTER 5

Vesryn didn't sleep. He spent the entire night tossing or staring at the ceiling. He knew what he had to do, but even with the Fate string, trusting a fae with his name opened a black pit of terror in his gut. The fact the humans had controlled the fae for Ages was the exact nightmare he wanted to avoid.

But what choice did he have? After being enslaved by the humans and then trapped in the ley lines for three centuries, he couldn't expect the fae to trust anyone, and fighting Fate was as terrifying as giving his name.

With a groan, he rolled over and buried his face in his pillow.

Fuck.

He'd have to hand his sword over and tell Duaia he'd no longer be a guard. He couldn't risk having access to Synne once he gave the fae his name. Still, he wanted to speak with Julius in the morning to make sure he was making the right choice.

When first light finally came and Vesryn reached Julius' office, Faelan was standing outside as if waiting for him. As Julius' mate and personal aide, that wasn't too surprising, but before he could say anything, Faelan held up a hand.

"You must make this decision on your own."

Vesryn bit back a soft hiss of frustration and glanced at the door. He wanted to storm inside and demand Julius tell him what he knew, and how much he'd shared with Faelan or anyone else, but he didn't dare challenge Faelan. Julius had made it clear years ago that Faelan spoke with the same authority as him in matters of his Sight. What good was having a Seer if he didn't share anything about his visions? But he also knew the toll those visions could take, despite how well Julius hid the symptoms from even Callith.

"Is he all right?" he finally asked.

Faelan offered a faint smile. "I'll take care of him."

Vesryn nodded and glanced at the door one last time, worried that something far larger was going on, but if there was, he obviously had no part in it. Which might have been disappointing if he let himself dwell on it; if Fate was going to make a mess of his life, he would have at least preferred it to be for something significant.

He stepped back and turned for the training grounds.

He spent the early hours defeating one elf, dwarf, beastkin, and human after another in mock combat. It didn't help clear his head or take the edge off the unease and frustration simmering beneath his skin, but he hoped by the time he went to bed that night, he'd at least be too worn out to lie awake again.

It wasn't until he spotted Faelan to the side that he realized how much time had passed. Usually he would already be in the throne room guarding Synne, but with Elwin taking his place, he had far more spare time than he was accustomed to. He tossed the dulled sparring blade to the next in line and picked up his shirt and a towel on his way to Faelan.

"What's wrong?" he asked, wiping the sweat off his face and chest before pulling his shirt on.

"Synne would like to have lunch with you."

Vesryn raised an eyebrow, but he didn't question it and grabbed his sword as he followed. After seventeen years, he rarely kept up with Synne's antics. The only thing he knew well was where she was likely to be hiding when she didn't want to be found.

Instead of going to one of the small nooks the princess preferred, Faelan led him to an indoor garden. The same one where Aster had finally revealed himself as the one behind the destruction of the ylren trees and the resurgence of shadow magic. The fountain had been restored from Duaia destroying it with a fireball, but Vesryn swore he could still feel a lingering chill in the air. Like shadows creeping along his senses.

Synne waited at a small table, and Vesryn spotted Elwin several paces back, but the feline nodded to him and disappeared when Vesryn caught his eye. The lack of Kithiel at Synne's side was surprising.

"What are you up to, Princess?" he asked, sitting across from her. He propped his sword against the table within easy reach.

"I should be asking you that."

Vesryn kept his expression calm despite his urge to wince. He knew she was perceptive, but he rarely had the displeasure of having that perception turned on him. "What do you mean?"

Synne narrowed her eyes at him. He braced himself for a scathing remark, but she huffed and poured them both a cup of tea. "I know you're bound to the fae."

"And how could you possibly know that?" Had Haru said something before he left? But no, the answer was far simpler.

"Juls."

Vesryn swore under his breath. For someone who guarded his own secrets so closely, Julius seemed too willing to expose the secrets of others. "And?"

Synn gave him a pointed look, but it was obvious how hard she was fighting against rolling her eyes. "And the fae won't stay here forever. When he leaves, you'll go with him."

He scoffed, adding a teaspoon of honey to his tea and stirring it. "He won't even speak to me."

She hummed softly, stirring a bit of honey into her own tea without looking up.

After serving as Synne's personal guard for so long, Vesryn was intimately familiar with her mannerisms. He didn't even need to ask to know she'd spoken with the fae. He breathed through the sharp frustration in his chest. Of course the fae had spoken with Synne. She was the heir to the Sun Throne, the most important person currently in the city.

"Did you give him your name?"

Synne picked up her cup. "Yes."

"Calaesynne!" What in the darkness had Elwin been thinking? He should have stopped her.

She glared over the top of her cup. "I won't treat him as an enemy because of old legends. We helped free him, and we stopped those responsible for enslaving and trapping him in the ley lines to begin with. He has no reason to try to control me. He has far more important things to worry about."

Vesryn glared at her. He missed when she was younger and the worst he had to deal with was her sneaking into the Wound to watch the celestial lights. Now she was ruling Ylrendorei in her older brother's place while Callith and his bondeds worked to restore the Wound.

"Besides," she continued before he could properly chastise her, "after what he went through, I don't blame him for being wary. But you're still bound for a reason. You can't deny Fate."

He knew that all too well. Even if he tried, he'd end up where She— They?—dictated sooner or later, likely broken and bloody. Whatever he'd been chosen for, surely it couldn't be worse than fighting for the future of magical creatures. Especially when they'd only won because they had a dragon on their side.

"I'm releasing you from my service."

Vesryn flinched. A physical slap would have been less painful. "You're what?" he snapped, flexing his hands into fists as he channeled his anger into his fatigued muscles. "That is not your choice to make. I'm not leaving."

Even as he said it, he knew that was a lie. The sudden, sharp pang beneath his ribs was proof of that. He may have decided to give the fae his name, but he still couldn't accept that he wouldn't stay. Even if that part of him that had never felt like he belonged here was growing larger by the day, no longer contained to the quiet whispers he'd forced it down to years ago.

He closed his eyes as he forced a breath into his aching lungs. He was going to leave his home, his family and the only friends he'd ever known. He was going to leave them to follow a fae who despised him into the Wound.

"Fuck," he hissed, distantly aware of warm arms around his shoulders.

"Ves, I love you as a brother. You will always have a place here."

Vesryn remained silent, focused on controlling his breathing.

"Don't shut me out."

When he was on the verge of breaking, he pulled away, unable to heed her words.

He would be surrounded by silence with only his own thoughts for company soon. He may as well get used to it now.

He made his way to Duaia's office as if in a daze. He may have decided to step away from his duties, but it still stung to know Synne could dismiss him so easily. He reached the throne room floor and spotted Duaia's mess of bright red hair, before scowling when he saw her speaking with Zaos.

Duaia turned as he approached, eyebrows lifting in surprise. "Done with lunch already?"

"I didn't eat," he said, barely controlling his anger as he thrust the sword out for her to take. "I've been relieved of duty. Please give this to Callith when he returns." Callith's father had given him the sword when he first joined the kingsguard. It seemed only fitting that it was returned to his son.

Duaia took the sword with a frown. "Why? What's going on?"

Vesryn looked at Zaos. "You didn't tell her?"

"Of course not."

"Tell me what?" Duaia demanded.

Vesryn flexed his fingers, already feeling naked without his sword. He let out a slow breath. "A Fate string binds me to the fae."

Duaia startled, looking from him to Zaos and back again as if waiting for one of them to admit to a jest. When neither of them did, she pinched the bridge of her nose and swore. He couldn't help the faint twitch of his lips as crude, ancient Elvish spilled from her lips. "Does Cal know?"

Vesryn winced and looked away. "Not unless Haru told him after they left."

She swore again, her red hair twitching with tiny sparks of blue, before she blew out a harsh breath, dispelling the excess magic gathering around her. She looked between them again before waving a hand as if shooing away a pest. "I'll see this returned to Cal. Go take care of your fae."

Zaos failed to stifle a laugh and fell into step beside Vesryn when he turned. Once they were on the stairs, Zaos nudged him with an elbow. "Well? Did you speak to him?"

Vesryn couldn't stop the resentful curl of his lips. "He won't speak to me unless I give him my name."

Zaos hummed.

He was as familiar with those hums as he was with Synne's. He stopped in the middle of the stairs, narrowing his eyes at Zaos' back until he stopped and looked over his shoulder. "You truly think I should give my name to a *fae* so easily?"

"Yes," Zaos replied, lifting a hand to stop Vesryn's arguments. "Ply me with wine and I'll explain."

"You just want your fucking ylren blossom wine back," Vesryn muttered under his breath, ignoring Zaos' laugh as he stalked past.

When he reached his rooms, he headed for the few bottles he kept on hand, all of them a step above the cheapest elven wine available and none of them full. Dwarven ale was far too potent for his tastes, and the two times he'd had siren brew were enough to last him the rest of his lifetime. And he certainly didn't dare risk human liquors, especially after the past weeks.

He poured two glasses of pale amber wine and handed one to Zaos before sinking onto the sofa next to him. He drew his leg up and angled his body to stare at his old friend expectantly.

Zaos took a sip of wine before mirroring him. "So I did some research."

"Of course you did," Vesryn murmured, taking his own sip.

Zaos ignored him and continued. "Most of the stories with fae using names in nefarious ways are usually members of the Summer Court."

"And you think he's not?"

Zaos shrugged, swirling his wine before taking another sip. "No descriptions I've ever found mentioned wings. I'd bet money he's a Wild fae."

Vesryn raised an eyebrow over his glass. Zaos wasn't one to gamble, even if he knew he could win. "Why?"

"It was the Wild Court that created the Thrones," he said, pointing a finger at Vesryn with a glare when he groaned.

"That's all myth!"

"Because that's what happens when history is forgotten. Why else would old tomes reference a Wild Throne? It was only after humans began wielding shadows there was ever a mention of a Shadow Throne. If the Light Throne became known as the Sun Throne, why can't the Wild Throne have become the Shadow Throne?"

"Stop saying throne," Vesryn muttered, then blocked the small pillow Zaos threw at him. "What if you're wrong?"

"I'm not."

"If you *are*."

Zaos tipped his head back with a long-suffering sigh. "Then you have to decide if you trust Fate enough to keep you safe."

He snorted and drained the rest of his wine. "I absolutely don't."

Zaos dropped a hand to Vesryn's knee and squeezed. "Then trust me," he said quietly.

Vesryn pressed his hand over Zaos'. "Of course I trust you. Which is why if I die, yours is the first ass I'm haunting as a spirit."

"I don't believe in spirits."

"You will."

Zaos shook his head with a laugh. "Stop acting like you're going to die. You'll be fine. Give the fae your name and figure out what he plans to do to restore his throne."

Vesryn looked up with a jolt. "You think that's what this is about?"

"That's my best guess." He looked away as he tossed back the rest of his wine.

Vesryn narrowed his eyes, pinching Zaos between his thumb and forefinger.

"Ow!" Zaos jerked his hand away with a glare.

"What aren't you telling me?"

With a grimace, Zaos stood and refilled both their glasses before setting the bottle on the table within easy reach. "The Thrones keep the balance, yes?" When Vesryn nodded, he continued. "They strain the chaos from the magic by separating the most distinct and powerful elements. We thought the Shadow Throne was destroyed, but it wasn't. Even if it had been, the fae's essence in the ley lines was keeping shadow magic restrained."

Zaos took a long swallow of wine before asking, "What do you think is going to happen, now that the Throne is truly destroyed and the fae is no longer holding all that magic in check?"

"Chaos." Fuck. That was one of the favorite horror stories that circulated in the academy. The end of all magic and life in the realm, thrown out of balance and devolving into chaos.

Vesryn tipped his glass back and drank it all. "Why me?" he demanded, holding the glass out for a refill. "You're the battlemage and historophile."

Zaos narrowed his eyes, but he didn't comment as he emptied the bottle into their glasses and set it aside. "Obviously you have something I don't that's needed."

"Decent hair?"

"You can be such a dick, do you know that?"

Vesryn lifted his glass in sarcastic assent before swallowing half his wine. "Fuck. I need something stronger."

Zaos snorted. "What you need is a nap before you go tell your fae your name." He snatched Vesryn's glass and emptied it into his own.

"Not my fae," he muttered.

"All right."

He smacked Zaos' arm with the pillow before hugging it to his chest. He slumped against the back of the sofa as silence wrapped around them like a favored blanket. Eventually he shifted closer to rest his head on Zaos' shoulder. "Will you miss me?"

"Of course I'll miss you. So will everyone else." Zaos reached up to run his fingers through Vesryn's hair, deliberately mussing it before smoothing it back out. "When you're done saving the realm, you'll come back home and we'll celebrate."

Vesryn closed his eyes as Zaos continued stroking his hair. He really hoped that was true.

HE WOKE with his head in Zaos' lap and an open book hovering over his face. When he squinted at the cover, he didn't recognize it. "Please tell me that's not more fae research," he murmured before yawning.

"Dinner should be here soon."

Vesryn snorted softly and sat up to fix his hair. He let his arms drop to his lap as he stared through the bottle and glasses on the table. He forced out a slow breath, jumping when Zaos closed his book with a loud snap.

"You'll be fine," Zaos said, tossing the book onto the table and standing when there was a knock on the door.

He couldn't help being wary of food and drink after Aster poisoned their elders with tea, but Duaia had assured them that all the staff were cleared of suspicion.

Zaos stopped the cart near the table and picked his book up, and Vesryn startled at the flicker of old magic before the book seemed to disappear.

"What—"

Zaos grinned at him. "When I talked to D earlier, she mentioned that the magic we thought we'd lost was only being restrained by the fae. Like the shadows. Which suggests that I'm right about him being a Wild fae."

Vesryn hummed softly as he reached for the old magic. He'd forgotten what it used to feel like before the war. Everything in the days and months after was a blur of shock and grief and horror. The loss of most of their skilled mages, warriors, and elders was a cut that still bled to this day, as painful as the sight of the Wound that had torn across the realm.

By the time they realized magic itself felt and behaved differently, they'd assumed it was another side effect of the war. But when the fae finally broke free of the ley lines, claimed Aster's corpse, and wrapped it in a cocoon, the realm changed. Magic changed. Or rather, magic returned to its natural state.

He released the magic and stood, focusing on the more important part of Zaos' words. When he lifted the lid of a pot, he found it full of a hearty stew. "You remember that baby rabbit you found when we were very young?" He ignored the glare Zaos leveled at him as he picked up a bowl. "Mamma, mamma! Look at this baby bunny we found!" he mimicked in a young, high voice.

"Shut up."

"Didn't matter that it had a long tail. You were sure it was a rabbit." He ladled stew into his bowl and picked up a chunk of warm bread before looking up. "What did it turn out to be?"

"You made your point."

"A *rat*."

"Yes, and that rat lived a very comfortable several years," Zaos said with a sniff before snatching his own bowl.

"So you finally admit it was a rat." Vesryn smirked as Zaos muttered idle threats under his breath and sat down to eat, then dipped his bread into the stew. When the bread was gone, he absently stirred the last of his soup with a quiet sigh. "I'm going to need supplies," he finally murmured. It'd been centuries since he ventured beyond the gates, and he refused to acknowledge the tiny flicker that might have been excitement. He wasn't even sure where to start preparing for an extended journey through the Wound.

What were they going to do for food and water? At least Callith had Haru and his ice magic, and Rashi with his nature magic. He was certain their king at least wasn't starving, wherever he was, but Vesryn didn't have that kind of support.

"I'll get Faelan to help with putting things together," Zaos said. "At least now you won't have to worry about carrying everything, with magic back as it should be. I can't believe you gave up your sword, though."

"It wasn't mine." That sword used to belong to Callith's uncle, one of the best warriors of his time but lost in the war like so many others. He didn't dare say he couldn't be trusted with a blade once he gave the fae his name. He hoped Zaos was right and his fear would be misplaced, but he couldn't take that risk.

Zaos hummed softly, but he didn't say anything further.

When they'd finished eating, Zaos took his leave, and Vesryn stood to stretch as he moved to the balcony. He leaned against the railing and looked out over the gardens. The air was chilled with the oncoming winter, and he welcomed the mild sting against his skin.

He turned his attention to the red string on his finger, wondering what the fuck Fate expected of him. He wasn't a ruler with power, he was a guard. An elf of no import. His magic was weak. His only skills were combat and tracking down troublesome heirs. What could he possibly do for a fae who hated him?

He followed the glimmer of the Fate string up and to the left, to a higher balcony of the palace. His heart leapt into his throat when he saw the fae standing on the ledge. "Don't—" he started to call out, terror seizing his chest as the fae tipped forward. "No!"

Vesryn gripped the railing, unable to pull away as he watched the fae plummet towards the gardens below, helpless to do anything to stop him. Callith would have found a way. Would have called on the palace threshold and wards to cushion the fae's fall, but Vesryn didn't have access to them.

As he watched, certain his bonded was about to die, the fae's wings snapped out to their full extent. His descent stopped and he lifted higher into the air, the brilliant orange of sunset momentarily swallowed by raven-black feathers.

Vesryn's knees gave out, and he sank to the balcony floor, pressing a hand against his racing heart with a bit-off curse.

The fae flew past in a blur with a rich laugh of delight that was quickly ripped away by the wind.

This fucking fae would be the death of him.

He turned and collapsed against the railing. This had to be a punishment, but for what he couldn't fathom. Not saving Callith's parents? Sharing pleasure with Callith? Not dying in the war? He closed his eyes and pressed his fingers against them with a helpless laugh.

Fuck.

He slumped even further and watched the sway of the Fate string as the fae circled higher, flying around and around the ylren tree. The sun sank below the horizon and the sky darkened before the string finally stilled, and he was surprised to find that it didn't stretch out above him to the fae's room but below to the gardens.

Trepidation fluttered in his gut as he stared at the string, but he had nothing left to lose. Whether he was more relieved or disappointed by that, he couldn't quite decide.

With a deep breath, he pushed to his feet and headed down to the gardens.

Chapter 6

Fey tipped his head back as he landed near some night-blooming flowers, breathing in cool, fragrant air. He flexed his wings, relishing the mild ache in his muscles. For the first time he could clearly remember, he felt far more like himself, even if his own name still eluded him.

He tucked his wings and lifted his hand, studying the three gently glowing seeds he'd found among the ylren blossoms so far. It wasn't enough, but the other trees were sure to have more. As much as he despised Fate interfering, he knew he could at least trust that he would find as many as he needed to seal the tears he found. Unless Fate intended something else completely. One could never tell.

He slipped the seeds into his hollow to keep them safe and viable until he had clothes with a protected pocket that could hold them close while they fed on his magic.

He walked through the gardens, taking comfort in the ylren tree, flowers, and dawntrees around him. They weren't nearly as numerous as the Wild Court in the fae realm, or even where the Wild Throne had been, before humans ripped apart the forests and expansive gardens, replacing them with stone and iron and decay. But the quiet languor of their magic as the season changed was familiar enough to be soothing.

When he reclaimed the throne, restoring the land would need to be one of the first things he did.

The remnants of the Wilds were far to the northwest, on top of the largest ley line in the realm. Where chaos once ruled, the Wild Throne had thrived. It once sat in the heart of a forever-young ylren tree, but humans had destroyed it and built a fortified castle in its place, and around it had grown a city of stone and iron and silver to drive out the creatures that originated from the fae realm.

He could still feel echoes of the burning ache of the iron collar and shackles, his skin raw and splitting from countless years at their mercy.

A shuffle behind him made him turn, and he tensed when he saw the elf who held the other end of his Fate string.

The elf stared at him for a long moment, his throat working as he swallowed, before he let out a harsh breath. "Vesryn Rydel."

Surprise rippled through him, his wings rustling as he straightened. He tasted the power in Vesryn's name. A true name, like every other given to him by an elf. "Vesryn Rydel," he said softly. "Kneel."

Vesryn sucked in a sharp breath before kneeling as the twist of magic wrapped around him. It was barely a whisper of compulsion, but Vesryn sank to the ground as if suddenly bearing too much weight to stand.

Fey swayed back a step, his heart racing as he pushed himself into the air, his wings snapping wide to carry him higher. He had never used his powers in such a way before. Not that he could remember. That simple twist of magical power was a heady sensation after being at the humans' mercy for so long. After being trapped in the ley lines for so long. Bereft of any control over his own life.

It was also terrifying, how easy it would be to use that power. To twist and bend Vesryn into his personal protector, rip away his ability to even think of harming Fey or seeking revenge or pleasure. Except he didn't want a slave or a pet. He refused to become like the humans who had turned his entire existence into a nightmare for Ages.

He circled the tree faster, catching the drafts to take him higher, spinning through the air and relishing the feel of the wind rushing over his feathers, the cold stinging his face. The humans had never allowed him to fly. He was thankful that his wings were intrinsically part magic, or they would have wasted away long ago.

He landed on his balcony and gripped the railing to catch his breath, his heart still beating too fast and painful in his chest. He closed his eyes and breathed until he calmed, releasing the light touch he still held on Vesryn's name. When he glanced over the balcony, he could see Vesryn still kneeling in the gardens. He tightened his grip on the railing as he watched, silently willing the elf to get up and prove he was still capable of independent movement.

Finally, Vesryn stood and left the gardens, and the slow stretch and sway of the string told Fey that the elf was inside the palace and moving upstairs.

Fey watched the string until it seemed to be stretching to a room below his own, then stepped onto the railing, drawn by something not quite instinct. Using Vesryn's name in such a way left a bitter taste in his mouth, and as much as he didn't want an elf or anyone else bonded to him, the elves here had been nothing but kind to him. He owed them more than to treat one of them as he'd been treated.

He stepped off and glided down to the lower balcony, landing on the railing and crouching for balance at the same time the elf stepped up to the door.

Vesryn froze, his eyes widening as his breath stuttered to a halt.

Fey couldn't help the way his attention snagged on the green of the elf's eyes, a deep rich green of healthy foliage he remembered from home. He dropped his gaze and slowly lowered his legs to the floor. "I have no desire to control you," he said quietly.

The elf scoffed and drew in a ragged breath. "Making me kneel was to teach me my place, then?" he asked, his voice tight.

"No, I…." He turned his head away, leaning back as he gripped the railing and gazed out over the city. He did not like this feeling, of knowing he could easily invoke the compulsion magic in Vesryn's true name. It was a double-edged blade, since knowing his true name was the only thing that truly kept him safe from Vesryn. "I needed to know it would work."

Vesryn crossed his arms, his gaze a heavy weight on Fey's face for a long moment before he blew out a breath. "You have my name. Does that mean you will speak to me now?"

"Yes."

He hesitated a moment before stepping back, waving an arm in invitation as he turned. "Wine?"

"Yes." When was the last time he'd had wine?

Fey scanned the room, admiring the large bookcase filled with tomes. He accepted the glass of pale amber wine, wrinkling his nose as he sniffed the liquid. It smelled sharp, like fruit instead of flower nectar, and the unpleasant burn when he swallowed made him cough.

Vesryn raised his eyebrows. "Not to your liking?" he asked, sipping his own wine.

"It's different from what I remember." He took another sip, watching the elf settle on one side of a sofa. Since none of the furniture looked made to accommodate wings, he hopped onto the back of a sturdy chair, gripping it with his talons as he crouched over it.

The elf's eyebrows twitched higher, but when he spoke, it was to ask, "What do you plan to do?"

Fey spun the glass between his fingers and studied Vesryn. His plans weren't a secret, but he couldn't help but worry what the humans would do if they learned he intended to reclaim the magic they'd stolen. He settled for a different truth instead. "Restore balance to magic." He tilted his head when the elf tensed and leaned forward.

"Chaos?"

His wings rustled with surprise, sure that the dangers of chaos had been forgotten long before he closed the veil between their realms.

Vesryn swore. "How long? Before magic starts ripping everything apart."

"Long enough," he said, finding the elf's disbelieving expression amusing. "That is a possibility if balance is not restored, but only one throne is missing." Granted, it was the most powerful, the first one created, but the other thrones had been made for this purpose. To keep the elements separated. One missing was a danger he couldn't ignore, but the balance wouldn't collapse all at once.

More than days or weeks, but when he tried to say centuries or decades, the words refused to pass his lips. "Years," Fey amended. Not as long as he'd hoped, but if he couldn't restore the throne before then, he wouldn't be able to restore it at all. He took another small sip of wine. "There will be warning signs first. In the weather and the land."

Vesryn slumped into the sofa, draining his glass like an elf sentenced to execution. "Bastard will be insufferable after this," he muttered. He eyed the few wine bottles on the table against the wall with an air of desperate need for a refill before setting his glass on the table instead. He flexed his fingers, staring at the glass as if afraid to look at Fey. "So what do you need from me?"

Fey tilted his head, tempted to say he didn't need anything, especially since he wouldn't be taking the elf with him into the Wound. But he still had at least a few days before he was prepared to leave. There was no sense in risking disagreement now. "The princess is providing supplies."

Vesryn nodded and flexed his fingers again before looking up at Fey. "You intend to restore the Shadow Throne?"

"I intend to restore and reclaim the *Wild* Throne."

"And how will you do that?"

"I don't know." He took another sip of wine, decided he didn't like it enough to finish it, and tossed it to the table. A gentle twist of wind magic ensured it sailed through the air and landed without spilling or breaking.

Vesryn watched the path of the glass before turning his attention back to Fey. "So you're going to walk into the Wound and hope you find a throne?"

Fey narrowed his eyes at the elf, bristling at the tone. "No."

Vesryn raised an eyebrow. "No?" When Fey didn't bother to respond, he sighed. "This isn't going to work if I have to fight for every conversation."

He looked away, feigning intense interest in the tomes on the shelves. He wasn't sure he remembered how to have a conversation.

"What am I supposed to call you anyway? Raven?"

Fey turned back to the elf with a glare. "Fey."

"Fae?"

His wings twitched, hearing the wrong pronunciation, even if it was slight. "Fey."

"Fay."

"Fey," he said, drawing out every sound and inflection.

"That sounds—" Vesryn shook his head. "Fey," he echoed.

"Yes."

That earned a faint smile. Fey had no idea what was amusing, but the elf looked good when he smiled. "Wilds keep you, Fey. If you don't want to tell me about the plan you don't have to reclaim a throne that no longer exists, what will you tell me?"

"You are not a pleasant elf," he said, blinking when Vesryn laughed.

"I'm an acquired taste." Vesryn leaned forward to remove his boots before stretching his legs out on the sofa. "If we are going to be stuck together, we should get to know each other."

Fey wanted to say they wouldn't be together long, but the words wouldn't form. "Why did you give me your name?"

Vesryn blinked, his lips twitching into a mockery of a smile. "I was told to trust you."

"By the princess?"

"No. And as acting ruler of the kingdom, she should have known better," he muttered.

Fey tilted his head as he studied Vesryn. He looked annoyed, but there was fondness in his words. "You care for her."

"Of course."

When he'd been trapped in the ley lines, he'd sensed a discontent within the kingdom. He knew some of it stemmed from the enslavement ring Draekor's follower managed to put on the previous king. He'd listened to that elf's pleas for help to the Sun and Winds and Fate. For years, Fey had tried to draw attention to the ring. He had even tried forming a fake Fate string, but it snapped before he could attach it to anyone. He'd known better than to tempt Fate by trying again, but he was sure Fate held it against him anyway.

Especially when he was the one who'd finally answered the king's desire to be free, even if it meant death.

"You think she is a good ruler?"

"Yes. The entire family is amazing." Vesryn buried his fingers in his hair and propped his elbow on the back of the sofa. "You're not going to tell me anything, are you."

He could have said there was no reason to, but again the words wouldn't come. "You can ask one question."

"And you'll answer."

Fey nodded, and when Vesryn hummed, he braced himself to be asked for his true name. Only the fact that he couldn't recall it was any comfort. But the elf surprised him.

Despite invoking his true name earlier, there was no hostility or anger when he asked, "When do you intend to leave?"

"Soon." Once he finished collecting the viable ylren seeds and had the supplies he needed, there would be no reason to linger. So long as he found a way to access his wild magic enough to coax seeds into blooming and growing swiftly enough to provide food.

The sooner he traversed the Wound and closed what tears he could find, the sooner he could restore his home. It was surely nothing but ruins now. When Sorren had sacrificed him against the throne, the power that ripped across the realm and created the Wound had come from the ley line beneath them. Whatever was left of the stone and iron castle, he hoped it had been reduced to ash. He did not look forward to tearing down the human city before he could restore the wilds.

"You are quite deep in thought."

Fey turned his attention back to Vesryn and found the elf watching him with half-lidded eyes. "I should let you rest." He straightened and hopped off the back of the chair.

"Sun's light upon you, then," Vesryn said, remaining stretched out on the sofa.

Fey left the way he'd arrived, launching himself into the cool night and dipping lower, twisting through the air before rising higher. Instead of heading back to his own rooms, he ventured farther from the palace as he flew over the city to one of the other ylren trees. It was significantly smaller, but he could sense the tiny sparks of fae magic scattered throughout the branches before even landing in them.

The city was quiet beneath him as he carefully picked the viable seeds, which was the only reason he heard it. A quiet *sss... sss... sss*, like something slowly dragging across the ground. He turned to scan the street as he tucked the seeds away, tilting his head as he tracked the sound.

He drifted lower, hovering above the ground. The noise came again, and he followed it to the opening of a dark alley. His lip curled as he caught the stench of death.

He should leave it for a guard, but there was no one around, and as much as he hated Fate's touch, he knew there was no such thing as coincidence when They were involved. Landing, he tucked his wings in tight before stepping into the narrow alley. He ignored the chill that swept over him, the smell of rot and decaying foliage growing worse as he moved deeper into the dense shadows, until he had to take shallow breaths through his mouth to keep from gagging.

The path turned and led farther into a maze of twists and turns between buildings. His wings brushed against the walls as they pressed closer together. Unease filled him, but before he could decide if he should find another path, a loud hiss made him freeze. His fingers twitched as he reached for the hollow holding his spear, but before he could open the space, something lunged out of the shadows and struck at his face.

A strange, high sound escaped his throat as he twisted away. The long, too-thick body of a snake narrowly missed him before it quickly turned and angled another attack at him. He cursed as his back hit the edge of a building, ducking and pushing away at the same time the snake slammed into the wall above him.

He raced for the exit of the alley, but he must have taken a wrong turn because he came to a dead end. He snarled and turned, a primal twinge of fear creeping up his spine as the yellow glow of eyes slithered towards him. "Fuck," he hissed. The alley was too narrow to spread his wings, but he crouched and launched himself into the air anyway. He caught the side of a building with his talons and pushed higher.

The snake struck at him again, catching his foot. With a grunt, he careened into the top edge of a wall and flipped onto the roof. There was a sharp wrench of pain and a snap of delicate bones as his wing caught on something, but he forced them to expand as another hiss came from right behind him. He stumbled across the roof with a harsh curse, lifting into the air for a few moments before his wing gave out and he crashed to the ground, thankfully onto a main road rather than another alley.

Sunstones glowed from the next street over, shedding enough light for him to see the giant snake head and bared fangs as it came over the building, aiming for him again.

He hopped back and into the air, and the snake struck the ground where he'd been standing. Instead of trying to fly again, he drove his talons into the back of the snake's neck. The sharp scent of blood filled the air as his claws broke through scales. The snake thrashed with a horrible wet hiss, the other end of its body sliding from over the building and whipping from one side of the street to the other.

"Fucking," he hissed, digging his talons in deeper, "hate—" a twist of his feet in opposite directions, "—snakes." With a powerful wrench, he ripped the snake's head off. Or most of it. Enough for its long body to jerk and twitch, slowly coiling around itself and finally going still.

He closed his eyes for a moment, panting for air as he carefully pulled his talons free. He stepped back, swiping a spray of blood from his cheek. "Fuck," he breathed, finally taking in the size of the giant snake. Even coiled, it was sprawled the length of an entire building. "Basilisk," he snarled.

The tears between the realms must have blown open wider than he'd thought for a basilisk of that size to have made it into the city already. And he was starting to think he hadn't been much of a fighter even before the humans enslaved him.

He heard yelling and the pounding of many feet somewhere close by and straightened, more than happy to leave the mess for someone else, but a hiss from nearby made him freeze. He stifled a groan and closed his eyes. Of course there were two.

He kept still and twisted his hollow open around his hand. The spear appeared there a moment later, and he immediately spun, lifting the weapon to meet the snake as it was closing in on his head. Too fast, the snake reared back before it could impale itself on the spear, rising higher until it was looking down at him. When it opened its mouth, its fangs glistened, drops of venom clinging to their tips.

Behind him, the footsteps thudded to a stop, replaced by shouts and the sound of drawn weapons. He wasn't sure how much help they could be, especially since this one looked older and far bigger. It must have been hiding among the roots of the ylren tree to have gotten this far into the city.

The snake flicked its tongue as its head swayed side to side. For a moment, he wondered what Fate would do if he was eaten by a basilisk before he ever stepped past the walls of the city, but then the snake's fangs were aiming for him and he was forced to jump back to avoid them. Stone pebbles flew into the air as the snake struck the ground and began pulling its tail close for another strike.

A buildup of magic behind him let him know someone was over their shock, but he wasn't prepared for the light magic that infused his weapon a moment later. The spear's red glow brightened like a sunstone, and he felt the heat from it as the metal warmed.

"Move!"

Fey pushed into the air as golden fire filled the street. The intense heat reached him even where he landed on the roof of a building. Below him, the snake thrashed as the flames enveloped most of its body, smashing into one building and then another before falling still. He almost believed that might be it, that the snake had knocked itself out, but a few moments after the magical flames whooshed out, the serpentine body twitched. And then its head rose into the air again, its hood flared.

"Oh fuck," Fey hissed. It wasn't a basilisk. It was a giant cobra.

No sooner had he thought that when the snake opened its mouth and spit venom at the guards. One of them didn't turn away fast enough and screamed as the venom hit their eyes.

With the cobra focused on them, Fey saw his chance and launched himself off the building. He lifted the spear, intending to cut its head off. Instead, the snake whipped its head around to focus its slit yellow eyes on him. He tried to change his angle, but his wing was all but useless.

An orb of light struck the cobra's eyes, blinding it long enough for Fey's spear to slice through its head as easily as water, but not before a fang sank into his arm. He lost his grip on the spear as it disappeared into the cobra's gut. When he hit the ground, he staggered, a cold numbness seeping towards his fingers.

Then the band of spikes on the spear activated, and part of the cobra disintegrated into a rainfall of blood and bits of scaled flesh, most of which landed on Fey.

"Fucking snakes," he muttered, turning towards the commotion of the guards and Zaos, whose hands were still wreathed in light.

"What in fucking darkness," Zaos snapped, looking Fey over before turning to shout, "Someone get D, now!"

Fey snarled in annoyance as his vision blurred, fumbling for the part of the snake head attached to his arm and gritting his teeth as he pulled the fang out. He dropped it to the ground and reached for the spear, only to miss as the ground tilted at the wrong angle. Then he was blinking at someone's feet, with hands on his shoulders keeping his face from landing in the foul-smelling mess around them. When he tried to stand, the hands kept him in place.

"Don't move. There's a healer on the way."

He didn't need a healer, though the numbing cold spreading through him should have been more alarming. "Spear," he said, reaching for it again, only for his hand to flop uselessly at his side.

"You can get your spear after D heals you."

"I'll be fine. Fate won't let me die so easily."

Zaos snorted. "I'm not sure even Fate can save someone from their own folly. You two are made for each other," he muttered. "Oh good, there she is."

Fey didn't need him to say as much to know the sorceress had reached them; he could feel the crackle of her magic as easily as he could smell the tang of power in Zaos.

Her surprised swearing was loud and extensive. There was a brief flare of healing magic before she moved closer and bestowed the same healing to him.

He clenched his teeth against a shout as pain lanced down his arm, accompanied by a disturbing sizzling sound, as if she was burning the venom out of him. The pain faded after an endless moment, and his vision cleared shortly after.

Then the soft green glow around her hands moved to his wing. The gentle magic spread over his feathers and sank into his bones and back, easing the sharp, throbbing pain.

Fey breathed a sigh of relief as it faded and flexed his wings. Healing magic was one thing he'd always longed for, those long centuries trapped by the humans, but wild magic was powerful enough without that ability.

"Human vipers weren't enough, now we have giant basilisks in the city?" Duaia snarled, nudging part of the mess around them with her foot. Now that he'd gotten a look at her, she looked like she'd been dragged out of bed, her nightshirt hastily tucked into her trousers.

"Cobra," Fey said, getting to his feet to find his spear. It took a few tugs to free it, and he resisted the urge to flick pieces of meat off it. Fate may have decided to torment him, but with his current luck, the spells would activate on the first swing and take out the guards. Instead, he tucked the spear into his hollow and turned back to the others.

Zaos wrinkled his nose as he looked Fey over. "Please do not track that mess into the palace. Or anywhere else."

Fey looked down at himself and picked a chunk of scales off his arm. He didn't even want to know what was in his hair and feathers. "Do you have water?" He could have tried summoning a small rainstorm, but this close to the ocean, it might end up volatile enough to destroy a few buildings. If it even worked.

Duaia had no such reservations. Magic pooled around her before a large bubble of water formed between them.

Fey expected her to dump it over his head in a mockery of a shower, but she surprised him as the bubble elongated and swirled around him like a funnel. It started with his hair and moved down his body, the clear water quickly turning murky. When it reached his talons, she guided it away and over the buildings, leaving him far cleaner, though still in need of a proper scrubbing; he could feel the tacky blood splatters still stuck to his cheek.

He glanced at Zaos and raised an eyebrow.

For some reason, the elf found that amusing. He grinned and waved a hand towards the palace.

Fey glanced at Duaia when she fell into step beside him, but she didn't speak until they'd left Zaos and the guards behind.

"This is all because of the strange magic fluctuations, isn't it," she said. "Something happened when you broke free of the ley lines, and now a creature not seen in Ages finds our city."

He wasn't surprised she could sense the tears and the fae magic flooding from them. As a sorceress, her affinity for all the elements would be far stronger than most. "Yes. The veil has torn open in several places across the realm." There was no way to tell how many creatures had come through the tears. He didn't sense one in the city, but for any that had opened in the Wound, this city was the largest source of food nearby. "The snakes likely found an underground path through the roots."

Duaia frowned and glanced away, towards where the large building of iron and silver was visible over the other buildings. "I guess we shouldn't tear it down now."

"No," he agreed. They would likely need it in the days to come.

She leveled a heavy stare at him and stopped walking, and he returned it in silence. "You will do what you can to fix the veil?"

"Yes," he said, tensing as the magic of a promise snapped into place inside him.

Fuck.

Chapter 7

VESRYN HEARD about the giant snakes from nearly every guard or
noble he passed in the morning. By the time he reached the kitchens,
two snakes had multiplied to a dozen, all the size of a young ylren tree
or bigger, with fangs longer than a full-grown elf. All slain by a winged
fae in the cloak of night.

He grabbed a piece of fruit and a chunk of warm bread for breakfast.
He was tempted to seek out Fey and get the true story, but a wide-eyed
Synne accosted him before he even made it back to the stairs. Kithiel and
Elwin lingered nearby, looking unconcerned enough to calm the sudden
spike of Vesryn's nerves.

"Where's the trouble?" he asked.

"No trouble. I've been looking for you."

He narrowed his eyes, suddenly wary. "Why?"

Synne gave him a brilliant smile that didn't fool him in the least.
"The clothier arrived, and I'm terribly busy with the frantic nobles and
snakes and butchers. Could you show the clothier to Fey, please?"

Vesryn knew full well how futile it would be to ask what her
intentions were, so he stifled a sigh. "Of course."

He finished his breakfast as she led him to a nearby sitting alcove
where the clothier was waiting. "Elina," he said, pleasantly surprised. She
was a feline beastkin and sister to Elwin. She was also one of the most
popular clothiers in the kingdom. Last he'd heard, Elwin was boasting
how she had a waiting list long enough to keep her busy through the next
two seasons.

Elina smiled and stepped into a quick embrace before peeking
around Vesryn and pointing an accusing finger at Elwin. "Mother wants
to know why you haven't visited," she said, picking up a large bag that
Vesryn knew was spelled to hold far more than its size suggested.

"I've been busy," Elwin replied.

Vesryn snorted softly when Elina didn't look convinced. "Shall
I show you to our guest?" he suggested before they could get into an
argument.

"Yes, thank you." She slipped her arm through his as Vesryn guided her upstairs.

Once they were away from the others, she tightened her arm around his with a soft, high-pitched sound of excitement. "This is such an honor. I can't believe Princess Calaesynne requested me. Have you met the fae yet?"

"I've spoken with him."

"And?"

And he was completely at Fey's mercy if he decided to invoke Vesryn's name. He still wasn't sure if that was likely to happen or not. Fey had seemed more scared than anything when he'd left Vesryn kneeling in the gardens, which had been a blessing. He'd expected some kind of test to make sure he'd given his true name, but he hadn't been prepared for his body's reaction to being ordered to his knees. Despite the fear of being controlled, heat had flooded through him with embarrassing swiftness.

And when Fey immediately ran, Vesryn had been left there, kneeling on the cold ground, confused and relieved and irritatedly aroused.

Elina poked his arm. "What's he like?"

Vesryn forced a teasing smile. "I'd hate to ruin the surprise."

She shook her head but didn't press further.

When they reached Fey's room, he knocked twice, then tapped his fingernails against the door to make sure he got the fae's attention.

The door swung open from a sharp tug, and Fey looked at him in clear dismay.

Vesryn couldn't help his grin, glad to return some discomfiture. "I've brought someone to make your clothes."

"May the Wilds keep you. I'm Elina," she said with a polite bow of her head.

Surprise flickered over Fey's expression before he stepped back and opened the door for them. "Wilds keep you," he said. "Call me Fey."

Vesryn followed Elina inside and wondered if his name was some kind of jest. He still couldn't hear a difference between it and fae. He propped himself against the wall with his arms crossed, watching as she pulled out bolts of fabric in dozens of colors and designs and leather, most in various shades of brown, black, and gray, from her bag.

Once they were all set out in overlapping piles on top of the low table by the sofas, she turned to Fey. "These are only some of what I have available. If none are to your liking, I can retrieve others."

It was almost amusing when Vesryn glanced at Fey to see him frozen as if in shock, until he realized this was likely the first time in recent memory that Fey had ever had clothes made specifically for him. He pushed off the wall and moved to the table, lightly dragging his fingers over the fabrics before resting on a supple leather dyed in blue like the ocean in a storm. "Try this one."

"Wonderful choice," Elina said, spreading the leather out. "Do you have a preference for style?"

Fey shook himself out of his stupor and stepped closer. "Something without sleeves. Easy to move in. With a pocket on the inside," he said, tapping his chest over his heart. He eyed the color choice, and Vesryn took it as a good sign when he didn't reach for a different one. He pointed to a sturdy black fabric. "Loose pants with that, but the bottom of the leg snug."

Then he picked through the leather, testing thickness and flexibility before setting aside a thick light gray one. "Bracers." He set a thinner black on top of it. "Long strips that I can use as a wrap in place of gaiters."

"Of course." Elina pulled out a thick book and flipped through pages of sketches. "Usually I would design something specific to your tastes, but the princess mentioned you would need this quickly," she said without looking up. She stopped on a page and turned the book around so they could see. "Something like this?"

The sketch was a simple sleeveless tunic in an older style, with a loose collar and only a few fasteners over the chest. The lower quarter hung open for utmost flexibility, if not protection.

Fey tilted his head as he studied it before nodding.

Vesryn raised an eyebrow. "That's going to be cold." He wasn't sure how cold the Wound would get when winter set in, but it would certainly be colder than Ylrendorei, where the warmth of the south seas offered some buffer against the cooler weather.

Elina waved a hand at him with a smile. "I can have them enchanted for warmth." Then she pulled out a smaller book, flipped to the first empty page, and scribbled notes, before looking through the sketches again. This time she stopped on a pair of pants that were loose and bulky around the thighs, before shrinking tight near the ankles. "I can make these shorter."

"Yes," Fey said.

Elina marked them down then pulled out a long string. "I'll need to take your measurements," she said before eyeing Fey's wings. "May I ask how you accommodate your wings when dressing?"

"They don't get in the way."

Her eyebrows rose, but all she said was "Oh" and lifted the string. "May I?"

Fey stared at the string for a moment as if he expected it to turn into a snake, before letting out a soft, resigned sigh. "Yes."

Vesryn poked through the fabrics and leathers as he watched them from the corner of his eye. He saw no evidence of a fight, with giant snakes or otherwise. Whether Fey had been injured or not varied according to the one telling the story.

He cleared his throat, straightening as Fey turned his attention to him. A strange shock like lightning tingled through his nerves as he met the fae's eyes. "There's gossip about you slaying a dozen snakes last night."

Fey frowned. "There were only two."

"Only two. Were they also only the size of a ylren sapling?" he asked dryly.

When Fey didn't answer, Elina said, "I heard they were large enough to provide more meat than a full fishing vessel."

Vesryn looked Fey over again, still seeing no sign of injury. "How did you kill them?" Fey lifted a leg and flexed his talons in answer, and Vesryn found himself unable to look away. He had found them as fascinating as the fae's wings when he'd perched on the back of Vesryn's chair, but knowing they were sharp and strong enough to kill a giant snake was like being ordered to his knees all over again. And he hated that he didn't hate it.

He looked away, focusing on the pile of fabrics until he found one in a deep red. It was silky soft to the touch, and he lightly rubbed it between his fingers as he waited for Elina to finish. He wanted to leave before the situation in his pants became worse, but he couldn't abandon Elina, even if he was sure Fey wouldn't harm her.

Finally, she stepped away and scribbled notes in her book, then looked at Vesryn. "What about you?"

"What about me?"

"The princess said I was to ensure you both had new clothes."

"I don't need any."

"Oh good," Elina said with a roll of her eyes. "I'll simply tell her that you declined my services, shall I?"

Vesryn winced. "No."

She snapped her string with a smug smile. "Then spread," she ordered.

Vesryn stifled a groan and held his arms out, letting her take his measurements. He glanced at Fey when he stepped closer and looked through the fabrics, before picking out the red Vesryn had been admiring.

"When can you have them finished?" Fey asked.

"Tomorrow evening. I was instructed to make them my sole priority."

"I'll plan to leave the next day, then."

Vesryn sucked in a breath, feeling like he'd been doused with freezing water. Even though he'd known this was coming, he'd expected to have more time. He wasn't ready. He doubted he would ever be ready.

By the time Elina finished and packed up her supplies, Vesryn was nauseous, his stomach twisting in on itself. He walked her to the stairs, where she patted his arm and stepped away.

"I'm fine from here. Are you all right?"

He smiled through the numbness. "I'll be fine," he said, grateful for the lack of ache beneath his ribs. He may not be fine for days or weeks, and may not stay fine after, but it wasn't a lie. Considering he was at Fate's mercy, that was all the reassurance he could expect.

WHEN THE knock on Vesryn's door came that evening, he expected Zaos, but he found Julius there instead. His already tight stomach twisted with more dread as he stepped back to let the Seer in.

Julius clasped his arm and squeezed, then remained standing as Vesryn closed the door. He looked tired, his green eyes pale enough they almost appeared white.

"What have you Seen?"

He focused on Vesryn with a tight, brief smile. "Too much…." He hesitated, letting out a slow breath. "Everything is about to change," he said quietly, a gentle thrum of power beneath his words. "But you will endure."

Vesryn knew enough about Seers from watching Julius grow up to know there was rarely any comfort to take in his words, and if Julius felt he needed to hear them, he would likely get to a point where he would need to remember them.

"For how long?"

"Until you can't."

He let out a humorless laugh, wondering why he thought that answer would be different. He blinked as Julius stepped close and pulled him into an embrace, swallowing hard as he returned it. "Why does it feel like I won't see you again?" he whispered.

Julius tightened his grip before stepping back, resting his hand on Vesryn's shoulder. "I can't clearly See that far." An irritated scowl touched his lips before he shook his head. "This almost feels like Aster and Justice all over again," he said, rubbing his eyes. "Thankfully the future isn't blank, but you do play a part in stabilizing it."

"And yet you can't tell me how I'm supposed to do that."

Julius offered a wry smile. "I'm sorry."

Vesryn shook his head. "I know the risks. Giving someone enough information for them to act on it can tip everything the wrong way." When Callith learned of Julius Seeing Synne taken by an assassin and went to his mother, the queen confronted the man herself and was killed. Callith still carried that guilt, and Vesryn didn't want that for himself.

Julius stepped back and looked around the sitting room. Most of Vesryn's belongings were in the spare room, all the various items collected through the centuries. Like the several lopsided vases and plates from when he and Zaos tried their hands at pottery. But most of his books and some art pieces lined the walls of the sitting room.

Julius' gaze lingered on the few bottles of wine. The same touch of magic filled the air as he turned back to Vesryn. "Don't forget to take the ylren wine."

Vesryn wanted to ask how he'd know when to use it, but a familiar pinched expression stopped him. He knew Julius' visions tended to cause headaches, sometimes severe enough that he would fall unconscious, though as far as he knew, that hadn't happened in years. "I won't," he said instead.

He was still relearning how to quickly access his personal hollow of magic, but it got easier each time he reached for it. He'd spent that morning going through all the items he'd had stored there three hundred years ago. He didn't recall ever collecting seashells, but at some point, he'd apparently tried to gather every shell to wash ashore. He certainly couldn't remember what he'd collected them for, but he intended to sneak into Zaos' room in the morning and scatter most of them under his sheets and inside his pillows. Once he did that, he'd have plenty of room for the ylren wine, clothes, some books, and what supplies Faelan had gathered for him.

Whatever he had to leave behind would go to Zaos, or whoever became his permanent replacement on Synne's guard.

Julius nodded and studied Vesryn long enough that he knew there was more, and that he wouldn't like it. Even if Julius' words were vague, they rarely promised anything to look forward to. Who needed a warning about something good?

"You're the foundation," Julius said quietly. "For everything to come."

Vesryn grimaced. "That's too much to expect of one person."

"Two," Julius said firmly, squeezing his shoulder. "Fate bound you for a reason. You both are needed. And you shouldn't be unarmed." He unfastened the sheath around his thigh and handed it over.

Tucked inside was a simple blade, a long dagger rather than a sword like Vesryn was used to, but it was a welcome gift all the same. New weapons were in as short supply as food, though with the Wound no longer threatening their borders, he was sure the city would be thriving again within a few years.

Julius hesitated like he wanted to say more but couldn't find the words. Instead, he clasped Vesryn's arm and left. He only made it a few steps before he turned back. "The wine is for your darkest hour," he said, the weight of power in the words raising bumps of flesh on Vesryn's arms. "Not before."

Vesryn swallowed hard and nodded, gripping the door to keep himself upright. He watched Julius disappear down the hall and then the stairs, and still felt like he would collapse if he tried to move.

"I'll be fine," he whispered, closing his eyes with a shuddering breath when the words were true. No definitive time. No duration. No expectation of before or after. At some point in the future, he would be fine.

He would be fine.

<h1 style="text-align:center">Chapter 8</h1>

Fey's clothes and a bedroll were delivered late the next afternoon in a wrapped package, with a smaller box tied with ribbon. When he opened the box, he found small circles of soap in various scents, some soft sea sponges, several bottles of oil, and two bottles of fragrance. One was sharp like spices and made his nose itch. The other had a gentle wood scent, a blend of ylren and dawntree, with a floral undertone that reminded him of home. He closed his eyes as he breathed it in before rubbing a tiny drop between his wrists.

He placed everything back into the box and set it aside before spreading out the clothes. Then he stepped back to stare at everything laid out across the bed, amazed that Elina had completed them so quickly. He rubbed the supple leather shirt between his fingers before carefully dressing. His wings flickered to insubstantial shadows as he pulled it on, the back of the shirt rearranging with a touch of magic to sit comfortably between and around the base of his wings. The pants were snug in the waist, billowing around his knees and thighs and tightening around the top of his calves.

When he picked up the bracers, the dim light of the sunstones highlighted the subtle design of feathers pressed into the light gray leather, and the shape of them curved like wings over his arms. The thin strips of black leather wrapped easily around his calves, and a buckle helped ensure they stayed secure.

Fully dressed, he retrieved the handful of ylren seeds he'd finished collecting from all the trees. When he tucked them into the pocket on the inside of his shirt, they immediately tapped into his magic, drawing it into them to remain viable and grow stronger.

In this realm's First Age, the ylren trees had been planted alongside the thrones to tap into the ley lines. To keep the thrones stable until they were occupied. Hopefully, a ylren tree alone would suffice if he couldn't figure out how to create a new Wild Throne.

A knock at the door stopped him on his way to the balcony. He glanced at his finger, but his Fate string wasn't stretching through the door. When he opened it, he found the Seer standing there. He tilted his head and stepped back to let the elf inside.

"I have your supplies," Julius said, holding up two skins of water in one hand and a cloth pouch in the other.

When Fey opened the pouch, he found a wrapped stack of dried basilisk meat, the sun magic used to dry it so quickly still clinging to it, and several smaller pouches filled with seeds. Each pouch was labeled with the name of a fruit or vegetable or, in the case of the fae plants, with a rough sketch of the fruit it produced.

"Is that truly all you need?" Julius asked.

Fey tucked the water and seeds away with the rest of his supplies. "Unless you know of something I'm forgetting."

Julius' lips twitched, not quite amused but resigned. "I do need to ask for seeds in return," he said, and Fey managed not to scowl.

He'd found less than three dozen viable seeds and hated to lose any of them, but he knew Julius wouldn't be asking if he hadn't Seen the need. "How many?"

"At least seven. But hopefully none will be needed."

He collected the seeds from his pocket and held his hand out to let Julius pick the ones he needed, unsurprised when he took six of the largest ones with the most vibrant glows. In return, Julius held out an empty seed pouch.

Fey put the remaining ylren seeds inside it and tucked it back into his shirt pocket.

"As much as you don't want to admit it, you *are* bound to Vesryn for a reason." Julius met his gaze and held it for a long moment before ducking his head in a polite bow. "Wilds see you through your journey."

Fey watched him leave before noticing the princess lingering nearby. He'd almost forgotten his promise to her. "You decided on your question?"

Calaesynne smiled and stepped closer. "Yes. Juls said I should ask now if I wanted an answer."

He glanced after the retreating elf, wondering just how much he could See. He'd never met a Seer himself, but the more powerful ones tended to rival even Fate's abilities. "And?" he asked, turning his attention back to the princess.

"Is it true fae aren't born like elves or humans or most other creatures?"

Fey blinked at the odd question, waiting a moment to see if she would ask for specifics, but she remained silent as she watched him expectantly. "Yes." When he said nothing more, he saw the moment she realized her mistake. "Wilds keep you," he said, closing the door before she could beg for more information. Discussing fae propagation was the very last thing he'd ever want to do.

He stepped away from the door with a sigh. He would need to leave soon. Tonight or in the morning. He had everything he would need, even a spare set of clothes like the ones he wore and an extra cotton shirt in a loose style like the sleep shirts he'd been using. He'd gathered all the viable ylren seeds. There was no reason for him to linger, especially with the risk of something else coming through the nearest tear and finding its way into the city.

Duaia and Zaos might be enough to protect the city for now, but there were things far more dangerous than a basilisk or cobra, and it wouldn't be long before the fae courts started sending scouts through. He'd rather deal with a hundred snakes than another fae.

The sooner he left, the safer the realm would be.

That decided, he gathered the rest of his new clothes and the box from the bed, tucked them away with everything else, and stepped out onto the balcony. The sun would set soon, but he could see well enough in the dark. The only things left were to ensure Vesryn didn't follow him and to try to call on his wild magic again. He wouldn't get far if he couldn't turn the seeds Julius had given him into food. He had the honey he'd saved, but that would last a week or two at most.

He glided down to the gardens and landed near some wilting flowers. He could sense their seeds and potential for life in them, and he hoped regaining use of his wings was the last piece needed to reach his Wild Court magic. He crouched in front of a plot of herbs and reached for some lavender, still valiantly holding on.

The tiny seeds tingled in his palm as he reached for his magic. With a slow exhale, he nudged them into blooming. Wild magic pooled around his hand, ensuring water, light, and nutrients were available as the seeds cracked open and sprouted.

A soft laugh of relief escaped him as he tipped forward onto his knees. Wild magic swelled up inside him, filling him with the power to call on the rains and the winds, on the fires deep inside the earth. His magic wasn't complete, he could still feel the void where his fae magic should be—the innate magic unique to nearly every fae—but this was enough.

He cradled the lavender in his palms as the sprouts grew into full plants, flowered, and wilted, dropping several new seeds in their place.

With a breath, he dispelled the magic and scattered the seeds in the flowerbed for the next season.

That done, he turned his attention to Vesryn. He lifted into the air and flew to the elf's balcony, where he rapped his knuckles against the doors.

There was a sound like books dropping to the floor and a curse before Vesryn yanked the doors open with an expression of annoyance. "Yes?"

"I am leaving," he said, ignoring the twist of something like guilt in his chest when Vesryn paled. He knew the elf belonged here, but because of Fate's interference, Vesryn thought he had to venture across the Wound and leave his home behind. "Vesryn Rydel, you will not follow me."

Vesryn sucked in a sharp breath, his shock vanishing and his verdant eyes darkening with his anger. "What?" he snarled, drawing himself up to his full height.

Fey hadn't noticed before that Vesryn was tall enough that he needed to tip his head to look up when they were standing so close. "Wilds keep you," he said, stepping back and hopping onto the railing.

"Wait," Vesryn said, but Fey ignored him. He had nothing else to say.

He tipped forward and spread his wings, letting the cool wind catch him and lift him higher into the sky. Instead of circling the tree and returning to his own room, he turned for the wall of the city. And the Wound beyond it.

He heard Vesryn shouting and cursing behind him, but he'd made his choice. There was no turning back now.

He passed the wall, the Wound stretching out in front and to both sides of him as he left Ylrendorei behind. He reached out to the fae magic slowly filling the void his death had caused. There was a tear to the east, the flow of power far greater in that direction. It was out of the way, but there was no point in saving a realm from chaos if creatures killed everyone instead.

He turned towards the rush of magic, tipping his face into the warmth of the sinking sun. Without the scents and sounds of the city and the press of thousands of lives around him, he realized he was truly alone for the first time since he could remember. With no chance of anyone learning his name, much less using it against him.

He pulled his wings in and dipped into a spin, catching himself close enough to the ground that he could drag his fingers through the short grasses taking root there. The future of the realm might be in his hands, but for the first time in Ages, he was finally free. Doing what he'd been born to do: keeping the balance of magic.

Was that what his purpose had been? He still couldn't remember much before the moment he'd given his name to that human. He knew he hadn't been close in line for the throne, and he'd never wanted to rule. Even now the thought of wearing a crown and sitting on the Wild Throne filled him with dread.

He only felt truly himself when he was flying, with the wind rushing through his hair and over his feathers. The warmth of the sun on his face, or the gentle light of the moon silvering the edges of his wings. As the sunset began to fade, he was sure that this was where he belonged.

CHAPTER 9

Vesryn snarled as he slammed the doors of his balcony before stalking down one side of his sitting room and up the other. He kicked aside the books he'd dropped when Fey's knock had startled him.

"You will not follow me?" he mocked with a sneer. "Fucking fae." The next time he saw the bastard, and he knew he would because the Fate string was still there, he was going to pluck every single black feather out of his wings and use them as pillow stuffing.

By the Wound. What in fucking darkness was Fey even thinking? Ordering Vesryn not to follow was pointless. He knew he couldn't stay. He'd already accepted the fact that he would leave here. Whether Fey was trying to protect him or deny Fate didn't matter.

Vesryn wasn't going to risk Fate dragging him into the Wound by force, but did he need to leave now, or could he wait until morning? He didn't have wings. He wouldn't be able to make it far before dark, and the thought of wandering the Wound at night made him shudder. Especially after giant snakes had found their way into the city. What else was lurking out there, waiting for an unsuspecting elf to become its next meal?

He sank onto his couch and slumped forward, pressing the heels of his palms into his eyes until he saw spots of colors.

He was doomed. Utterly and completely.

Venturing into a wasteland hadn't been a terrible idea when he thought he'd have company, but alone? That was unbearable. And who knew how long it would take to catch up to Fey, if he even could. How long would the magic that compelled him to obey last? Would Fey fly the entire way? Vesryn had no hope of walking that kind of distance on his own; he barely remembered any survival skills he'd learned. The supplies Faelan had given him would run out within weeks, if not days.

He slid his hands into his hair and curled his fingers tight, focusing on the bite of pain to control his breathing.

He would be fine. Eventually. Even if only for a moment, or sometime in the distant future, he would be fine.

The knock on his door was a welcome distraction. "Enter," he called, looking up as Zaos came in, his brow creased with worry.

"I heard Fey was seen flying into the Wound."

"He left," Vesryn said, slumping against the back of the sofa. "He came here to order me not to follow him."

Zaos raised his eyebrows before frowning. "He used your name."

Vesryn laughed and let his head fall back against the cushion. "I thought if I gave him my name, he would control me. Make me do something horrible like he'd been forced to do. I never thought he would use it to leave me behind."

Zaos sat next to him and blew out a loud breath, and Vesryn let himself tip to the side until he was resting his head on Zaos' shoulder. "Why don't we leave together?" Zaos asked softly.

"What? You can't leave." There was no way Duaia would be able to manage everything by herself, and there weren't many battlemages in the city. Certainly none as skilled as Zaos. Vesryn saw Zaos rubbing the base of his pinky, a habitual gesture he was prone to from time to time. Except Vesryn realized that was the exact spot that a Fate bond would attach to.

"No," he said, sitting up to face Zaos. "How long?"

Zaos winced and looked away. "Do you remember when we were young and I left one morning, making my way east?"

"You made it all the way to Syll Taesi before anyone found you."

"I was following my string."

Vesryn stared in silence, at a complete loss for words. Finally, he managed a rough, "You've had a Fate string your entire life, and not once ever thought to tell me?"

"It's not like that," Zaos said quickly. "I thought they died."

"*What?*"

"I stopped in Syll Taesi because the string disappeared. It flickered and then it was… gone." Zaos shook his head, rubbing the base of his finger again. "For years I thought they'd died. But then it came back around the time we went into the academy."

Vesryn remembered. Zaos said he'd fallen ill. "You disappeared for a week."

"I followed it, but it disappeared again before I could get much further than the eastern border. Every ten years, it returns for a week or so before it vanishes again."

"How is that even possible?"

Zaos shook his head. "It shouldn't disappear unless they die, but some kind of spell could mimic death," he said, though he sounded doubtful.

Vesryn looked at Zaos' finger. "It's there now?"

"No." Zaos let out a slow breath as he flexed his fingers. "But if the pattern holds true, it should appear this spring."

Vesryn shivered at the strange ripple of realization that passed over him. What were the chances of the Wound being restored the same year that the connection returned? That a fae appeared to restore a stolen throne? "And you want to be as close as possible to where it leads when it does. Do you know where?"

"Fairly certain, yes. It always reaches up, as if into the mountains to the far east."

He slumped into Zaos' shoulder again with a grumbled, "Were you planning on coming with me this entire time?"

"Maybe."

Vesryn snorted and pinched Zaos' arm. "Thank you for telling me."

"To be fair, I told you before, but you were far more drunk than I thought you were."

He closed his eyes with a groan. "The first time you gave me siren brew?"

Zaos laughed. "How did you guess?"

"The only times everything went black and I have no memory are the two times I drank it." He reached for Zaos' hand, lightly tracing his thumb across the base of his little finger where the string should be. He couldn't believe Zaos hadn't told him while he was sober. He might have tried to keep his own string appearing a secret, but he hadn't made it even two weeks. He couldn't imagine keeping that kind of secret for centuries. Of not knowing if your bonded was dying over and over again or if they were trapped in some kind of malicious spell.

No wonder Zaos hadn't been bound to the fae. His skills were needed elsewhere.

"Are you packed and ready to go, then?" Vesryn asked, biting his lip against a grin. He'd barely escaped Zaos' room earlier without someone seeing him.

"You mean despite the hundreds of tiny shells that nearly got stuck in my ass?" he replied dryly, and Vesryn gave up trying to hold back his laughter. "By the Wound, you are such a dick. Your fae is going to stab you before he ever reclaims his throne."

Vesryn scoffed. "He'd have to come within reach of me first," he muttered, tensing when he caught Zaos' knowing grin. "What?"

"You didn't deny he's yours."

He scowled and looked away, glad that he'd never been pale enough for a flush to be obvious, but Zaos knew him well enough to notice it anyway and snickered.

"You like him."

"I would have to spend more than an hour with him to know that."

"Fair enough," Zaos conceded with a chuckle. "But at least you find him intriguing, yes?"

"Why do you care?"

"Because if Fate bound you to someone you despise, what hope do I have?"

Vesryn turned to him with a frown, but Zaos flicked a dismissive hand before he could say anything.

"Not everyone can be so lucky as our king. Those three were made for each other."

Vesryn glanced at the shimmer of red around his finger. He couldn't deny much of his apprehension had faded when Fey left him kneeling in the garden. He hadn't simply turned and left—he'd fled, as if afraid. Though he still wasn't sure if it was fear of Vesryn or fear of himself. Either way, he was sure his name at least was safe with Fey, but anything more was a risk. No matter how attractive or intriguing the fae was, he doubted he would have the chance to find out.

He was convinced he'd die of thirst somewhere in the Wound, long before he ever caught up to the bastard.

CHAPTER 10

THE WOUND was depressingly void of magic. Fey had known it would be bad, but stepping foot on the first truly barren land he found was like stepping on a cursed grave. Cold like a hungry abyss, eager to devour anything that crossed its path.

Even with the tears bleeding fae magic into the realm and wild magic no longer being restrained, it would take close to an Age to return the Wound to its former splendor. The vast plains of flowers and sweet grasses. Woods with floors of pale red moss and tiny silver fireflies that glowed bright enough to be visible even at high sun. The marshes with the blue-skinned nymphs. The tiny burrowing creatures with soft gray pelts and large ears.

He remembered one of the shadow kings dragging him along on one of his many warpaths along the western coast. The salty air and giant waves crashing against black sand and sheer cliffs. The height had been dizzying, and he'd tried slipping off the edge a few times, but there was always a guard ready to grab him and haul him back.

There'd been a cove where a song of sirens lived. The king had ordered a slaughter, taking their scales and fins to add water magic to his shadows. Thankfully, that king hadn't been particularly talented, and he'd depleted all of the scales without mastering any new spell.

He remembered all that with disturbing clarity, but nothing from before. There were hints of hazy memories trying to surface, but nothing vivid. He told himself it didn't matter. He didn't need his name or his past to seal the tears or restore the throne. Even if he could remember, he was sure that kind of knowledge was never something he'd been privy to.

If he was truly meant to create a new throne, he would find a way when the time came.

FEY FOUND the first tear on his second day in the Wound. It shimmered in the air like a cut between the realms, magic bleeding both ways, and the land around it was filled with lush purple fairy moss. The entire area was covered in a thin blanket of sparkling pale red dust.

Pixies. Worse than snakes and far more irritating.

He bit back a soft snarl of distaste as he stalked forward. "You do not belong here," he called, nudging some of the snowdrop flowers with his talons. Almost immediately, the air was filled with annoying chittering and the flitting of tiny wings. He hissed as a swarm of pixies formed around him, grinding his teeth as he resisted the urge to swat them through the tear. "Leave!"

"Who is he to tell us to leave?" a high-pitched voice piped up from somewhere above his head.

"Ugly fae," shouted another.

"Hideous!"

"Was it your mother or father who fucked the crow?" another cackled. A moment later, a sharp tug yanked one of his feathers free.

With a snarl, Fey reached into his hollow and pulled out the spear. It might have been far too powerful to use against something like pixies, but it would be a mess either way if they didn't go willingly. "Leave before I rip your wings off!"

The pixies' shouting rose higher, until it was little more than a furious buzzing in his ears. When one of them ripped out a few strands of his hair and one dared steal another feather, he swung the spear.

The spells flared as its aim held true, even against a target so small and quick.

He felt when the spear found its mark with a faint pop of vibration and sound, before the spikes activated, reducing the pixie to a small burst of blood and pixie dust.

The rest of the pixies froze, hovering in the air in shocked silence, before erupting into terrified screeching. Every last one of them flew for the tear, shoving each other in their haste to escape.

Finally the noise faded and he let out a soft huff of relief. "Overgrown mosquitoes," he muttered, retrieving a ylren seed from his pocket. He stabbed the shaft of the spear into the ground as he considered using the pixie blood, but he wasn't sure if that would allow the pixies to continue using the tear. Instead, he cut the tip of his finger, pressed the seed into the drop of blood, and crouched to push it into the ground.

He poured a bit of water over it and added a twist of his magic, then stood and stepped back. He didn't have long to wait for the magic to flare and take root, a long, slender sprout of a ylren tree slowly winding out of the dirt. Once it latched on to the tear and the flux of magic between the realms, it grew faster, thin branches spreading and reaching higher, the trunk expanding until it blocked and then encompassed the tear. It would do nothing to stop the flow of magic between the realms, but it would stop anyone or anything from passing through without destroying the tree.

By tomorrow, the tree should be large enough for even that to prove difficult.

That done, he retrieved the spear and a large clump of fairy moss to scrub it clean.

"You would make things much easier for me if you showed me how to control you," he muttered. Not that he wasn't grateful to have such a powerful weapon at his disposal. It hadn't tried to decapitate him, and it hadn't resisted being used when he drew it against a target, but he'd spent hours cleaning it of blood and bits of scales and flesh after fighting the snakes, and he didn't have that kind of time to spare if he encountered more creatures.

He narrowed his eyes when he felt a ripple of amusement from the spear, along with the sense that the spear wasn't meant to make anything easier.

Once he finished cleaning the pixie residue, he checked the surrounding moss and flowers to ensure no others were still hiding. He found none, but when he reached the edge of the clearing where the foliage gave way to barren earth, he did find side-by-side snake tracks. Two wide, wavy trails leading away from the tear and towards the city.

He walked around the entire clearing and found no other tracks or signs of anything but the two snakes and pixies. He tucked the spear away again and focused on the ebb and flow of magic around him. There was another tear farther to the east, but it felt small enough to ignore for now. He couldn't risk getting distracted by the tears yet. He'd close what he could on his journey northwest, but the rest would have to wait until he restored the throne.

He turned to the north instead, where a much larger tear was threatening to burst open even wider.

CHAPTER 11

EVEN KNOWING they would have to part ways, having Zaos at his side made leaving Ylrendorei easier. But when they woke up after their first night in the Wound, the Fate string that had been reaching to the east the day before was now guiding him north.

Vesryn closed his eyes so he didn't have to see it. There was no going back; he knew that. The city wasn't even visible behind them any longer, and the other smaller cities that made up the kingdom were scattered along the south coast.

"What's wrong?" Zaos asked.

He forced his eyes open to focus on his friend. They'd known each other long enough that he didn't have to say anything.

Zaos clasped Vesryn's arm. "You'll be fine. This is where you're meant to be."

"Yeah," he whispered, wishing he truly believed that. Fate may have chosen him as a puppet, but what happened to the puppets when they were no longer needed?

"We'll meet again," Zaos said firmly, tightening his grip on Vesryn's arm when he tried to pull away. "Say it."

"Zaos—"

"By the Wound, just say it."

Vesryn swallowed hard, twice, before finally managing a soft "We'll meet again." He closed his eyes with a sob of relief when the words held true, pulling Zaos closer and slumping into him. "Fuck," he breathed, wrapping his arms around Zaos in a tight embrace.

"I can't believe you ever doubted that," Zaos said against his hair. "Of course we'll meet again, and I expect you to have properly wooed your fae by the time we do."

Vesryn rolled his eyes and pulled back. "And I expect you to tell only good stories of me to your bonded."

Zaos tilted his head back and forth as if considering. "I don't think I know any."

"That's fine. I'll have plenty to tell them when we meet. I think I'll start with the rabbit."

Zaos glared before he began gathering up their meager supplies. By the time they broke camp, the sun was clearing the horizon.

Vesryn kicked more dirt over their campfire as he lingered, unable to be the one to walk away first.

Zaos gripped Vesryn by both shoulders and gave him a light shake. "May the Sun's light never forsake you."

He nodded and grasped Zaos' arms as he repeated the blessing, and then it was time to go. He watched Zaos turn and continue east, towards the mountains not even visible on the horizon. Then he looked north where his string pointed.

When he finally stepped in that direction, he couldn't take a second step, his entire body seizing up and refusing to continue. It felt exactly like when his body had obeyed Fey when ordered to his knees.

"You absolute fuck," he snarled. The compulsion must not have activated yesterday because he'd been following Zaos, but he didn't have that excuse now, and it worried him that even with two nights of time and distance between them, the compulsion still worked.

He closed his eyes and breathed. There was a way around this. He had to believe that, because if Fate had to get involved any further, it would not be to his benefit.

The Shadow Throne had been far in the northwest, and that would be Fey's destination. He turned a bit more to the west, keeping the reach of the string to his right, and blew out a harsh breath of relief when his body moved without resistance.

He walked for hours without seeing anything. There was nothing but patches of grass and weeds and long stretches of bare, cracked gray dirt. If not for the familiar path of the sun and the Fate string on his finger, he wouldn't know where he was going.

No landmarks. None of the old villages or towns or small lakes that once filled the plains between Ylrendorei and the singing forests to the north. Thankfully, there were also no strange or bloodthirsty creatures, but his fingers still itched for a proper sword. He hated that he'd left it behind, but he hoped Callith would see it as a reminder of Vesryn's loyalty despite walking away from his oaths.

He hoped his king had passed through the Wound safely. That he was still restoring parts of it with Rashi and Haru. Maybe even escaped to the northern forests to meet Rashi's family, or into the icy mountains to meet more dragons. Wherever Callith was, surely it was better than this.

His FIRST day alone in the Wound may have been uneventful, but by the third, he was convinced that he never should have stepped foot past the city walls. Fuck Fate and Her grand schemes and whatever game She was trying to win.

Vesryn was tired and thirsty, and he was starting to chafe and smell. He wanted a shower and his bed and some company, and not even for sex. It was very readily obvious that he'd taken for granted the fact he lived in a community with others he trusted. He'd never wanted for companionship, whether it was someone to share a drink or a bed with, and now he was *bored*. Even the marvel of the recovering Wound had lost its appeal, and the fear of being attacked by snakes or worse faded considerably when he could see to the empty horizon in any direction.

Three days on his own and he was ready to beg Fate to put him out of his misery.

He'd finished the last of his water when he'd stopped to rest at high sun. There were no clouds in the sky or even a hint of rain. If he didn't find a source of water soon, his fears of dying alone in the Wound were sure to come true, and then he would have to choose between haunting Zaos or the fucking fae who'd left him behind to die.

CHAPTER 12

Fey landed and tucked his wings in as he reached a small nexus in the ley lines. Spread out around him was a field of flowers with a spring and a few trees, with another small copse farther away. He could feel the residual light, frost, and nature magic from the elf king and his bondeds. Wild magic was there too, a faint shimmer of the pure white energy unique to unicorns.

He couldn't resist the urge to linger within the echoes of powerful magic, with the sense of elation and peace infusing the spellwork still clinging to the area. It soothed a forgotten piece of himself even as it chafed like an iron collar. He would never find such peace because he didn't deserve it. Like he didn't deserve the Fate bond forced on him.

When he glanced at the string, he expected to find it dimmed with distance. Instead, it shone bright and pure as if Vesryn was there in the Wound. Following him.

With a frown, he lifted into the air and turned, studying the horizon behind him. There, barely visible in the distance, was a moving figure.

He hovered in the air, watching for several long moments, but the figure didn't grow much larger. Still several hours away, then.

"Fucking elf," he muttered. He'd ordered Vesryn not to follow. He'd even made sure to use Vesryn's name to enforce the order. How had he ignored the compulsion? Fey should have commanded him not to step into the Wound at all to ensure this didn't happen.

He landed with an annoyed twitch of his wings. Did he wait for the elf to reach him? There was a tear nearby, but that could wait. He was sure he'd made good progress despite the distance to the few tears he'd sealed already.

He knew he was stalling. Not only here, but by using the tears he came near to avoid traveling directly to the northwest. He knew he needed to restore the throne, to reclaim the wild and shadow magic from human control, but now that he was moving, he dreaded returning.

He'd watched the humans cut out the Wild Throne and burn the first ylren tree to take root in this realm. Rip apart the gardens full of every flower that grew in the fae realm's Wild Court. Been bound and helpless as they used their newfound magic to destroy everyone and everything he called home. He may have finally put an end to Draekor's bloodline, but the damage done by his ancestors was a permanent scar on this realm.

Fey doubted he was strong enough or capable of healing it. Or if he even had the right to try. There'd been no true fae in this realm for Ages. There was no reason for a fae to reclaim the throne. He could restore the balance and then find someone else to claim the throne.

Was that what Fate intended for Vesryn? Why else bind Fey to an elf? Except the elves already ruled the Light Throne. Claiming another would risk the balance as surely as the destruction of another throne.

He should move on before Vesryn reached him, but he knew the elf would surely die if left on his own. This was the first source of water he'd found since leaving the city, and elves couldn't summon rain like he could. He slumped against the tree, glaring at the Fate string.

He would rest and wait, and when Vesryn finally reached him, he could force the elf to turn back. He did not want a Fate bond. He did not want help. He certainly did not want an elf as a companion as he traversed the recovering wasteland he'd created.

His wings rustled as he turned his attention to the clearing, and he dropped his hands to the soft green-blue moss around him. When he closed his eyes, he focused on the thrum of the residual magic in the area.

He flexed his fingers, calling on his wild magic. Air condensed into a tiny storm in his palm, with a dark gray cloud and sparks of lightning that covered his skin in tiny drops of rain. He dispersed it, burying his fingers in the moss instead. The earth beneath him trembled, long fissures cracking it apart and stretching to the edge of the clearing before filling back in. Deeper beneath the earth he sensed the burning, liquid rock, but he didn't dare draw it closer to the surface.

Wild magic answered his call more easily each time he reached for it, but the innate, personal fae magic he'd been born with remained out of reach, much like his name.

With a grumbled curse, he settled against the tree and closed his eyes to wait.

He must have fallen asleep, because he startled awake at the sound of approaching footsteps. He instinctively reached for his spear before he realized it was Vesryn standing in front of him. He squinted against the sunset turning the sky red and gold and opened his mouth to order the elf to return to the city, but the words refused to form.

As Vesryn drew a few steps closer, Fey saw the elf looked horrible and smelled worse. "Do you have water?" Vesryn asked, his voice as rough as his lips were chapped.

Fey offered one of his waterskins, and then the other when Vesryn drained the first. He waited until the elf sank to the ground with a groan to ask, "How are you following me?"

Vesryn focused on him with narrowed eyes. "I was heading northwest where the Shadow Throne used to be."

"Clever," he murmured. Almost as clever as a fae.

"Thank you," the elf said dryly. He took another sip of water before wincing. "Is there a water source here?" He looked around the clearing as if finally noticing the healthy, thriving plants.

Fey nodded to the small spring hidden among the roots of the trees. "There, but water won't be a problem," he said before tensing at the implicit invitation for Vesryn to join him on his journey north. Even if he'd wanted to, he couldn't send the elf back when he looked one wrong step away from death. Not if he was determined enough to come this far despite running out of water.

Vesryn eyed him warily before taking another slow sip. "It won't?"

Fey picked up the empty waterskin and formed a small rain cloud over the mouth of it. Within moments the water overflowed and he dispelled the magic before handing the skin back to Vesryn, who was watching with raised brows.

"I thought you had air magic."

He drew his knee up, resting an arm over the top of it. He was hesitant to share anything about himself with anyone, but he had Vesryn's true name. And who was the elf going to tell out here? "Every fae has an innate magic they are born with, and magic granted to them by their Court."

"And summoning rain is which?"

"Wild magic."

Vesryn sealed the waterskin and leaned back on his hands. "And your innate magic?"

Fey looked away, towards the tear he could see shimmering in the distance. "I don't remember," he said before pushing to his feet. He heard Vesryn scrambling to follow, but he didn't bother to tell him to stay.

He saw the tracks of the unicorn as he neared the tear. He might have hunted it down, but a unicorn was only dangerous when threatened, and the lingering magic of its passing was at least as old as the magic that created the clearing. It could be all the way to the coast by now.

"What the fuck is that?" Vesryn hissed, his footsteps coming to a halt.

"A tear between the realms," Fey replied, circling it. Several things other than a unicorn had come through, the traces of their magic lingering around the tear, but nothing that he could identify. This tear was larger than the others, more than big enough for a girallon and a manticore to pass through together. Big enough that, once he planted a ylren tree, they would need to stay through the night to ensure nothing else came through.

He pulled a seed from his pocket, one of the larger ones that glowed a healthy, shimmery quicksilver. He cut his finger, coated the seed in his blood and magic, and pressed it into the ground. Then he called on a small storm to soak the earth. He waited for the first sprout to break through before turning back towards the clearing.

Vesryn remained standing there, watching the ylren tree grow into a small sapling with his mouth agape. "What in darkness just happened?" he breathed, reaching out as if to grasp Fey's arm before stopping himself.

Fey stepped to the side to ensure there was distance between them. "I planted a ylren tree."

"With your blood."

"How else would you plant one?"

Vesryn opened and closed his mouth like a fish before shaking his head. "Right then," he muttered, eyeing the ylren tree once more before heading back to the clearing. "Are we making camp here?"

As much as Fey hated to stop, the clearing was a nice change from the dirt and rocks he'd been sleeping on. He settled back in his spot against the tree with a resigned sigh. "Yes." He ignored the elf's gaze as he retrieved several pieces of fruit and a strip of dried meat for each of them from his hollow.

Vesryn accepted his share, sniffing both as he settled against his own tree. "You're not going to try to force me back to the city, are you?"

"I should," he muttered under his breath, but when he glanced at his finger, the Fate string was bright and pure, and there was a pulse of satisfaction, as if Fate were there, watching. "No," he said, a bitter bite to his words.

The elf sniffed the snake meat again before taking a bite. "Neither of us wants to be here, but I don't want to die because you keep trying to deny Fate. What am I needed for?"

Fey pulled his legs in. "I don't know yet."

"What was the ylren tree for?"

"To block the tear against more creatures coming through."

"Like the snakes."

Fey nodded, turning a piece of fruit over in his hands before setting it aside. "The tree will allow fae magic to return to the realm but keep creatures from passing through."

"And I'm guessing these tears appeared when you broke free of the ley lines."

"Yes."

"And blocking them is as important as restoring the Wild Throne."

Fey hesitated, looking towards the tear for a long moment before using a twist of magic to dig a small pit for a fire. He knew both were important, but how much effort did he put into finding each tear? Should he go directly to the ruins of the Wild Throne instead? Focus on restoring it before hunting down the tears?

Vesryn waited until the flames caught before pressing further. "Am I here to ensure you don't get distracted by the tears?"

He narrowed his eyes at Vesryn, annoyed that he was likely right. More irritating was the elf's laughter and the impulse to smile in return. He scowled instead, poking the flames until they were large enough to keep the encroaching chill away. "We'll stay here tonight."

"Sure," Vesryn said, shifting closer to the fire as he finished eating. "Now can you summon one of those rain clouds big enough for a shower?"

Chapter 13

Vesryn would never take a hot shower for granted again, though he certainly wouldn't mind using Fey's rain clouds while they traveled. The fae had even controlled the temperature enough that he wasn't freezing by the time he dressed. He'd never been so grateful for enchanted clothing as he was now. His new clothes had kept him warm enough that his lack of sleep was from the uncomfortable ground.

He still expected Fey to order him back to the city. Or maybe he'd wake and find himself alone again. Except he couldn't see the point in that; with the Fate string connecting them, there would be no hiding from him.

He settled on his bedroll and wiggled his toes near the fire. As exhausted as he was, he was all but desperate for conversation. He almost offered to share the ylren blossom wine, but he knew this was nowhere near his most desolate moment. That was a sobering thought. Maybe he would have a far happier life if Fey did send him back to the city. Except Zaos was gone, and if things were truly changing, if a new Age was about to begin, nowhere would be peaceful soon.

The war three hundred years ago was devastating, but if Julius was right, the entire realm would likely become unstable. And if he was truly the foundation for what was to come, he couldn't bear that weight alone.

"What will it take for you to trust me?" Vesryn asked. He'd already given his name; what else could a fae possibly want or need from someone?

"Nothing," Fey said quietly, surprising Vesryn when he continued. "I can't trust you when I can't trust myself."

There was nothing he could say to that, other than the numerous questions he wanted answers to. Instead, he stretched out on his bedroll and turned his attention to the stars. "You could," he offered after a long moment, "considering you know my name. And what do I possibly stand to gain by betraying you? There's no one else here." He certainly had no idea how to create or restore a throne, even if he'd had the magical capacity to do so. Or knew where it needed to be, or how to claim it if it was restored.

He didn't expect an answer, so he didn't wait for one before rolling onto his side to sleep.

VESRYN OPENED his eyes, unsure what had woken him, but with his heart racing as if from a nightmare. He kept still and listened, but the only sounds were the faint howling of the wind and the crackle of the dying fire. Fey was on the other side, sitting propped against the small tree. His eyes were closed, but his breathing wasn't the steady rhythm of sleep.

He closed his own eyes again to get some more rest when he heard it.

"Help me!" Synne's voice echoed from the distance, high with fear.

Vesryn sat up with a curse, reaching for a sword he no longer had as he scrambled to his feet. "Synne!"

He didn't bother with his boots, barely getting untangled from the light blanket before he raced into the darkness. He only made it a few steps before Fey spoke from behind him.

"Vesryn, stop."

He snarled as his body stumbled and froze. No matter how hard he tried to move, his legs remained planted on the ground, his arms hanging uselessly at his sides. "Release me!"

"Please, help me!" Synne yelled again, sounding somehow both closer and farther away.

Fey stepped up beside Vesryn with a confused frown. "What are you hearing?"

"Synne! Either let me go or help her!"

In the distance, Synne screamed, a sharp, high shrill that cut off abruptly.

No! Vesryn choked on a desperate breath and strained against the magic holding him in place until something threatened to snap inside him.

"Stop fighting," Fey ordered, staring at him with wide eyes.

All the tension in his body vanished, but the fear and anger burned hotter, threatening to consume him from the inside. He focused on Fey, whose wings rustled as he took a step back from whatever he saw on Vesryn's face. He tried to hold on to the anger, but it broke when Synne screamed again as if in pain. He sank to his knees and curled forward. "Make it stop," he begged, covering his ears with a sob, though he could still hear her screaming.

He'd failed her. Failed Callith and Julius and Duaia. Cursed the kingdom to fall and crumble to ruin. He shouldn't be the foundation of anything. He didn't even have a functional magical core.

Fate and Julius both had to be wrong to put any trust or hope in him. He wasn't needed. He should just—

He reached for the dagger he kept on his thigh, but his body refused to move, still bound by Fey's orders.

When he glanced up, Fey was gone.

FEY ORDERED Vesryn to stay where he was and not to move, though he wasn't sure the elf could even hear him anymore. He pressed his magic into the compulsion before lifting into the air to get a look at the surrounding area.

He glanced at the elf to make sure he hadn't moved, tightening his grip on the compulsion even further to ensure it held, before flying in the direction the elf had started to run. Towards the tear and the small copse of trees beyond it.

There was a handful of creatures he thought it could be, but most of them required large bodies of water to live. There was little of anything beyond the clearing—some scattered bushes and tall grasses, but no pools of water anywhere he could see.

A quick glance at Vesryn showed him facing the trees more than the tear, so he flew closer and circled them. There was magic here, but it felt like nature magic. Something the elf king's fox might have created before they moved on.

He landed nearby and studied the trees, but he didn't see anything out of the ordinary. Six, seven trees. Grass. No flowers or moss. He reached for his spear anyway, but it evaded his grasp and he cursed. When he tried again, he snatched the sword instead. "What good are you going to be?" he muttered, eyeing the dull and rusted blade, the chips along the edges. But it would have to do.

"You do not belong here!" he called, stalking along the edge of the trees. Instinct told him not to step within their circle. "Show yourself!"

Nothing new had come through the tear; he was sure of that. Whatever was affecting Vesryn, it had been there before either of them arrived. Had been watching them, waiting for its chance. With a snarl, he swung the sword at the thinnest branch of the nearest tree. Despite the dull edge, it sliced through easily enough.

He stopped and waited for anything to react, but only the faint whistle of a breeze through the branches answered him. "What do you want?" he shouted, slicing another branch off the next tree. "Did Fate send you?" Something new to punish him? To punish Vesryn? He'd accepted the elf joining him; was that not good enough? Vesryn didn't deserve whatever torment he was enduring because of Fey, not when he'd done nothing but try to answer Fate's call.

Warmth seeped into his hand. When he risked a glance down, flecks of embers seemed to be peeling off the sword. Unlike the trees in the clearing, still imbued with enough magic to retain green leaves, these trees were bare, as if the magical void of the Wound had sucked all the life out of them.

Fire would reduce them to ash within moments.

He moved to the next tree, the flames around the sword growing thicker and brighter with every step. When he sliced a branch off, there was still no response, even when both ends caught fire. The flames were tiny and dispersed to smoke before he took another step.

The next tree gave him pause. It was larger than the others, thicker, the wood somehow darker in the unmoving shadows.

Behind him, Vesryn screamed.

Even as Fey turned to look, he knew it was a trap. The crack of splitting and bending wood was loud in the following silence, before Vesryn screamed again, the sound breaking as if ripped from a torn throat. Except Fey could still see the elf where he'd left him, huddled on the ground, just past the light of the fire.

"Fuck," he hissed, fighting the sudden overwhelming need to get to Vesryn. He forced himself to turn back to the trees instead.

"Fey!" Vesryn yelled, his voice thick with pain.

The sword grew hotter in his hand, on the verge of burning, and he focused on the discomfort of it. When he finally tore his attention from Vesryn, he focused on the trees again, only to find Vesryn standing in front of him, a collar of glistening red slowly spreading across his throat.

Help him, help him, help him echoed in his mind to the same rhythm as his quickening heartbeat. But he couldn't. That wasn't Vesryn. Not the real Vesryn.

"You killed me," Vesryn said, stepping closer. His face transformed into others that used to torment Fey's dreams. His parents and siblings, lesser fae of this realm's Wild Court. All killed by his hand. The guilt that should have been there was oddly absent. "You killed us."

"Yes." And he thought maybe he would do it again.

Then the face changed again, to a stranger he knew intimately but couldn't remember. "You killed me."

"No," he whispered. He clutched at his chest, though it did nothing to stop the ache of loss.

The stranger moved forward, reaching a hand out, fingers curled like claws.

Agony pierced through Fey's gut. When he looked down, a long thin branch was sticking out of the side of his stomach.

The illusion in front of him wavered and vanished, and a tree in the vague shape of a two-legged creature stood before him. Its extended arm was the branch that stabbed him. It cracked and snapped in two as the creature moved back, leaving the branch in Fey's side. Then the rest of the tree's branches shifted, each one turning sharp at the end, before they all arrowed towards him.

Fey stumbled back with a desperate wingbeat, narrowly avoiding being impaled again. He ignored the spill of hot blood down his side, gritting his teeth against the pain. "Fuck." A leshy. He'd never seen one up close before. They tended to prefer the dense forests.

He jumped back again to dodge another volley of sharp branches. One clipped his wing with a bright lance of pain as it ripped through, but it still felt functional. He wouldn't last long like this without his spear. "Can you spit flames?" he hissed, tightening his grip on the sword.

The sword responded with a series of pulses that were undoubtedly vile insults.

"Fucking fae weapons," he muttered, throwing himself to the side and snapping his wings out to take flight. He kept low to the ground as he headed for the other side of the trees. He stretched his arm out as he neared one and was relieved when flames instead of flecks of embers engulfed the dry wood.

An enraged shriek echoed from the other side of the copse, so he did the same to the next tree, before stumbling to a stop and catching himself on one knee. The fire caught and spread as his vision swam like when cobra venom filled his veins, but he was certain he wasn't poisoned. It was likely the blood leaking out of him. He could taste it on the back of his tongue.

The flames swirled in front of him, the only warning he had before a sharp, tiny branch whistled through the air like an arrow. It caught against his ear as he reflexively jerked back. His sword arm twitched and lifted as if pulled by the sword, the blade knocking more arrows aside, where they crumbled to ash in midair. Then he reached back and chucked it forward.

The sword vanished into the fire, and Fey cursed as he was left defenseless.

Another shriek rent the air before something heavy crashed to the ground.

Fey staggered to his feet, clutching his side as he made his way around the blazing trees. He found the leshy on the ground with the sword lodged in its chest, spitting fire. He dodged the flailing branches as he moved closer to grab the sword.

He twisted until he heard a resounding crunch and the leshy stopped moving. Its body twitched, and the legs reformed into a single trunk. The only sign it was anything more than a tree was the face above the spread of branches.

He braced himself against the sword for a moment as he gathered the strength to tug it free. The fire in the leshy's chest sputtered out without the sword to feed it.

"Fuck," he hissed, the pain in his side intensifying now that the danger had passed. The short piece of wood stuck in his side was slick and slipped between his fingers when he tried to pull it out. His vision wavered black, and nausea twisted his stomach from the pain, like thousands of splinters were burrowing into his insides. He couldn't help the choked laugh at the similarity to his spear's spikes.

Flames leapt from the sword to the wood, the blood coating it sizzling as it heated and turned to smoke. When he grasped it again, it slid free with a concerning wet squelch. He found himself on his knees again, clutching at the wound and wishing he'd asked for healing poultices, or at least something for pain.

Was he really going to die here? He already felt too weak to make it back to Vesryn. Would the elf even find him before morning? Or would the fire still devouring the trees behind him claim him too?

When the sword pulsed with power, he hoped it would at least put him out of his misery quickly and not insult him again. He wasn't prepared for the white flames that wrapped around him like a folded wing, or the healing magic that poured into the wound. The burn wasn't entirely unpleasant, but he was breathless by the time it faded, leaving him as whole and healthy as he'd been before entering the Wound.

The red jewel dimmed considerably, the restoration spell that had been there gone. Had it really been meant for him, or had he fucked up? They still had a considerable ways to go. Not that there was anything he could do about it now. Healing spells were beyond him, and that had been the most powerful there was outside of resurrection.

"At least you're not as useless as your friend," he muttered, hefting the sword as he pushed to his feet. His lips twitched when the sword pulsed with agreement. Then he turned to the dead tree.

The leshy was far too large to carry or drag, but he wanted Vesryn to see that what he'd heard wasn't the princess. So he set to work cutting out its head. Black ichor spilled from the severed limb with the cloying stench of wet, rotting leaves. He picked up the head by the thin grass-like mass sprouting like hair.

When he turned to head back to the clearing, the jewel in the sword flickered faintly, and he brushed his thumb over it. In response, it flared a bright white gold that felt warm and hungry. He didn't question the instinct to touch the sword to the leshy again. The moment they touched, the corpse ignited like kindling.

He hopped back from the intense heat. Within moments, the leshy was reduced to ash. A breeze picked up and scattered the remains, but a thin tendril of ash swirled around the sword and disappeared into the jewel.

Fey eyed it for a moment before tucking it away with the spear and hefting the head of the leshy. He took to the air and headed back to the clearing.

Vesryn was still sitting where he'd left him as he landed next to the elf. He was slumped forward, fingers bloodless where he gripped his arms, and when he looked up, his eyes were red-rimmed and full of a desolation that resonated with the dark void in Fey's own chest.

He wanted to burn the leshy all over again. As much as he didn't want the elf bonded to him, seeing him hurt was unacceptable. He dropped the head in front of Vesryn. "This is your princess," he said, wincing when Vesryn recoiled as if struck. "It was mimicking her voice. Using your devotion to her to influence you."

Vesryn stared at the ancient face carved into the tree-like flesh. He was silent for a long while before he shuddered and looked away. After another moment, he carefully got to his feet. "Thank you."

Fey scowled and stepped back. "You should never thank a fae," he said, turning back to their abandoned campfire. He poked the flames with a stick, coaxing them back to life.

Vesryn lingered a step inside the touch of light before sinking down onto his bedroll. "Because it means I owe you something in return?" he asked. He smiled faintly when Fey nodded. "That's fine. So long as it's you, I wouldn't mind owing something."

Fey stilled, staring at Vesryn across the flames, sure he couldn't mean that. Fey had done nothing to encourage that kind of reckless trust, and he didn't need it. He certainly didn't deserve it.

"Fey," Vesryn said, meeting his eyes. "I don't know why Fate thought I was the right choice for you, but I trust you with my name. Owing you a favor doesn't bother me."

He hated the way his stomach swooped and twisted. "It should," he whispered, looking away from Vesryn when the elf grinned.

"Are you going to make me strip and dance naked in some intricate fae ritual?"

"You mean sex?" Fey retorted, as surprised by his own words as he was by Vesryn's laughter.

"You have a sex ritual?"

Fey tucked his wings tighter against his back. "We have a few," he managed to get out as he poked the flames again, momentarily mesmerized by how the red sparks seemed to swirl in front of Vesryn like a lazy caress before flickering out.

"Perhaps you'll tell me about them sometime."

He shivered and met Vesryn's verdant gaze for a moment, the heat and interest he found there terrifying despite the answering curl of warmth in his stomach. "Perhaps," he whispered.

Vesryn wiggled his fingers in front of the fire before glancing towards the leshy head, barely visible in the dark. "What do we do with that?"

"I burned the rest of it."

The elf nodded. There was a weak twist of magic before a large flame peeled away from the fire. It danced through the air towards the leshy, where it immediately engulfed it in a brief, intense inferno. Like the rest of its corpse, it was reduced to ash and scattered with the next gust of wind. And like the sparks from the fire, some of the still smoldering ashes swirled around Vesryn before fading from sight.

There was an answering pulse of magic from the sword, as if it were reaching out for Vesryn or the flames and ashes, or both. Before Fey could decide what that might mean, Vesryn scrubbed his palms against his face.

"You may as well get some rest. I don't think I'm going to be able to sleep again."

Fey nodded and stretched out on his side next to the fire. He pillowed his head on a bent arm and closed his eyes. He was acutely aware of Vesryn watching him, but despite the tear nearby and the chance of something similar or worse than a leshy lingering out of sight, he wasn't worried about being attacked.

Somehow, he knew Vesryn would guard him as well as he'd guarded the princess, even without being asked.

CHAPTER 14

Something had changed.

Vesryn couldn't quite say what. Whether it was the fact they were leagues away from any kind of civilization, the only two creatures either of them could rely on, or if it was the aftermath of the leshy. Or the moment of connection the night before.

He knew he hadn't imagined it. It might have been brief and fleeting, but Fey had almost let his guard down. Had *almost* relaxed enough for more than a single slip of personality to show through. And oh, did Vesryn like what little he'd seen.

It wasn't often he found others comfortable enough to say what was on their mind around him. He was old enough to have earned some stature even if he wasn't anywhere near an elder's age, but as one of the few royal guards who had served the previous king and then the princess, most were careful to avoid getting too close to him, in case something they said made it into a ruler's ear. Zaos was one of the few who was comfortable enough to be himself, though it didn't hurt that he also held a high rank in the guard.

Once they'd checked the ylren tree, which had grown several times over in the night, and Fey was satisfied it was large enough to protect the tear, they moved on. Fey alternated between walking or flying, though it was quickly apparent he couldn't fly for long without leaving Vesryn far behind.

Vesryn had expected the fae to do exactly that, to keep as much distance between them as possible, only returning for meals or to camp. But Fey surprised him by flying ahead and lingering long enough for Vesryn to catch up or flying lazy circles above him. When he walked, he kept ahead of Vesryn but remained in speaking range, even if they didn't have much to say.

Rather, Vesryn had plenty to say, but he wasn't sure what would be acceptable and what might push Fey into leaving him behind again. Even if the Fate string made it impossible to lose him completely, he didn't want to wander by himself again. Still, he couldn't stand the silence any longer.

"How long do you think before we get there?" They were heading northwest, though the landscape wasn't changing. He thought he could see a shadow on the horizon that might have been the forests far to the north, but it was likely only storm clouds.

Fey slowed a bit and glanced back at him. "Weeks, most likely."

Weeks. He'd known that was the most likely possibility, but now that he'd had a taste of walking for days, he was not looking forward to weeks. If only he had wings. Or a horse. But supplies were scarce enough in Ylrendorei that they'd maintained only a dozen or so horses at a time. With more and more of the farmland needed for crops for the people, it was a delicate balance to keep enough livestock without starving both.

Now that the Wound was no longer creeping closer to their border and infecting their crops, he expected Afamrail would have a hundred new plots ready for spring planting, even if he had to dig them himself.

"Do you need to rest?" Fey asked.

Vesryn glanced at him with a smile and hoped he didn't look too surprised. "I'm all right." At least he was used to being on his feet for long stretches of time, even if most of that was stationary. "Though if you'd like to carry me while you fly, I wouldn't complain."

Fey scowled at him, though it wasn't so convincing when he flushed, and Vesryn couldn't help pressing his luck.

"Don't tell me that's one of your sex rituals?"

Fey's wings twitched, flexing as if they were about to snap open to their full span, before they tucked in tight again. He didn't answer, but Vesryn caught a glimpse of the tips of his ears and the way they'd darkened.

Vesryn bit his tongue against prying for details, though he couldn't help but wonder how exactly having sex while flying could possibly work. Before he could get too distracted by trying to imagine various positions, Fey stopped and turned towards the east.

He stopped beside the fae, lifting a hand to shield his eyes as he squinted at the horizon, but he saw nothing. "What is it?"

"A tear."

As much as he didn't like straying from their destination, he liked the idea of more creatures like the leshy wandering the Wound even less, especially if they found their way to a city or village. "How far?"

"Not far. We could be there by high sun."

"All right." He glanced at Fey when he didn't move and found him scowling at nothing. "What's wrong?"

"I sense fae."

"Fuck," Vesryn hissed, which was enough to catch Fey's attention.

When he glanced at Vesryn, his scowl twitched towards amusement. "Don't speak your name near them."

"One fae knowing my name is more than enough," he replied dryly, falling into step beside Fey as they headed east. "Do you know who they are?"

"No. If Fate is on our side, it will be someone from the Wild Court."

"And if we're not so lucky?"

"Anyone else."

Vesryn brushed his fingers against his dagger, hoping he wouldn't need it.

By the time they were close enough for Vesryn to feel the magic seeping through the tear, he'd counted seven figures. Tall fae who could have passed as elves if not for the ethereal beauty and exquisite armor and clothing. Even the leather and gold armor seemed to glow with magic so intricately woven into them that it looked natural.

Fey stopped several paces away, and one of the fae moved to meet them, a haughty tilt to his chin and a firm grasp on the sword at his hip.

He stopped in front of them, looking them over with a sneer of disdain. "Crow," he said, spitting the word like an insult. "You are not welcome beyond the veil."

Fey straightened and lifted his chin. "And you are not welcome here."

The sneer returned, and the fae bared his teeth in a mocking smile. A few of the other fae drifted closer, hands on their weapons.

Vesryn tensed, resisting the urge to step closer to Fey. With his wings, moving closer would only hinder them both in a fight.

"You dare defy the Summer Queen?"

Fey tilted his head. "I see no queen here."

"Insolence!" The fae drew his sword, the metal singing as it slid free of the scabbard. "The Summer Court has come to claim this realm's throne. Where is your queen?"

"Dead."

The fae narrowed his eyes. "The king?"

"Dead."

"Who holds the fae throne?"

"There is no fae throne." Fey's wings shivered, and while Vesryn was still learning the various ways they twitched and what they meant, he was sure Fey's otherwise placid expression hid amusement.

The Summer Court fae took a menacing step closer, seeming to tower over Fey despite their similar height. "Explain."

For a moment, Vesryn was sure one of them would resort to violence, but then Fey answered. "The Wild Throne was destroyed."

The fae paled and stepped back, looking across the mostly barren landscape, his eyes wide with horror. "When?"

"Less than a moon ago."

He cursed and turned to his men, barking orders too quickly for Vesryn to follow. The other fae broke into motion, their weapons drawn, and only when they moved towards Fey did Vesryn comprehend that one of the orders had been to seize the crow.

Vesryn wrapped his fingers around his dagger as the first fae closed in. They apparently had no expectation of resistance, because with a quick draw and stab, his blade sank easily into the fae's throat. He pulled it free, tightening his grip against the spill of hot blood over his fingers. When he turned to the next fae, he caught the wide arc of Fey's spear in the corner of his eye, and the fae that crumpled beneath it.

Then he was being pressed by two fae with swords far longer than his own dagger. He spared a quick glance to place the remaining three and found one by the tear as if waiting to retreat, and the leader and the last surrounding Fey.

Vesryn stepped back to keep either of his attackers from getting behind him, then moved in a wide circle to keep Fey and the others in his line of sight for as long as possible. When the two moved for him, it was obvious they were used to fighting together. One focused high while the other went low, and Vesryn was forced back to avoid being sliced in pieces.

He kept moving, deflecting when he couldn't dodge. Blocking when he couldn't deflect. His new bracers absorbed the attacks as if made of mythril rather than leather. He managed a few glancing blows as he parried. He drew blood on one's arm when they pulled back. Left a deep cut on the other's hand with a quick flick of his blade. A bad angle on a block resulted in a sharp stinging gash across his forearm.

He resisted the urge to push an attack even when he saw an opening, getting a feel for their movements as best as he could. But this wasn't a friendly spar. He didn't have long before they would grow impatient.

As one came in, sword lifted to cut him from shoulder to hip, the other quickly rushed behind Vesryn. He didn't have time to hesitate. He dropped his dagger as he lunged forward and down, inside the fae's reach. He grabbed their arm and twisted as he stepped to the outside. Off balance, it didn't take much force to push the fae into continuing forward, into the other fae's attack.

Metal pierced armor in a smooth glide aided by spellwork. Vesryn didn't wait for the surprise to fade. He hooked his dagger with his foot and flipped it into the air. He snatched it before the fae freed his sword and buried his blade in the fae's neck. It wasn't the cleanest attack, but it was one of the quickest ways to ensure they didn't get up again.

Once he was sure both fae were dead, he turned in time to see Fey burying his spear in the leader's chest. The other fae was already on the ground, which left the one by the tear, who was already retreating.

Vesryn snagged the dropped sword beside him, hissing in surprise at the flare of magic burning his skin, and threw it like a lance. The fae disappeared through the tear before it hit, but the sword sailed through after them. He could only hope it found its mark.

"That was reckless," Fey said, coming to stand in front of him.

"Which part?" he asked, smiling when Fey's lips twitched.

Then Fey glanced at the tear with a scowl. He reached into his shirt and pulled out a ylren seed, hesitating before holding it out to Vesryn and dropping it into his palm. "Use your blood."

Vesryn eyed the seed and the faint translucent yellow glow surrounding it with a touch of awe, hardly able to believe such a small thing could produce the largest trees in the realm. "Why mine?" he asked, dragging the seed through the tacky blood drying on his forearm.

"Hopefully yours will keep other fae from being able to manipulate the tear from the other side."

He hummed softly as if he understood, a habit he'd developed while listening to Zaos for hours on end. When he tried to hand the seed back, Fey motioned to the tear, so he moved closer and crouched in front of it. This close, the spill of magic from the fae realm warmed the air with a scent like the palace gardens in full bloom on a hot spring evening.

He swallowed against the sharp twist of longing for home and dug a hole with his thumb before dropping the seed inside, then covered it and stood.

Fey summoned a small storm to water it; then they turned to the fallen fae. There was no sense in not searching them, especially when no one should be able to come through the tear soon.

Vesryn knelt next to one and wiped his dagger clean on a bit of leather before sheathing it. Then he started removing the armor. He didn't recognize the metal, but it looked like a mesh of gold and mythril. Whenever they found a way back to the city, it would certainly fetch some decent coin, for the novelty alone if not the materials. He sensed Fey standing nearby and expected a protest or order to stop, but after a moment, Fey turned to do the same to the others.

When they were done, they had a large pile of armor, a few small bags of coin, five swords and three smaller daggers that only Fey could touch without triggering spells on them, and two bags of supplies with fresh bread, cheese, dried meat, skins of water, and three bottles of wine. The last earned what Vesryn was sure was an excited twitching of feathers.

He stood once they had everything stored away in their hollows. When he glanced back at the tear, the sprouting ylren tree had already grown to cover the lower part of it, so tossing the fae back to their home realm wasn't an option. "Do we bury them?" he asked, turning to Fey. "Burn them? Some fae funeral ritual?" He controlled his smile when Fey narrowed his eyes at him.

"No," Fey said, lifting a hand with a twist of magic. A moment later the ground trembled all around them and cracked open. Two large pits opened up and swallowed the fae, then closed over top of them. Other than the two small mounds and remaining footprints in the dirt, there was no indication they had ever been there.

"That was terrifying," Vesryn said, his voice faint. He was used to seeing Duaia and Zaos work powerful magic, but neither of them had ever instilled in him the fear of being buried alive.

Fey looked almost smug before he began to walk away, heading back towards the northwest.

After a final look around, Vesryn fell into step behind him.

CHAPTER 15

FEY DIDN'T like how reckless Vesryn had been. The Summer Court wouldn't have killed them.

They wouldn't have killed Fey at least. Even if the Wild Court were seen as lesser fae by the other courts, they were still fae. Killing each other outside of declared war had been an archaic practice Ages before Fey was even born.

They may have killed Vesryn, though, and that thought angered him. Vesryn was only here because of the Fate string. He didn't deserve to be targeted by everyone and everything they came across.

Was this another of Fate's attempts to punish him?

Except as he walked, he knew he was as close to lying to himself as he could get. Vesryn's reckless actions bothered him, but not as much as the fact he'd acted to protect Fey.

The Summer Court had been coming for him, not Vesryn. The elf hadn't been protecting himself.

Why? No one had ever protected him before, at least not that he could remember. Most of his life before being enslaved was still fuzzy, but he couldn't believe that the rest of his family didn't try to save him. Except they were fae of the Wild Court. They could have easily taken care of one human, even with Fey under the human's control.

"No one tried to save me," he whispered. His steps faltered as that truth sliced through him. "No one could have saved me," he added softly, though that truth wasn't any easier to hear. He swallowed hard before trying, "No one would have tried to save me even if they could."

Somehow that didn't come as a surprise, but the sharp ache in his chest still hurt.

The contempt from the pixies he'd chased off was to be expected, and even the Summer Court's insults weren't surprising, but he knew they weren't the only ones. Even within the Wild Court, he hadn't been welcome.

Was that why he'd given his name to a human? Because he knew it would lead to his family's destruction? Why couldn't he remember?

"It'll be dark soon," Vesryn called, pulling Fey out of his thoughts.

He stopped and looked up, finding the sun nearing the horizon as it set. Surely they hadn't been walking that long. They had stopped to rest briefly at high sun, but he wasn't tired at all. Then the wind picked up and the chill of the breeze made him shiver before the warming enchantments activated. It was far cooler than it had been. Autumn was giving way to winter, and the days would grow shorter still.

He scanned the landscape for any sign of trees or shelter, but there was nothing. Only barren landscape in every direction. Grasses and weeds were in abundance, and he spotted a few brambles that they gathered for wood.

They found a level area to make camp for the night, and Vesryn waited until the fire was blazing before asking, "Are you all right?"

Fey ignored him as he retrieved one of the packs they'd taken. He pulled out the wrapped flat bread, still fresh enough to be soft, and set it near the fire to warm. The dried meats followed. Then he found one of the bottles of wine and opened it. The sweet, honeyed scent made his mouth water, and he took a deep swallow, his eyes closing in bliss. When he opened them again, he found Vesryn watching him with an amused smile.

"So it's only my wine you don't like?"

Fey licked his lips, warmth suffusing his limbs when Vesryn's gaze lowered to catch the motion. Instead of answering, he offered the bottle.

Vesryn took it, sniffed it, then met Fey's eyes again as he took a sip. He licked the mouth of the bottle with a soft hum before handing it back. "I concede defeat."

Fey grasped the bottle with numb fingers, hesitating a moment before bringing it to his lips again. He knew he couldn't taste Vesryn on the glass, but that didn't keep his ears from burning. When the fire warmed the food enough for the scent of herb-filled bread and meat to fill the air, he pulled out a wrap of soft cheese filled with pieces of tart red berries.

Vesryn moved closer to sit beside him as they filled their bread with the meat and cheese. He drank from a skin of water while Fey sipped more wine.

Maybe it was the wine going to his head or the warmth of the fire and food that should have reminded him of a home he'd never truly had, but he couldn't help asking, "Why did you protect me?"

Vesryn stopped with his arm lifted for another bite. "What?"

"They weren't interested in you until you killed the first one," he said, watching the flames instead of Vesryn.

"Why wouldn't I protect you?" Vesryn asked before taking another bite.

"You could have run."

Vesryn snorted. "That will never happen," he replied. When he paused, Fey glanced over to find a surprised look on his face, though it disappeared when Vesryn noticed him watching. He smiled and winked and finished eating, which Fey found far more distracting than he should have.

He bit into his own bread, though he barely tasted the tangy sweetness of the cheese or the rich smokiness of the meat. The wine made him warm and relaxed, and he knew that was dangerous. Especially when it was only the two of them. He offered the bottle to Vesryn, but he shook his head with a soft laugh.

"I've been warned I shouldn't indulge in wine."

"Why?" he asked, fascinated by the flush spreading up Vesryn's neck.

The elf cleared his throat and tossed a piece of brambles into the fire. Finally he answered. "I'd rather not make a fool of myself."

Before Fey could decipher his meaning, Vesryn stood and spread out his bedroll, then lay down on the other side of the fire. Disappointment was a strange sensation. He couldn't help staring at Vesryn, at the glow of the flames highlighting all his sharp angles. The dip beneath his throat. The strong muscles of his arms and hands. The shirt pulled taut across his chest. The powerful thighs.

As if aware of Fey's eyes on him, Vesryn rolled over to put his back to Fey and the fire, but not before Fey caught the growing bulge in his pants.

And then he was distracted by the broad shoulders and back and the tight leather-clad ass.

He tore his gaze away from Vesryn and glowered at the Fate string instead. The magic thrumming beneath the connection was as annoying as it was insulting. He was a Wild fae, reviled and despised even among his own Court, and Vesryn was an elf. Even if they touched and completed the bond, there little hope of this leading to anything that would last.

He stoppered the wine and put it away before moving back far enough to spread out his own bedroll. He stretched out with his back to the fire. "Pleasant dreams," he said softly, closing his eyes to rest.

THE SUMMER sun was warm on his face, the shadows of clouds passing over where he was stretched out in the sweet blue-green grasses. A pale yellow butterfly trailing flecks of fairy dust landed on the flowers nearby. Somewhere in the distance was the sound of sparring and the rush of the waterfall that fed their streams.

Fey should have been cleaning the stables or tending to the gardens, but the weather was too perfect to waste on chores. Someone called his name, the unfamiliar voice muffled and distorted, and when he sat up, the stranger who approached was shrouded by the sunlight behind them.

Are you happy here?

He snorted quietly, shielding his eyes with a hand as he squinted up at the stranger. Anyone who knew who he was wouldn't care enough to ask that. "No." But where could he go? He wasn't welcome in the fae realm, and he couldn't expect the other races in this realm to treat him any differently. His raven wings were a sign of dark fortune. The only reason he was allowed to stay here was because of his blood ties to the Wild Queen. "Who are you?"

If you want to meet him, give your name to a human.

"Meet who?" he asked, scrambling to his feet as the stranger turned to walk away. "Who are you?" he called, his heart racing. He'd never told anyone about him, the bright fae who haunted his dreams in fantasies too detailed to be anything but memories of a past life.

"Wait!" But the figure was already fading into the distance.

Give his name to a human? That was the most absurd suggestion he'd ever heard. Fae weren't in the habit of giving their names to anyone, even other fae.

Something struck the back of his head, and he spun in time to see two younger fae laughing. They scooped up another rock to throw at him.

"Get back to work, crow!"

"Earn your place or we'll roast your wings!"

Fey snarled and picked up his own rock, but when he stepped forward to throw it, the landscape twisted and changed.

He found himself standing on a cliff overlooking a bloody battlefield. Countless fae were spread out below, cut off from each other and surrounded by a never-ending flood of dark creatures. They seemed made of fire and smoke, with living storms that crackled with sickly yellow lightning inside them. Chaos incarnate.

"We can't win this," he said, turning to the fae beside him.

The Second Daughter of the Wild Queen. She was tall, with hair spun of blue fairy moss and eyes of reflected moonlight, her skin sun-kissed autumn. Two large-pronged antlers stretched from her head, a spiderweb woven around one, sparkling with spots of collected morning dew. A small songbird nest rested in the other, two bright blue eggs tucked inside. "We will win," she said, turning towards him, but her gaze focused past him. "It is already done."

Fey turned then, seeing him, and the relief in his chest twisted into dread.

Bright gold-red eyes smiled at him as the fae approached, though his expression sobered as he looked at the princess. He stopped beside Fey, dipping his head into a respectful nod.

"You are ready?" she asked.

"No." Fear made Fey's breaths short as he gripped the front of the fae's fine leather tunic. "Don't do this."

The fae cupped Fey's cheeks with too-warm hands. "It's the only way."

"It's not," Fey snapped. They could go back to the fae realm. Even if there was nothing there for them, at least they would be alive. They'd be together. There was no need to tame this realm. Let Chaos keep it.

The fae tilted his head with a faint smile. "Do you trust me?"

Fey bared his teeth in a snarl, wishing he could say no. "Fuck you," he hissed instead.

The fae leaned closer until their lips touched, a featherlight kiss full of promises that would never see fruition now. "I will find you again," he said, reaching for Fey's hand that held his spear.

"It will only work if it is both of you," the princess said.

The fae jerked back as if struck, before turning a dark look on her over Fey's shoulder. "That was not part of the bargain."

"The bargain was for chaos to be unraveled. You each hold one side of a balance. The balance must shatter, not be tipped."

Fey closed his eyes as a bitter laugh escaped him. Pawns. That was all they had ever been. Gambits in someone else's play for power. He turned to face the princess, lifting his chin as he spread his wings in a futile attempt to protect his bright fae. "When I return, I'll destroy everything you've built." The power in the promise cracked through him, almost painful with its intensity.

The princess smiled. "But it will have been built. That is all that matters."

If not for the warm arms around him, he may have launched himself at the princess. Instead he lifted his spear and pressed the tip against his own chest. A gentle push was all it took, the spells igniting for the blades to pierce through his body and into the fae behind him.

A small cosmos of magic exploded from them as the spear cracked their cores open, throwing them from the cliff. The powers of death and rebirth erupted over the battlefield, over the chaos-infected land, across the entirety of the realm, ripping apart the creatures below and the chaos that bound them.

FEY WOKE with a choked scream dying in his throat and the taste of blood on his tongue.

He sat up enough to look around, shivering from the heavy chill of the night, but there was no sign of dark creatures nearby. The only sounds were the crackles of fire and Vesryn's occasional snore. He pressed a hand against his chest as his heart slowed from its racing pace. There was a lingering ache as if he'd been stabbed, but surely that was only his imagination.

He couldn't believe the dreams had been memories. He hadn't been born before this realm was tamed, unless…. "This isn't my first life," he whispered, then squeezed his eyes shut at the enormity of that truth.

There were few essences that remained intact from one life to the next. Not even Fate was burdened with such a curse, locked away in Their tower, the title passing from one Fate to the next.

His wings were the mark of the Raven, the harbinger of death. An entity feared by most and revered only by those with the desire to start or win a war. He'd assumed his wings were a curse that passed from one fae to the next like Fate. Not a curse that he was born into over and over again.

The Raven was one side of a balance, the other side his bright fae, the Phoenix. The only creature with the innate power of rebirth. Which meant the Fate string binding him to Vesryn was surely a lie. Vesryn was an elf, not a fae, and he certainly didn't have powerful magic. The only magic he'd seen Vesryn use was to move a flame to burn the leshy.

Fey scoffed a laugh and curled on his side, drawing his arms and legs into himself beneath a wing for warmth. "Fuck you," he whispered, ignoring the flicker of power around his little finger.

If he somehow survived restoring the throne, he might have to hunt down Fate and ensure the title was never claimed again.

Chapter 16

Vesryn woke to a dying fire and a chill in the air. He groaned and rolled over, blearily reaching for the embers and using his limited magic to coax them back to life. Then he retrieved his cloak and burrowed beneath it for more warmth, the enchantments struggling against the sharp drop in temperature. Only when he'd warmed did he sit up to find the land covered in frost.

Winter's first bite glittered in a dozen shades of sunrise gold all around them. When he glanced over, he found Fey curled on his side, facing the fire, mostly hidden beneath a wing. He knew the fae was old, more than thousands of years; fae had vanished from the realm Ages ago, and Fey had seen the Wild Throne taken by the humans. But he had the ageless beauty that marked most immortals, and asleep, he lost some of the sharp edges that made him seem cold and withdrawn.

The illusion didn't last long. A few moments later, Fey stirred. He blinked a few times before focusing on Vesryn, something like disappointment crossing his features before his expression shuttered. He sat up with a yawn and pulled out some of the pilfered bread and meat without meeting Vesryn's eye.

Apparently, whatever moment they might have shared the night before was gone.

They ate in silence and then continued north, the sun warming the air enough that Vesryn put away his cloak before high sun. His few attempts to draw Fey into conversation were met with silence, and he stifled a growl of frustration. This was as bad as traveling alone. He wasn't sure what he could have possibly done in his sleep, especially after only a sip of wine.

"Fey," he said, managing not to snap, "are you ignoring me because of something I did or said?"

Fey hunched his shoulders in a way that pressed the top of his wings together like a shield before he let out a long audible breath, finally slowing enough for Vesryn to fall into step beside him. "No," he said after a drawn-out moment.

Vesryn watched Fey from the corner of his eye. "Is that the truth?"

Fey finally deigned to look at him, even if it was a scowl. "Fae cannot lie."

He hummed softly, sure he'd heard that somewhere before, though he'd never quite believed it. He might experience pain or discomfort when lying, but he could still lie. Though, like with the lack of the sun's blessing, he was sure he was the only elf with that affliction. "Are we to be enemies until we restore you to your throne?"

"You are not an enemy."

That was at least somewhat comforting. Vesryn lifted his left hand, wiggling his fingers to draw Fey's attention to their Fate string. "This suggests we should be something more than simply not enemies."

Fey's scowl deepened and he looked away, glaring at the empty horizon stretching out before them. "This bond is a l—" he started, his steps faltering. "The bond is not a lie," he said slowly, stopping as he looked at Vesryn, his scowl twisting into a look of confusion.

Vesryn stopped and turned to face him. "Why would it be a lie?"

"You're an elf."

"Is that a problem?"

Fey stared at him in silence, as if searching his face for signs of something he'd missed. "I don't know," he said quietly before he resumed walking.

What the fuck. Vesryn blew out a harsh breath and glared at the sun, wishing he could find answers in its light, but whatever guidance other elves ever found in it had never reached him. The sun was still as elusive as always. Just like magic. He hoped wherever Zaos was that he was faring better, but Zaos had always done fine on his own, preferring old, dusty tomes and quiet spaces over loud company.

He closed his eyes. "I'll be fine," he murmured, clinging to his mantra, but the spark of discomfort in his chest nearly undid him. It wasn't pain, so it wasn't exactly a lie, but he'd had centuries to learn the nuances of his particular curse.

Something was going to happen soon. And it was going to hurt.

THEY WALKED for days.

Vesryn's throat became sore from talking to himself or singing or humming. Anything to fill the silence. On rare occasions, Fey would speak more than a few words to him. If he hadn't known better, he would almost think the fae's ice was thawing.

In the distance, barely visible along the horizon, he thought he could see jagged bumps, slowly growing bigger every day until they rose high enough to nearly touch the sun's low winter path.

He lost count of the number of tears they sealed. They found at least a dozen, though most of them were small enough that nothing too dangerous could pass through. They spotted a unicorn once in the distance. It stopped to watch them pass before resuming its own journey east.

Every day was a grueling walk as the weather grew colder and the days grew shorter. Then the landscape changed.

The ground turned soft long before the tall weeds became visible and the fog crept in. The chill felt alive, clinging to Vesryn's skin and sticking in his lungs. Between one step and the next, the dense fog swallowed them completely. He stepped closer to Fey, hardly able to see him even with the black wings threatening to hit his face.

He tensed as he heard something moving around them, far too quickly to be anything natural. Or maybe it was the fog distorting the sounds. Soft clicks came from one side, then a whispering, shuffling sound, before more clicks came again from another direction.

"Fey," he whispered.

"Quiet," the fae hissed back, but a moment later he stopped.

So did the strange clicks.

Something close to terror slithered up Vesryn's spine. He had no doubt they were being hunted. He didn't know anything more than the old stories of the creatures that once haunted the night, but he knew this must have been how his ancestors felt in Ages past.

His fingers itched for a proper sword, though he wasn't sure what he expected to do against something he couldn't see. He tried to remain quiet, but even his breaths sounded loud in the unnatural silence.

Continuing on would give their position away, but they couldn't stand here forever.

He flexed his fingers as he scanned the fog. Was that a shadow in front of them? He stepped to the left to get around Fey, but he froze as the fae's wings twitched. The rustling of feathers was as loud as a yell.

The fog in front of them swirled, and Vesryn moved on instinct, throwing himself in front of Fey. If he'd had a longer sword, maybe he could have blocked the attack, but all he had was his short dagger and his arms, and he raised them in front of himself.

Too high.

There was a short whistling sound, like an arrow shot from a powerful bow, and something long and slender sank into his chest. Aside from the initial pinch of pain, he didn't feel it.

A moment later he didn't feel much of anything at all.

Fog swirled around him as he sank to the ground as if his legs were no longer there.

"Vesryn."

He blinked as Fey appeared in front of him. He opened his mouth to tell him to run, not to worry about him. He'd followed the Fate string knowing he'd likely die in the Wound, but he hadn't thought it would be before he did anything worthwhile.

He didn't manage to say anything, couldn't even seem to draw breath as his vision faded. The last thing he saw was those wide, brilliant violet eyes.

Chapter 17

"Vesryn!" Fey yelled, gripping the elf's shirt. "Vesryn Rydel, don't you dare fucking die," he snarled, but he knew it was too late.

He used the bunching of Vesryn's shirt to pull out the tiny spine embedded in his chest, a dark tinge of poison still clinging to it. He tossed it aside with a snarl and reached for his spear, but the dull sword all but leapt into his hand instead.

He stared at it for a moment, his eyes dropping to the gemstone in the hilt. The fire magic inside it swirled as if alive. He knew better than to question ancient fae weapons; they all bordered on possessing sentience. He pressed the sword against Vesryn's chest, hoping the echo of the restoration spell still thrumming inside the stone would be enough to keep him alive.

Then he retrieved his spear and turned. Whatever creature was hunting them was still there, waiting for a chance to stick a poison dart in him. He couldn't give it that chance.

He crouched as he spread his wings and quickly launched himself into the air. The sight wasn't any clearer from above, but he didn't need much. With his free hand, he called gales of wind to scatter the fog. The screeching howl of a sudden, powerful windstorm drowned out everything else. Wisps of fog were ripped away, though the thicker, denser blanket close to the ground remained intact.

A quick, shadowy movement in the thick whiteness caught his eye and he threw the spear, trusting it to find its mark.

Its inherent red glow brightened as the spells sparked to life, casting a blood-tinged haze on the fog before it sank out of sight. A moment later there was a sharp crack, like the spear had pierced something hard and thick, before a terrifying shriek rent the air. It died off abruptly as a twist of magic preceded a wet, squelching crunch. Then a horrible stench like rotting, poisoned meat wafted up to him as the fog began to settle and disperse.

He needed to get back to Vesryn, but he couldn't assume there was only one creature. He hovered in the air as he listened, but he heard nothing beyond the quiet howling of wind.

After several long moments, the fog finally thinned enough to see, and a giant black creature slowly became visible. It looked like some kind of spider, only with a hard shell and a long tail that ended in a thin spike. The land was covered in gray mud and brown, dying grasses, with scattered pools of stagnating water.

When there was no sign of another creature, he turned back for Vesryn, only to find the elf's body covered in white flames.

"No." *No, no, no.* He dropped in the air before his wings slowed him enough that he didn't break anything as he landed hard beside Vesryn. He slapped the sword away, the flames around it sputtering out as it landed on the ground, but the ones around Vesryn continued to burn.

"Fuck," he hissed, waving a hand over them to put them out, but they shifted around his hands as if evading his touch, and he realized they weren't hot. Despite the way they were slowly reducing Vesryn's body to ash, there was no blistering skin or stench of burning flesh. But even as he watched, Vesryn's skin darkened and crumbled like a spent log on a campfire.

No…. This wasn't supposed to happen.

Fey slumped on his knees, helpless to do anything but watch the flames consume Vesryn. Until all that was left was a line of ash.

When would Fate stop punishing him for refusing the Fate string? The bond wasn't supposed to be a lie….

When he glanced at his finger, the Fate string was faint and flickering, but it was still there, though it no longer reached beyond his finger, as if its anchor no longer existed.

He looked at the ashes and the tiny flames sputtering out in their center. Should he gather them or let the wind scatter them? Or sit and wait for…. What? What was he expecting to happen?

Vesryn was an elf, not a fae, and the only entity he knew of that could return from ashes was the fae of rebirth. The Phoenix.

The sword flared with a pulse of energy beside him, the jewel in the hilt glowing bright.

Could it really be so easy? He wasn't even sure he believed his dreams, much less myths, but what did he have to lose? When he picked up the sword and placed it across the ashes, the jewel glowed as bright as the sun before going dark. Nothing more than a glittering drop of drying blood.

Fey watched and waited. And waited. And waited. But nothing happened.

When a breeze picked up, he expected the ashes to scatter, but they remained intact, a soft vibration of magic wrapped tight around them.

With nothing left to do, Fey stood and walked the area to ensure there were no other threats lurking. The dead creature was still there, and retrieving his spear from its body took far longer than he would have liked. When he finally pulled it free, it was covered in green ichor. He buried the carcass with a twist of the earth, then cleaned his spear with a small, fierce storm and strong winds.

A glance back showed nothing had changed, so he continued on to the mound of dirt in the distance. Inside were several eggs. As much as he hated destroying them, it would be far worse if more of these creatures spread into cities. When he was finished, he buried them, then returned to Vesryn's ashes, still intact, and sat.

He retrieved a small jar of honey and the last of the bread as he settled in to wait. Hope tried to spark in his chest, but he shoved it down.

Hope could only lead to disappointment, and he'd had more than enough of that to last him until the end of time.

Chapter 18

Fire betrayed him as a scorching heat devoured him from the inside. Flames filled his fractured core until the heat shattered it completely. Pain that wasn't completely physical ruptured through Vesryn's entire being, ripping away all thought and feeling and sense of self, reducing him to ash.

The sweet relief of silence and nothingness left him breathless, except he no longer had lungs to breathe. No eyes or ears or limbs. Was this death? All life returned to the ley lines when it ended. There was a sense of something large and bright hovering beyond his reach, but he had no idea how he was supposed to get there.

When he'd told Zaos he would haunt his ass if he became a spirit, it had been in jest. Surely whatever broken magic that caused him pain when he lied hadn't twisted his ability to die in peace.

What was the point of his Fate string if he was going to die here? Fey hadn't needed him. If anything, Vesryn would have died long before now without the fae's help.

He didn't want to die. Even if few elves had lived to see their twilight years in recent centuries, he'd thought he would at least see a thousand. Yet here he was. Broken and shattered and nothing more than a flicker of awareness.

"Vesryn Rydel, don't you dare fucking die!"

He didn't hear the words, but he felt the resonance of them, felt the sharp tug of the compulsion from the fae invoking his true name. He might have laughed in relief if he'd still had a body.

But he still had something. The fire that shattered his core returned, surging through what remained of his essence and piecing him back together from flames and ash. Somehow, sensation and taste and sound and smell returned all at once.

His lungs seized, and he rolled to the side as he coughed. He blinked his eyes open and found the world around him brighter than it should have been, colors that shouldn't exist bleeding through the ground and the air, as if the realm itself was an intricate painting given life. When he looked at his hands, flecks of ash fell away, disappearing into the wind and leaving behind smooth, sun-kissed flesh. His hands, but not. If he looked close enough, if he tilted his head and focused on his wrists from the corner of his eye, he would have sworn he saw feathers of white flames burning beneath his skin.

"Vesryn."

He looked up, blinking at Fey. "Oh," he breathed, mesmerized by the bright-dark glow of him across the fire. He was surrounded by and made up of colors like sunset golds and reds and the deep blacks and blues of the midnight sky. Kisses of silver and caresses of violet.

Fey's wings rustled, a nervous sound, before he offered Vesryn a skin of water.

When he reached for it, he realized he had a sword clutched in his hand. The blade was rusted, chipped and gouged along the edges as if it were old and uncared-for. The hilt looked like wings spreading for flight, and a jewel in the pommel glowed bright with what looked like living flames. His sword, but not.

"This was mine," he said, but the words didn't come from him. A memory that didn't feel like his, or at least not from this life, filled his mind. An endless battlefield against dark creatures that rose up from the depths of the earth and thrived in the heart of storms. A war of attrition against chaos. Wings of liquid white fire and a sword filled with a sentient blaze. A victory that came with a price and a promise.

The jewel pulsed with magic and recognition, and Vesryn instinctively reached for it. He heard Fey telling him to stop, but there was no power in existence that could stop him from reclaiming what was his.

When he touched the jewel, a large drop of too-bright essence came free with an explosion of power. Pain burned through his gut, forcing him to the ground as he writhed and screamed in agony. And then it was gone, nothing but a memory lingering in his cold sweat and labored breaths, in the warmth filling him from his restored core.

He pressed a trembling hand against his stomach, but there was no blood or gaping wound. Of course there wasn't. The pure, dense magic of his core was back where it belonged. It had waited Ages for him to be reborn again, locked away in his weapon, in the deep, dark silence of a tomb filled with the echoes of death.

Memories spilled into him as he stared at the night sky. Memories of a past life—past *lives*. A bright creature able to bring back lost souls or guide them into a peaceful rest. Reborn after every death, unable to truly die.

Until the Second Daughter of the Wild Queen forged a pact with him. To give up his core and halt his rebirths, letting the reincarnation magic run wild, to be controlled enough to seal the ever-returning chaos, allowing this realm to be tamed.

And in return? a voice that once belonged to him echoed in his mind. *What could you possibly offer me in return?*

Peace, came the smooth reply, with the power of a promise, and all the elegance and arrogance of a ruling fae. *And the power to keep it.*

A pact forged in blood and flame and betrayal, because sealing his magic could never be enough to stop chaos long enough to tame it. Death had to be controlled as well. Two scales of a balance as old as the stars.

But as willing as he might have been to sacrifice his own core for a reprieve, he'd have never asked that of his raven.

His raven?

Vesryn released his grip on his sword, letting it rest on the ground as he pushed himself upright again. He focused on Fey with a frown. That name felt wrong, though he didn't have a better one to replace it with. It was as wrong as the shimmer of a Fate string on his finger. Something that shouldn't exist between them. Fate shouldn't be needed to draw them together; their joining was as inevitable as the setting of the sun and the rising of the moon.

Where the Phoenix brought the promise of life, the Raven was a living omen and portent, a harbinger of calamity.

His raven. Meant to call him back from an unnatural death. And as stubborn as ever, if a Fate string was what led them here.

Vesryn lifted his hand with a smile and wiggled his little finger. "Are you so hopeless that Fate needed to intervene?"

Fey's eyes widened. "You're not r—" he started, his words cutting off with an audible hitch. "Who are you?" he demanded, a scowl overtaking his expression.

That was an interesting question. Several names rose up inside his mind, echoes of countless memories within them, but they weren't his. Not in this moment. He still felt like Vesryn. Still thought of Ylrendorei as his home, of Zaos as his closest companion. Maybe that would change as the memories settled, but for now, he was still "Vesryn."

He paused when he felt a twinge of discomfort in his chest. "And the Phoenix," he amended, nodding faintly at the corrected truth.

"How?" Fey whispered. "I see you in my dreams, but I don't remember you."

Vesryn smiled faintly, running his fingers through his hair. His white hair. He was momentarily distracted by the familiarity of the change before focusing on his raven again. "You never do," he said, tilting his head when he felt the urge to *pout*, of all things. He ignored that urge as he focused on Fey again, studying the changes and similarities from the last time they'd been together, standing on a cliff at the beginning of this realm.

The pull inherent in the Fate string, the need to touch and complete that connection between them, was an uncomfortable sensation beneath his skin, but he was more concerned by the fact Fate was involved at all. He'd suspected someone had been influencing intentions from the shadows—why else would any fae think to subdue this realm? But what could Fate hope to gain from this elaborate scheme? Or was this an effort to prevent an even larger disaster than chaos itself?

He hated not knowing what part he was supposed to play. Especially if Julius was right and Vesryn's choices would set the path for things to come.

Fey's wings rustled as he leaned forward, offering the skin of water again.

Vesryn accepted it with a smile, resisting the urge to let their fingers brush. To forge the missing connection between them. Not only the Fate bond, but the one that had existed as a natural link since their creation. The balancer between their scales. He knew better than to rush his raven. Like a wary or wounded animal, he'd have to wait for Fey to come to him.

He took a deep swallow of water and tipped his head back to study the sky. So many Ages had passed that the stars were different from what he remembered, even though they were exactly the same as he'd grown up with. The ebb and flow of new memories settling inside him was odd but familiar, and for once he felt whole. He'd found the piece of himself that he'd always thought was broken instead of missing.

"What now?" Fey asked softly.

Vesryn blinked and looked at him as he took another sip of water. "We continue north. Fix your throne. Maybe you remember me and that you can trust me along the way."

Fey flushed behind his glower, looking away long enough to procure a stick with small berries on it, which he tossed at Vesryn.

He dropped the waterskin to catch it. "Twilight korlans?" he asked, plucking one of the dark blue stone fruits off the branch and carefully taking a bite. He regretted it a moment later as his eyes watered from the tart, sour taste. He turned his head to spit the bite out and flicked the other half at Fey. "These aren't ripe," he choked out, grabbing the water and taking several swallows.

"They're ripe," Fey objected. He took a bite and raised an eyebrow. "It tastes fine."

Vesryn grimaced and drained more water, then tossed the rest of the fruit back. "What else do you have?"

Fey sighed and offered a large yellow fruit instead.

Vesryn sniffed it before sinking his teeth into it, letting his eyes close with a soft hum of bliss as tangy sweetness exploded over his tongue. He devoured it within a few bites and tossed the pit back. He licked the drops of juice from his fingers and feigned ignorance when Fey watched him. "Do you have a sharpening stone?" he asked, wiping the remnants of moisture on his pants before picking up his sword.

It felt good in his hands. Even better than the one he'd wielded for the last few centuries. This one had been made for him, forged from the stone of a falling star, though its beauty was lost beneath the rust and years of neglect. He looked up when Fey sank his fingers into the dirt, watching the twist and curl of violet-tinged magic as it called a palm-sized rock up from deep in the earth.

He propped his chin on his fist as Fey shaped it into a sharpening stone. "I do love watching you work magic," he murmured. "It always feels like a gentle kiss of rain."

Fey slanted a narrow-eyed look at him before throwing the stone at him.

Vesryn caught it with a soft laugh. The familiarity he felt for his raven was strange, especially as it blanketed the awkward silences and unsteady footing that still existed between them.

He splashed some water over the stone, picked up his sword, and settled into the task of cleaning and repairing it. The slow, sharp rasps of stone scraping metal mingled with the crackles of the fire. The repetitive motions soothed him into a quiet meditation despite the weight of Fey's gaze on him. He let the silence linger and deepen as he let the memories swell to the surface.

Wars, mostly. Everyone wanted his powers to save their fallen soldiers or families, or to rain destructive fires down from the skies over their enemies. Especially when the raven's appearance ignited the festering fears or hatred enough for a society to act on them. But they'd had peaceful times too, if short-lived.

He paused to wet the stone again and glanced up to find Fey still watching him. "What dreams do you have of me?" he asked, ducking his head to hide his smile when Fey's wings twitched. "Anything interesting?"

Fey huffed and drew a leg up to wrap his arms around. "Mostly the end, I think," he said after a long moment. "We're on a cliff with strange creatures overwhelming our forces below."

"Ah. Not a pleasant dream, then."

"Dreams are rarely pleasant," Fey murmured.

The stone skipped against his sword when Vesryn's grip faltered, but he recovered quickly. "I'm sorry I wasn't there." As one of the few winged fae, the raven was always subject to contempt and scorn. Fear always encouraged the worst in someone, even if fae liked to pretend they were above such base emotions. When he had his raven by his side, he could mitigate the damage, but he'd been locked away.

He'd assumed they would both sleep through the Ages until this realm was stable enough for them to return. He should have known better, but he'd never quite learned the patience to deal with the word games most fae lived by. Knowing his raven had been trapped here for Ages with no one to look out for him hurt more than any life ever could, and he hated not having an enemy in sight to seek retribution.

"You're here now," Fey said softly.

Vesryn looked up and silently cursed the fire between them. The distance between them. Physically and within time. The Phoenix may have regained his sense of awareness, but he was barely a memory to Fey. Little more than a ghost in a dream. For now.

"I'm here."

CHAPTER 19

SHORTLY AFTER they broke camp in the morning, Vesryn realized the magic he'd been sensing since he woke up was moving closer. "Something's coming," he murmured, lifting a hand to shield his eyes as he looked to the east and slightly north, where the singing forests should be. "Is there a tear that way?" He should have been able to locate them as well as Fey now, but the energies within the Wound were in so much flux, he couldn't make much sense of anything.

"Most likely," Fey replied, "but too far away to worry about right now."

"Close enough for the Summer Court to be sending a search party?" he asked.

Fey stopped and glanced back at him before looking to the east, his lips tilted down with displeasure. "No," he said and resumed walking.

Vesryn raised an eyebrow and followed. Yesterday he may have accepted that as an answer, but now he had the advantage of recognizing when his raven was not sharing something. "You know who it is," he said, waiting for Fey to deny it. But of course he couldn't. "Are you going to tell me?"

"Why?"

Vesryn tilted his head and glanced towards the magical presence again. It may have been a coincidence that it was coming closer, but who would be out in the Wound and in the same area as them if not the Summer Court? Word may have spread by now that the Wound was safer than it had been, but it would still take time to re-establish trade routes, much less begin reclaiming the land for living on.

"If there's danger, I should know."

Fey huffed quietly. "There's no danger here."

Vesryn tipped his head back with a drawn-out sigh. Even he could hear the blatant twist in those words, but he didn't press further.

If who or whatever he sensed was coming for them, they'd find out soon enough.

THE SUN was nearing the horizon when Vesryn saw a glint of something in the sky. He ignored it as some kind of bird, but it swiftly grew larger. A bright silver star moving towards them.

Fey stopped with a soft curse, though Vesryn's attention was thoroughly captivated as he realized it wasn't a bird at all. It was a dragon.

"Blood and bone," he whispered. He'd heard the gossip as it spread from those who had seen Haru's dragon form flying over the city, though he'd unfortunately had his hands full when the dragon had crashed into the throne room during their battle against Aster. He'd only gotten a few glances at Haru for himself before the dragon form reverted to his two-legged one.

As the dragon flew closer, the silver of his scales shone beneath the gold reflection of sunlight. He grew larger and larger until he circled overhead and then landed.

Vesryn stood in shock, taking in the long serpentine form, massive claws, and velvet-covered horns. Then he spotted Callith with a black fox in his arms. The fox leapt to the ground as Callith slid down from the dragon's back. Vesryn took a hesitant step forward even as Callith quickly closed the distance between them.

"Vesryn?" the king asked, looking from Vesryn to Fey in confusion. "What are you doing out here?"

He stifled an incredulous laugh and lifted his arms, surprised and pleased when Callith stepped into his embrace as easily as ever. "That's an interesting story. How did you even find us?"

Callith released him, looking up at him with a frown as he swiped his thumb below Vesryn's eye. "Your eyes have changed."

Vesryn tilted his head. "They have?" he asked, touching his own face as if that would let him see.

Callith snorted. "They're gold. Like sunfire. And your *hair*...." He shook his head and moved back a step as Haru and Rashi came up beside him, both standing on two legs. "I felt an elf die," he added, pressing a hand above his stomach where the poison stinger had hit Vesryn. "What happened?"

Vesryn winced. "We should sit," he said, glancing around with a wry twist of his lips. Nothing but dry and cracked dirt stretched out all around them, but Callith didn't seem bothered by that.

He glanced at Rashi, who grinned at Haru, and then the three of them called on their magic. Frost glittered in the air before the warmth of a burst of sunlight turned it into cool rain. A moment later, the thick scent of earth and petrichor filled the air. Soft grasses broke through the damp soil, followed by moss and flowers and a tree. Green spilled out from beneath them until they all stood in a large clearing that stretched for several paces in every direction.

Haru procured a large pack from one of his voluminous sleeves and held it open for Rashi to pull out small cushions for all of them. Callith took his own and sat, and Rashi and Haru settled with Rashi in the center.

"Sit," Callith said, "and tell me why I no longer feel a connection to you."

SUSPECTING THIS wouldn't be a short conversation, Fey built a small fire for warmth. Then he sat silently near Vesryn, who told the others of the events leading to them venturing into the Wound, starting with the Fate string that appeared when Fey had claimed Aster's body and recreated it as his own.

He let the conversation wash over him as he watched the Sun King and his two mates. The golden threads connecting the three of them hadn't been there the last time Fey had met them, shortly after he regained a corporeal form in the palace. The redwood crown around the fox's head hadn't been there either, but after watching Vesryn turn to ash and be reborn again as the Phoenix, he wasn't surprised to learn Rashi and Haru were heirs to the Nature and Frost Thrones.

The three of them had been on their way to Haru's home for Callith and Rashi to meet the dragon's family when the elf had sensed Vesryn's death.

Fey glanced at his Fate string and wondered what the fuck Fate was playing at. Three creatures with access to different thrones were mated, the Phoenix had returned after being sealed away since the First Age of this realm, and Fey was trying to restore and reclaim the Wild Throne. The only ones missing were Air and Sea, but he suspected Fate would drag them into this mess by laying a finger on them soon enough.

He pressed his thumb against his little finger where the glimmering red string wrapped around it, silently willing Fate to fuck off. In response, there was a pulse of something like the magical equivalent of a rude gesture. He dropped his hand with a huff and glanced up to find the dragon's amber eyes focused on him, or rather, his finger. He expected some kind of question or maybe a snide comment about him not deserving a Fate string, but Haru said nothing. Simply tilted his head with a curious look before turning his attention back to his mates.

"Are you going to return to the city?" Vesryn asked.

Callith glanced at his mates before shaking his head. "Not immediately. We'll still go to the mountains, then see how much of the land we restored has spread. For now, that's still our main focus."

"The land would heal faster if you tapped into the ley lines," Fey said, then tensed as all four of them focused on him.

Rashi leaned forward with an eager look. "We've been doing that when we find a nexus. You're saying we can do the same wherever we are?"

"Yes," he said, before realizing they didn't know what he was referring to. The lines were the primary source of magic in this realm, and the way they stretched across the entire realm was intentional. Six large pools of raw power, connected together by the ley lines, with smaller pools scattered between. Six thrones were made to draw on that power and keep the elements separated. While it was true that it was far easier to work powerful magic while close to the ley lines, they could be tapped into from anywhere.

But it was even harder to reach them from here. The physical land of the Wound wasn't the only aspect of it that was a wasteland; the ley lines that should have been thick rivers of energy were barely more than a trickle, and even the nearest nexus felt more like a puddle after a light rain than the deep pool it should have been. The newly opened tears and the restored flow of magic from the fae realm were helping to restore the ley lines, but that could only do so much.

Fey looked between the three of them. An elf king ruling the Light Throne, a fox connected to the Nature Throne, and a dragon, one of the most powerful creatures natural to this realm, with a connection to the Frost Throne. Any one of them should have been able to tap into the ley lines of their own throne from anywhere in the realm, but together?

He hoped Fate knew what They were doing. There'd always been an unspoken rule against tying the thrones through mate bonds for this very reason. Two connecting wasn't dangerous, but three or more came close to tipping the balance back towards chaos, and the amount of power three thrones could pull together could do enough damage to create a new Wound. Or restore one.

Rashi closed his eyes and tipped his head back, his frown of concentration turning into a brilliant smile a long moment later. "I can feel it. Should we try it now?"

"No," Fey said, an urgency in his voice that he hadn't expected. His wings twitched as he wondered what he was missing. The influx of power it was sure to cause? It wouldn't be nearly as devastating as the Wound's creation. Backlash? They wouldn't be working a spell, merely guiding the power back to its set path. The thrones? What about the thrones?

"The thrones aren't in balance," he said slowly. "If you restore the Wound completely without the Wild Throne in place…."

Vesryn swore softly. "It'll accelerate the chaos."

Fey nodded.

Callith sighed and pinched the bridge of his nose. "We'll wait, then. How will we know when you've succeeded?"

"You mean without coming with us?" Vesryn asked with a soft snort, seeming unbothered by Callith's glare.

"You'll know," Fey said, though when he tried to say more, there was nothing. He wasn't sure how or what sign restoring the throne would give, but they would know.

Rashi didn't seem bothered by the vague promise. "So when you restore the throne, we should restore the Wound?"

Fey opened his mouth to say yes. "No," he said, his wings rustling with the same surprise showing on all but Haru's face.

"When then?" Callith asked.

"I don't know," he said, bracing himself for some kind of retaliation, but Callith only tipped his head back with a frustrated groan.

"Why do I feel like we're being used?"

"Because we are," Haru said, glancing at Fey's Fate string again, before the internal glow faded from his eyes.

Callith muttered a curse as Rashi patted his knee.

Fey glanced at Vesryn to find him staring into the fire, his thumb absently stroking the bracer on his arm. They were a copy of the wing pattern on his own bracers. Warmth fluttered in his stomach as he watched the slow, smooth glide of Vesryn's finger along a single feather, unable to keep from wondering what those fingers would feel like against his own wings.

That was something he shouldn't be thinking about.

Nothing had changed, except everything.

If his dreams were true, Vesryn was who he'd been waiting for. Who he'd betrayed his family for. Who the Wound was created for.

He pushed to his feet and walked away, ignoring the chill as he stepped outside of the reach of the fire. He moved to the tree that had grown large enough to lean back against. He crossed his arms as he watched the last of the sunset, shadows beginning to overtake the crimson fingers of light clawing at the land and sky.

Beyond their tiny oasis, the land was still barren, faint tendrils of magic the only sustaining force to keep the land from decaying further.

He'd caused this. Not to stop the humans and their wars, but because he'd been so desperate to find the bright creature who haunted his dreams that he'd trusted a stranger's cryptic words. Because after living so long as a chained and beaten animal, he'd been desperate for any escape, even through death. Was he a harbinger of calamity because of natural forces or because he chose to destroy everything in his path?

Footsteps behind him made him tense, expecting Vesryn, or worse, the elf king. But it was only Rashi. The fox offered him a large bun stuffed with what smelled like meat, herbs, and cheese, warmed from the fire.

He accepted it with a faint nod, soaking in the heat as he held it in a cupped hand.

"Are you all right?" Rashi asked, staring up at him with bright green eyes.

"I'll be fine," he replied before taking a bite, if only for an excuse not to speak more.

Rashi remained where he was, watching the horizon as the sun slipped out of sight.

This close, Fey could see the tiny branches scattered around Rashi's crown, sprouting even smaller leaves of greens and reds.

"Would it be rude to ask to touch your wings?"

Fey choked as he inhaled bread, nearly dropping the remains of his dinner as he coughed it out of his lungs. When he'd regained his breath, he turned a confused scowl on the fox. "Would it be rude to ask to touch your ears?"

Rashi grinned and flicked his ears forward. "No," he said, far too brightly. "Shall we trade?"

He scowled harder and risked a glance at the others, but they seemed absorbed in conversation.

Rashi stepped closer and bounced lightly on his feet, exuding the same excitement he'd shown when Fey first met him.

Fey sighed in defeat and carefully stretched a wing out.

The fox grinned and shifted even closer, tilting his head in offering before lightly skimming his fingers over Fey's wing and through his feathers.

Fey swallowed a hum of surprised pleasure and took another bite of the bun, then lifted his other hand to caress the soft fur of a fox ear.

"They're beautiful," Rashi murmured, gently ruffling the feathers before smoothing them out again.

"What are you doing, little fox?" Vesryn asked as he approached on silent feet. The dangerous edge in his otherwise teasing tone caused Fey's stomach to tighten, and he dropped his hand as Rashi hopped back.

The fox winked at Fey before turning to Vesryn with a smile. "Petting the fae," he replied lightly, then hurried back to the fire.

Fey watched him go and tucked his wings against his back again, acutely aware of Vesryn hovering within touching distance. He slipped his free hand under his arm to resist closing that distance. He studied Vesryn from the corner of his eye, licking a smear of cheese off his finger as he finished eating. His stomach tightened further when Vesryn's intense golden-red eyes darkened. "You're jealous," he guessed, surprised to find it was true.

Vesryn narrowed his eyes and took a step closer before leaning in, bracing a hand against the tree above Fey's head. "Because you touched Rashi?" he asked with a snort. "No. Because I don't have fuzzy ears to lure you in with." He tipped his head forward, close enough for Fey to shiver from the warmth of breath on his neck.

Fey swallowed hard against the urge to tell Vesryn he didn't need fuzzy ears. He was all too willing to touch him as he was. Except the Fate bond would surely do more than connect their essences, and once he started touching, he knew he wouldn't want to stop. He closed his eyes and tilted his head enough to inhale Vesryn's heady scent. Like woodsmoke and ginger. When he opened his eyes again, Vesryn was right there, close enough their breaths mingled.

Then Vesryn pulled back with a smug smile. "I can wait," he said before turning and making his way back to the others.

Fey managed to stifle his groan until Vesryn was out of hearing range, then slumped against the tree to let it out in one long breath. The pleasant heat curling through him made him light-headed, and he welcomed the chill breeze on his face. He tipped his head back and glared at the moon shining overhead with a quiet "Fuck."

Chapter 20

Callith and the others departed in the morning, leaving Vesryn to suffer Fey's silence alone once again. Not that he minded. Every night more memories settled within him, and with them came clarity.

Fey might be denying them both for now, but that wouldn't last long. It never did.

And the silence wasn't nearly as grating now that he could read Fey more easily. The fae might be quiet, but his wings alone were as expressive as any feline's ears or tail. So when Fey's wings rustled with a mix of surprise and alarm, Vesryn stopped and drew his sword, newly restored in full thanks to Haru's assistance the night before.

No longer dull or rusted, its sharp blade gleamed like quicksilver, the darker lines where the metal had been folded over and over again spreading along its length like ripples of water.

"What is it?" he asked, scanning the horizon.

"A tear," Fey said.

It took him a moment to locate the flux of magic, but when he did, he cursed. There was more than a tear. "There's at least twenty of them."

"Likely more by the time we arrive," Fey muttered, his wings twitching with agitation.

There was no avoiding this fight. Even if they'd wanted to, part of the mountain range loomed in the distance, and there was only one pass on this side of the forests. Even if the tear wasn't in the middle of that pass, the fae would find the path and be guarding it before they could reach it.

"Well?" Vesryn asked. Flying over the mountains wasn't an option even if Fey was willing to carry him. This part of the range was hidden in the clouds, far too high for them to easily fly over.

Fey flicked his wrist, his spear appearing in his hand.

Vesryn wasn't fond of the idea of starting a war with the Summer Court, but it was too late for that now. They'd declared war the moment they chose to fight rather than surrender the last time. "I'll draw their attention first. You should fly out of sight from above and then attack from behind."

Fey frowned at him, though he didn't protest the suggestion of an ambush. They needed every advantage they could get regardless of how dishonorable or cowardly it might seem. He crouched to push into the air but stopped and eyed Vesryn. "Can you wrap fire around my spear?"

He raised an eyebrow with a wry twist of his lips. "That sounds like something Zaos would do."

"He added light when I was fighting the cobra."

"Of course he did," Vesryn muttered. Zaos rarely had a chance to use his battlemage skills. He wasn't at all surprised to hear he'd joined that fight. Magic had never answered Vesryn before, but his core was restored now. It was still weak compared to what it should be, but flames formed around his fingers with ease. Moving them to Fey's spear was simple enough, but they died out when he tried to leave them there. He tried twice more with the same result, until his sword pulsed with impatience.

Fire swirled around the sword before engulfing the blades of the spear.

"Fucking braggart," Vesryn muttered, yelping when a large clump of embers hit his hand. Instead of burning, it felt like a bite.

Fey snorted quietly. "Fae weapons," he said before taking to the sky.

WHEN THE mountain pass finally came into view, Vesryn was alone. Fey had disappeared to the west to stay out of immediate sight, and from the slant of the Fate string, he was hovering somewhere high in the crags of the mountains, waiting for Vesryn to make the first move.

He kept his sword down as he moved forward, counting fae as they came into view. More than twenty. Twice that. He'd almost reached fifty by the time he was close enough to stop walking. The bright armor of the Summer Court spread out before him in a wave of gold, each fae standing impassive.

"Will you let me pass?" he called. In response, every warrior readied their weapon. He hadn't expected otherwise, and he wasn't keen on the idea of having an army at their backs while they tried to restore the throne, but he'd hoped to avoid a slaughter.

He tightened his grip on his sword and felt the thrum of magic as flames spilled down its blade. The cross guard changed, the wings growing and unfurling over either side of his hand. The red jewel brightened, a slash of black appearing in its center like an eye.

Some of the fae in front of him shifted back with unease, but others surged forward. Before the rush of battle claimed him, he saw the shadow of wings descend and heard the shouts of surprise. Then he was preoccupied with the fae surrounding him.

These weren't scouts or newly trained fae. The first he cut down had a mark he recognized as a ranked soldier in the queen's army. If there'd been any chance of avoiding outright war before, it was certainly gone now, but they would have to worry about that later.

He trusted his blade and instincts to see him through this fight. Blocks and parries, dodges and weaves. The thrill of battle burned through his body. His vision sharpened. His hearing heightened. He could taste the fae magic surrounding him, hear the sparks from metal catching fire, feel the hot splash of blood on his skin, smell the fear rippling through the soldiers as they realized who they fought. The flames of his sword cut through armor as easily as flesh, and he caught the wide arc of a swing of Fey's spear nearby. Heard the breaking of armor and bone alike, the wet crunch as the spikes activated.

A blade slipped through his defense, but the pain was a fleeting discomfort. His sword cut clean through the arm holding the blade, then separated the fae's head as well. He ducked a swing from behind, pulled the blade free from his side, flipped it over the back of his hand to reverse his grip, and stabbed behind him. From the punched-out sound of pain, he thought the blade had landed in a groin, but he didn't have time to confirm.

For the two he'd taken down, another four were there to replace them.

The battle was endless. A sea of similar cold faces eager to cut him down or capture him for their queen. Some things never changed, except he refused to be used as a tool again. By Fate or fae or anyone else. He was going to help his raven restore the Wild Throne, and then they were going to rule in solitude for at least a few years. They both deserved some peace after all this time.

Vesryn yanked his sword free of a fae's chest with a grunt. He flicked melted gold armor off the blade as he spun, looking for the next target, but all around him were the dead or dying fae of the Summer Court.

He snuffed the flames surrounding his blade and stood still, his chest heaving as he looked for his raven. There, across the blood-soaked battlefield, were two large wings spreading a shadow across a pile of corpses. As he watched, Fey jerked his spear free, the sound of scraping metal and tearing flesh audible in the expanding silence.

Vesryn lowered his sword and moved as if drawn by an invisible string. Except the string was fully visible and glimmered a translucent red between his hand and Fey's.

Fey turned towards him, meeting his gaze before scanning the area. Only when he saw for himself that the battle was over did he let his gore-coated spear tip rest against the ground.

As he drew closer, Vesryn saw the splatters of blood over the entirety of Fey's face and body. Something red and stringy clung to one wing and Vesryn grimaced, looking away as he came to a stop in front of Fey.

"You're a mess," Fey said.

Vesryn glanced down at himself to see he was almost worse. Now that the excitement of battle was fading, he could feel blood drying in unpleasant areas, along with aches too sharp to be minor wounds. His shirt was sliced on one side and soaked through with blood, but when he poked at the edges of the gash, the blood was already turning tacky. "I'll be fine," he said, glad when the words rang true.

Fey didn't look convinced, but he didn't comment as Vesryn surveyed the mess of bodies again.

He wasn't sure if any had escaped back through the tear, but once it was sealed, they wouldn't need to worry about anyone coming through behind them. There were too many to bother with looting them, and foot soldiers likely wouldn't have anything worth the trouble aside from their fae armor and weapons.

When he turned back to Fey, he found violet eyes staring at him. At his side where the worst of his injuries was. Anyone else and he could have healed the wound with ease, but for all his powers of healing and rebirth, he couldn't heal himself.

Fey stepped closer, his hand lifted as if to touch, but he stopped, his wings rustling with agitation and the soft whisper of guilt.

Vesryn held himself still, hardly daring to breathe. As willing as he was to wait for Fey to come to him, it was killing him to have his raven so close, but not nearly close enough. He flexed his fingers and slowly lifted his hand, palm up in offering. "Let me help you clean up."

Fey's breath hitched as he looked up, meeting Vesryn's gaze for an agonizingly long moment before slowly sliding his palm against Vesryn's.

Magic and awareness unfurled between them like a blossoming flower, the Fate string and the innate connection that had bound them through the Ages settling between them.

"There you are," Vesryn murmured, stepping closer and shifting his hold until he'd twined their fingers together between their chests.

Fey's other hand gripped Vesryn's shirt as he leaned forward, the spear pressed into their sides, his breaths coming short and stuttered. "How is this real?" he whispered. "How are you real?"

"That's not important."

Fey raised an eyebrow. "Then what is?"

Vesryn lifted his sword and used the tip of the blade to flick away the entrails in Fey's feathers. "How we're going to get you clean."

"I could summon some rain."

He hummed and squeezed his fingers around Fey's. "I love your rain showers." He tilted his head with a grimace as he glanced around the battlefield. "But maybe not here."

Fey blinked and scowled at the fae lying motionless around them, as if he wished he could slay them all over again. Instead, the earth trembled and opened up beneath them, swallowing the Summer Court fae before closing over them, though the bloodshed and signs of battle were far too extensive to remove completely. "We should close the tear," he muttered, and Vesryn stifled a laugh.

"Good idea. I don't want to be interrupted," he said, enjoying the flush across Fey's cheeks despite the glare.

Fey huffed and turned for the tear.

Vesryn followed, refusing to release his raven's hand even when Fey gave a weak tug, as if Vesryn couldn't sense the delight along their new bond when he tightened his hold rather than let go. Once they sealed the tear, he intended to clean every inch of Fey with his own hands. Twice. Nothing was going to stop him from finally indulging in having his raven all to himself again.

Except when they neared the tear, more fae were waiting for them. Instead of gold, the several fae taking up post around the tear were clothed in black and silver.

"Winter Court?" Vesryn guessed, seeing Fey's nod from the corner of his eye. That might bode well for them, but he wasn't putting hope in any fae court.

The fae finally noticed them as they drew closer, and one of them stepped forward. Tall and dressed in fine black leather with a black, silver-edged cloak billowing around his calves, he was obviously the one in command. Two guards flanked each side, their hands resting lightly on their sheaths. When they came within speaking distance, the leader looked at Fey, his eyes wide. Then he looked at Vesryn, at their hands joined together, and his pale complexion somehow paled further, his mouth falling open in shock.

"You know me," Fey said. "Know us."

The fae blinked and straightened. "Of course," he said, before eyeing Vesryn. "Though I believed *you* were only myth. No wonder all the courts are about to shit themselves."

Vesryn stifled a groan. All the more reason to seal the tears and restore the throne, before the Summer Court gathered in earnest. Or worse, joined forces with another court. "Who are you, and why are you here?"

The fae cleared his throat, tearing his gaze away from Fey's wings to focus on Vesryn. "I'm Ciarán. I came to help." He paused and glanced past them at the remains of carnage, then finally seemed to notice how filthy they were. "Though I see I wasn't needed."

"Why would you help?" Vesryn asked, but Fey stepped past him with a sound of surprise.

"You're the Prince of the Winter Court."

Ciarán smiled. "My reputation precedes me."

"I remember you. You used to visit my father."

"Yes, a long time ago." Ciarán glanced at Vesryn before clearing his throat again. "And I am here to help because the Summer Court intends to take this realm for themselves."

Vesryn raised an eyebrow. "You plan to stop them with so few?"

"I have a small contingent waiting at another tear, closer to the Wild Throne. It is inside Winter's territory. My guard will stay here and prevent the Summer Court from passing through."

Vesryn glanced at Fey, who nodded faintly.

"No need," Fey said, pulling a seed from his inside pocket. He turned to Vesryn and swiped it through the drying blood around the gash on his side.

The seed immediately lit up with a burst of magic and sprouted. He tugged his hand free of Vesryn's and hurried to the tear to plant it, but not before it grew to the length of his arm. If the last ylren trees had grown impossibly fast, this one grew even faster. With each blink it seemed to double in size, until it had completely swallowed the tear within its trunk. Only when it was the size of a mature dawntree did it slow, towering over their heads and blocking most of the sunlight.

Fey returned to Vesryn's side, close enough to brush their fingers together.

Vesryn didn't hesitate to clasp them again. "We should have sent the prince back through first," he murmured.

"I didn't think it would grow that fast."

Ciarán pulled his attention from the tree to look at them. "I intended to travel to the throne from here."

"That's not necessary," Vesryn said.

Ciarán raised an eyebrow and motioned to the tree. "As you can see, we have little choice now," he replied dryly.

Vesryn bit his tongue against telling the prince to find a different tear. He knew any potential allies could only help at this point, even ones so few in number, but he didn't like Ciarán, though he couldn't say why.

"You're welcome to travel with us," Fey said.

Ciarán's answering smile made Vesryn want to punch him in the face.

"It would be my honor to travel with the Raven and Phoenix," he said, bowing his head slightly before turning to gather his men.

So much for having some alone time with his raven.

Fey turned towards him with a faint smirk, leaning in close enough that his lips brushed Vesryn's ear. "You're jealous," he whispered.

Vesryn twitched back with a soft growl. He wasn't one to get jealous. Except Fey couldn't lie, and hearing it aloud, he knew it was true. He didn't want to share his time with Fey with anyone. Certainly not with Ciarán, who'd known Fey before the humans had stolen the Wild Throne. Who looked at Fey like someone who knew his raven's touch or at least had imagined it.

Fuck.

CHAPTER 21

Truth be told, Fey welcomed Ciarán's presence. It wasn't an excuse to keep from falling into Vesryn's touch in every way possible, but that was exactly what it was. When they'd touched and their essences mingled, he became aware of the depth of devotion and loyalty and something that couldn't possibly be love, because no one loved the Raven, the harbinger of calamity.

The overwhelming sensation of that connection settling into place between them also meant the wall blocking his memories began to crumble away. He vividly remembered being treated as less than fae by his own family. Now he understood exactly why he'd given his name to a human. He'd had nothing to lose, especially when there had been whispers of his father bargaining to sell him to another court to rid this realm of his poison. Before he could bring calamity to the Wild Throne.

How fitting that it had been destroyed anyway.

According to Ciarán, after Fey sealed off this realm, the fae realm assumed the worst—that the Raven had brought forth a calamity that destroyed everything. They weren't entirely wrong, but any guilt he'd carried for it was fading.

He was regaining more than his memories from before he gave his name to a human. Memories of other lives were coming back as well, and he knew he shouldn't have been reborn without Vesryn by his side. As overwhelming as their restored connection was, it also felt right. The most true connection he'd ever had with anyone. They were each other's anchor, two sides of a balance. They'd given up their magics to subdue the chaos with the promise they would return when this realm had been tamed.

For some reason, Fey had come back alone, without memories of his past lives, haunted by dreams of the Phoenix. Someone devoted to him, who treated him as an equal. Someone who loved him despite the curse of his wings.

Of course he'd sacrificed a family who hated him for a chance to get that back. He would have destroyed this entire realm and the next if it brought his phoenix back to him. But now that his phoenix was here, in the flesh, holding Fey's hand like it belonged in his grasp, it was too much. He needed more than a few moments to adjust.

They'd barely crossed halfway through the pass by the time night fell, and he and Vesryn still needed to clean themselves off properly. They'd only wiped off the worst of the mess and accepted a potent salve from Ciarán for their injuries before making for the pass. Most of the path was wide enough for two to walk alongside each other comfortably, with a few areas narrowing enough for only one to squeeze through.

When the light began to fade, they stopped to make camp. Ciarán's guards split up to start a fire, pitch a tent, and fill a pot with water and fresh vegetables they'd brought with them while Ciarán glanced over the two of them. "You should have enough time to clean up if you'd like." He rummaged through a small pack before offering Fey a dark glass bottle.

When Fey opened it, he breathed in the scent of ylren blossoms and something bright and tangy. He closed his eyes and sniffed again, not bothering to hold back his soft hum of delight, though it would smell even better mixed with Vesryn's scent. When he opened his eyes again, he found Vesryn watching him.

Want surged through him, and not all of it was his own. His mouth went dry as Vesryn's eyes darkened to molten gold, and he didn't have the will to resist when Vesryn stood and held out a hand in offering. He placed his hand in Vesryn's and followed him to the edge of the camp and farther, around a bend in the distance, so they were out of sight and hearing from the others. A few steps more and they found a small alcove in the mountainside for a bit more privacy.

Nerves twisted in his stomach as Vesryn released his hand and carefully shrugged out of his shirt. The bloodstains had well and truly set, and the slashed fabric had frayed with their long walk, but the gash in Vesryn's side was mostly healed thanks to the salve. Fey was grateful for that, but he was more interested in the dips and curves the shadows and fading light emphasized on Vesryn's chest and shoulders.

Drawn by Vesryn's bright flame, Fey reached out and trailed his fingers down Vesryn's arm, stepping closer when he turned to face him. The touch of Vesryn's fingers on his elbow was like the first spark of a lightning storm, energy singing through his veins.

"Fey," Vesryn murmured, leaning in to press his face against Fey's neck.

"No." That sounded wrong. But so did the name he'd been given in this life. "That's not my name."

"You remember now?"

"Not all of it…. But Nox feels more true than Fey." His first name, before he'd become known as the Raven or a harbinger.

Vesryn lifted his head with a smile. "The dark to my light."

He nodded and slid his hand up Vesryn's arm to the back of his neck. "But you're not Lux."

Vesryn leaned into the touch as he settled both his hands on Nox's hips. "I'm still Lux, but I'd like to stay Vesryn for a while longer."

"It suits you."

"Nox suits you. I always liked that name. Now will you please undress so we can get clean?"

"You don't want to undress me yourself?"

"Oh, is that an option?" Vesryn asked, shifting to back Nox against the rock wall. He plucked the bottle from Nox's fingers and set it on an outcropping beside them, then turned his attention to Nox's clothes.

His wings flickered as Vesryn pushed his tunic over his shoulders, becoming insubstantial long enough for the tunic to fall away completely. Vesryn's fingers trailed down his chest, causing every muscle to twitch in their wake, before making quick work of his pants.

Vesryn let out a happy sigh as his hands explored the bared flesh.

Nox relished the ripples of pleasure for a long moment before he slid both his hands down Vesryn's arms, lightly passing over the healing gash in his side to reassure himself it was closed, then tugged Vesryn's pants open and down, scowling when they caught on his boots.

With a snicker, Vesryn pressed a too-quick kiss to Nox's lips, there and gone again before Nox even registered the touch. Then he was gone completely, bending to tug his boots off and cursing as his pants hindered his efforts.

Nox didn't wait for him to finish and summoned clouds above them. He tipped his face back and closed his eyes as warm rain fell over them, then turned his head to hide his smirk when Vesryn yelped in surprise.

Boots thunked to the ground as Vesryn tossed them aside, followed by their clothes, and Nox offered a hand to pull him back to his feet, only to gasp as hot breath washed over his hip. His fingers tangled in Vesryn's hair instead, curling tight as he stared down at the elf. No, not an elf, and not a fae either.

Their essences were far older. Ancient. Primordial.

Nox could see the lines of power still settling inside Vesryn. Sunbursts of pure golds and reds and shattered colors, like looking through raindrops. The beautiful, bright creature that had haunted his dreams, restored in the body of an elf, kneeling before Nox like a besotted lover.

As if hearing that thought and determined to prove him right, Vesryn turned his head and dragged his tongue along the length of Nox's thickening cock.

A strangled sound of pleasure built in his throat, and he had just enough presence of mind to reduce the rocks beneath them into soft sand before he lost himself to the sensation. The wet tangle of hair around his hand. The strong fingers digging into his thighs. The warm rain falling against his skin. The hot breath and hotter tongue moving up and down his cock.

Vesryn's name left his lips as a desperate plea. He'd lived countless Ages without his phoenix's touch, done unspeakable things without his light for guidance, but all that guilt and despair, the obscene filth left beneath his skin by every human who'd touched him, the blood on his hands from breaking free in the only way available to him—all of it washed away beneath the waves of bliss crashing through him.

His fingers twisted tighter in Vesryn's hair, holding him steady as he rocked his hips. Vesryn's moan reverberated all the way to his core, and his eyes were blazing suns in the fading light when he looked up and swallowed Nox even deeper, his fingers bruising where they pressed into Nox's flesh to pull him impossibly closer.

Nox bent forward with a moan, burying both his hands in Vesryn's hair. His wings snapped out and forward to wrap around them both as intense pleasure shuddered through him. He moaned again as Vesryn swallowed his spend, heat splashing against his leg as his phoenix found his own release.

"Fuck," he breathed, ignoring the smirk Vesryn pressed against his stomach before following with a kiss.

"I would prefer a bed for that," he said, his voice rough as he pushed to his feet.

"You think we'll find one of those soon?"

Vesryn tipped his head back with a frustrated groan. "No."

Nox snorted and stepped into him, resting his forehead against Vesryn's shoulder as pleasure continued to spark through his body. Vesryn's laugh was a soft rumble beneath his cheek, followed by the scent of ylren blossoms and the firm press of fingers working a lather into his hair.

He closed his eyes with a hum of content and slipped his arms around Vesryn's waist, letting his phoenix take his weight while he waited for strength to return to his limbs. Eventually he straightened and poured some of the liquid cream into his hands to work into Vesryn's hair in return, then over his shoulders and chest and stomach, relishing the slick glide of his fingers over warm, firm flesh.

The cream must have had restorative properties or spells, because his aches and fatigue faded, as well as the remaining signs of their injuries. Even the gash on Vesryn's side had healed to a scab and old bruise by the time they rinsed.

Nox released his hold on the clouds, replacing the rain with a warm swirl of air to dry them before the chill could set in. It wasn't until they were dressing in their clean and intact spares of clothes that Nox noticed the foxglove blooming in some of the cracks and crevices around them, their subtle scent lost beneath the lingering ylren blossom of the soap.

Vesryn hooked his arms around Nox's waist and squeezed. "Those are new," he murmured. "Fae magic?"

Nox hummed an affirmative and brushed his fingers against the delicate sunset-orange bulbs. "They used to bloom in my footsteps," he said, tilting his head when Vesryn nuzzled against his neck.

"They suit you."

Nox relaxed into Vesryn's hold. He was loath to step out of the peace of his phoenix's arms after so long searching for him, but Ciarán would come looking for them soon enough.

"Do you have any oil?" Vesryn asked, stealing another too quick kiss when Nox gave him a questioning look. "For your wings."

Heat and nerves returned in equal measure, but he retrieved one of the bottles of oil from the box of supplies he'd been given and handed it over. Then he formed a seat of smooth stone in the center of the alcove, and Vesryn summoned small orbs of light that danced and swayed over their heads.

The first touch of fingers in his wings made him moan. Then Vesryn's thumbs pressed into the back of his neck and traveled down the length of his spine, digging into tight muscles. He closed his eyes and tipped his head forward, his moans deepening as the oil warmed with the sharp, heady scent of dawntree wood.

The silence was peaceful and lulled him into the hazy state between waking and sleeping. He knew the peace couldn't last, but he'd expected it to last longer than Vesryn finishing with one wing.

"We should move on while they camp for the night."

Nox opened his eyes with a frown. "Why?"

Vesryn hesitated as he worked oil into Nox's other wing. "I don't trust him."

"Because of how he looks at me?" He'd pretended not to notice, but he certainly did. Ciarán's gaze was like a physical weight every time the fae looked at him.

"No." Vesryn grunted softly as if in discomfort. "Not only that…. He never said he wasn't after the throne."

Nox tilted his head, finding it hard to focus on anything with Vesryn's fingers brushing every feather he could reach. But now that he thought about it, Ciarán hadn't spoken much about his intentions other than being there to help. Which was vague enough it could mean to help against the Summer Court, only to make a move for the throne himself. All of which seemed pointless when there wasn't even a throne to claim. But if anyone could have knowledge on how the thrones had originally been created, surely the Prince of the Winter Court would be one of them.

He kept silent as Vesryn finished with his wings, then leaned back into his warmth. "You don't think we'll need their help?"

Vesryn draped his arms over Nox's shoulders. "I don't know, but I think we should keep everyone away from the throne. And that'll be harder to do if they're there when you create it."

"I don't want to claim the throne," he whispered. Hadn't he already proven he couldn't be trusted?

"Neither do I," Vesryn murmured, resting his chin on top of Nox's head. "Should we give it to the prince, then?" he asked dryly.

Nox tipped his head back. "He'd be better than anyone from the Summer Court."

Vesryn turned a pained expression on him. "That's not exactly comforting. They're all fae."

Nox raised an eyebrow. "I'm fae."

"No, you were born among fae. We are nothing like them."

"Says the one still pretending to be an elf." Nox pushed to his feet and finished dressing, then turned to Vesryn expectantly. "Are we abandoning them?"

Vesryn glanced towards the dim glow of the camp, where the faint scent of cooking was emanating from. "Yes."

Chapter 22

Vesryn hadn't expected the path to become increasingly more difficult shortly after leaving the Winter Court fae and their prince behind. The entire pass was blocked by fallen boulders, and they were forced to climb until they found one of the old winding paths carved from the sides of the mountains. It was nearly eroded with time and disuse, the outside edge crumbling beneath their weight. If he believed the current Fate was watching their every step, he might have believed this was Their doing. Some test or punishment for fighting the bond for so long.

He summoned more orbs of light once they were far enough away not to draw attention to themselves. The more distance they could put between them and the fae before they realized what happened, the better. With any luck, Ciarán would give them as much time alone washing as possible, especially if he didn't want to risk interrupting something.

"Never would have expected to find your silence disturbing," Nox said after a long while of walking in silence.

Or climbing on Vesryn's part. He couldn't exactly miss the subtle flexing of Nox's wings or the powerful jumps as he cleared the larger obstacles strewn along the path.

"Oh, now you want to talk?" he asked with a soft snort. "*Weeks* of ignoring me, and now that I've had my mouth on you, you're finally willing to converse. Was that all it took?" He laughed as a handful of tiny pebbles rained down on him. "At least I don't have wings to clean that out of."

Nox turned to look at him and continued walking backwards on the rare patch of even ground. "Where *are* your wings?"

Vesryn shrugged. "Not powerful enough yet?" He could feel them beneath his skin, still caught the faint white glow of feathers in his wrists and arms from the corners of his eyes, but when he called on them, they couldn't push free. Like a chick still trapped in its egg. "When my core returned, it felt weaker than it should have. Likely from sitting in the Vault for Ages."

He tilted his head when Nox turned away, a guilty hunch to his shoulders. "Or is there another reason?"

Nox groaned and didn't answer for a long moment. "When I was fighting the leshy, it stabbed me."

"What?" Even if it was in the past, that didn't stop the surge of worry and fear.

Nox continued walking without looking back. "The wound was bad enough that the sword's restoration spell activated."

"Why didn't you tell me?"

"Would it have changed anything?"

Vesryn let out an aggrieved sigh. He couldn't say either way. He would have likely felt guilty knowing he'd been of no help. That it'd been his fault to begin with, falling prey to the leshy's tricks so easily.

As if sensing his thoughts, or more likely sensing through their settling bond, Nox glared at him over a shoulder. "It wasn't your fault."

"Are you only saying that to make me feel better?" The glare turned to a smirk, which was as close to a teasing affirmative as Nox was able to give. He shook his head with a laugh. "Zaos is going to be so pleased to learn you're as much of a dick as I am."

Nox's wings shifted. "You were close with him?"

"We grew up together," he said, tilting his head when Nox didn't say anything else, but he didn't have long to wait before Nox's curiosity won against his stubborn silence.

"You slept together?"

Vesryn hummed. "You prefer the truth?" he asked, drawing up short when Nox stopped and spun to face him with a scowl.

"I never want you to lie to me."

He winced and held his hands up. "I wouldn't have lied."

Nox narrowed his eyes.

"I promise," he said firmly. "I'll never lie to you." His breath caught as a sharp pain twisted beneath his ribs, intense enough to make his eyes water and his lungs seize. Fuck. No. He never lied to Nox, not about anything important. Not outside of affectionately tormenting each other.

Nox eyed him in confusion before his eyes widened in understanding.

"Nox, I swear. I would never intentionally lie to you about anything that mattered," he said, sagging in relief when the fading pain vanished completely. He caught himself against the jagged rocks of the mountainside as he hunched over and drew in a few slow, deep breaths. When he sensed Nox next to him, he looked up. "I'm sorry," he said, lightly grasping Nox's wrist when he stepped closer.

He had no idea what he could possibly lie about that deserved such an intense reaction, and he hoped he didn't find out for years.

Nox sighed and twisted his wrist until their fingers slotted together. "I trust you. Even if you haven't properly kissed me yet."

Vesryn huffed a shaky laugh, slipping his other hand around Nox's waist and tugging until they were pressed flush together. "You mean like this?" he asked, lightly brushing his nose against Nox's before kissing the tip.

The violet eyes that had slipped closed in anticipation cracked open with a dark look that made him laugh, though it was quickly muffled when Nox crushed their lips together, his hot tongue pressing past Vesryn's lips.

He closed his eyes with a moan and slid one hand into a wing and the other into Nox's hair. He shifted his hips, trying to back Nox into the mountainside for leverage and found his own back there instead. The rocks crumbled beneath his weight with a touch of magic, until it felt like leaning against a bed of sand.

There was his raven. The confident, commanding creature who wasn't afraid to take what he wanted.

Vesryn hummed into the kiss when the rocks changed further, offering him a place to sit. As soon as he did, Nox straddled his lap. He curved his body to avoid breaking the kiss while giving Nox room when he fumbled for Vesryn's pants.

Nox snarled against his lips in frustration, before finally getting a hand inside. His wings folded forward as he wrapped his fingers around Vesryn's length with a soft grunt of satisfaction.

"Fuck," Vesryn gasped, tightening his fingers in Nox's hair. He tipped his head back with a groan as Nox stroked him, shivering from the hot breaths against his neck. Nox growled and dragged his tongue against Vesryn's throat before biting.

He hissed with the burst of pain and gave a sharp tug on Nox's hair, but it was ignored as Nox pressed closer, burying his face against Vesryn's neck. His wings blocked out most of the light from Vesryn's orbs, encasing them in heat and darkness. Not to be outdone, Vesryn dropped his hands to Nox's pants and yanked them open before slipping a hand inside.

His raven's feathers rustled at the first touch of Vesryn's fingers, his wings folding closer as he pushed into Vesryn's hand with a pleading moan. "Not going anywhere," he murmured, relieved when the words held true.

Nox pulled back enough to look at him, his violet eyes aglow in the dark. "Promise."

"I promise." Their essences had always been linked. Even separated by death, they'd call to each other. "We were born of the same ash of the first star. We'll always find each other."

Nox crushed their lips together again and rocked his hips, pushing into Vesryn's hand. "Vesryn," he murmured, closing his eyes and resting his forehead against Vesryn's temple.

Vesryn wrapped his other arm around Nox's waist and ruffled a handful of feathers, matching the pace of his strokes to Nox's, their free hands roaming with the desperate need to touch. The only sounds were their breathing, growing faster and rougher, and the slick glide of their hands.

Nox broke first, spilling over Vesryn's fingers with a sharp moan. He dropped his head to Vesryn's shoulder, his own fingers going slack for a moment before he resumed stroking with determination.

He pressed wet kisses to Nox's neck and breathed in the rich scent of him. The green growing things found in the deep, dense parts of the wilds, mixed with the dawntree oil still clinging to his feathers. "Nox," he breathed before the pleasure peaked and he crashed over the edge.

Neither of them moved for a small eternity, sharing breath and slow kisses as their bodies cooled. At some point, Nox procured a cloth to clean them both, then settled more comfortably against Vesryn's chest. His wings lowered a bit, enough for a few slivers of light from the orbs to peek through. After a long moment, he said, "I wish we could disappear somewhere."

Vesryn turned his head enough to press his lips against Nox's forehead. "Maybe we can after the throne is restored." When chaos was averted and someone they could trust had claimed the throne. He'd drag Nox into the wilds where no one could find them for a few weeks or months. Or years.

Nox let out a snort of disbelief before falling silent.

Vesryn was content to sit there all night, but it was still dark when they finally continued on.

AT ONE point a rockslide blocked the way, and Nox resorted to hooking his hands under Vesryn's arms and flying him over the mess. Which was as endearing as it was annoying; if he'd had access to his own wings, they could have been on the other side and finding a way to recreate the throne by now.

Vesryn breathed a soft sigh of relief when the path began descending at a steady pace, but then the sky began lightening with dawn. They both stopped as sunlight broke over the land below.

He'd expected to find more barren wasteland like a continuation of the Wound. Maybe decaying ruins left behind by the humans when their warmongering began tearing the realm apart. Maybe extravagant, overgrown gardens, reclaiming their place after so long beaten back.

This was worse than even what he imagined of the lands of the Wild Court. Green as far as he could see. More than the green of large trees. Giant bushes with leaves as big as a girallon. Vines as thick as a dwarf, wrapped around nearly every tree and hanging from most branches. The only clear path through looked like a winding river, the water brown in the few spaces it was visible nearby.

In the far northern distance was a giant mountain with a single peak, though where the top should have been, it was caved in. A bright glow of red was visible for a few moments before it diminished beneath the brighter sunlight. In the valley between the mountain range and the single peak were the ruins he'd expected, the crumbling walls of the castle the humans had built were barely visible beneath the greenery trying to reclaim it.

Nox swore, looking from one end of the enormous valley to the other. "How is this possible?"

"It's been Ages," Vesryn guessed. And the loss of the Wild Throne likely had something to do with it. Even if the humans had still called this area home during the war, this felt chaotic. As he surveyed the area, he could tell the vines and foliage were slowly making their way up the mountainside. Given enough time, even the Wound might turn into this.

He was afraid to ask, but he did anyway. "Where do we go?" When he glanced at Nox, his gaze was locked on the mountain on the other side of the forest, and Vesryn tipped his head back with a soft groan. Fuck.

CHAPTER 23

Their descent was quicker thanks to a steep, winding path down the face of the mountain. Nox was tempted to carry Vesryn over the canopy all the way to the mountain, but he knew he wouldn't make it far before his strength gave out.

Before they neared the bottom of the path, the temperature warmed considerably, and a cacophony of noise threatened to deafen him. Insects, birds, a low, distant rumble and yowl of something that sounded large. It was overwhelming after the silence of the Wound.

He glanced at Vesryn as they reached the ground, his talons sinking into the thick moss and foliage. Without a word, they both drew their weapons. He blew out a slow breath and followed Vesryn when he started forward. He would have taken the lead himself, but he couldn't risk cutting a path with his spear. It'd be just as likely to target a tree and get stuck in it.

They trekked for what seemed like hours before there was a break in the canopy, and he took the chance to fly up to see their progress, only to find they were still close to the mountain range. And not heading directly towards the peak in the distance.

Dread threatened to consume him. This could take *weeks*, and he sensed at least three tears here. One towards the river but past it, and two where they were headed. All three were large. Much larger than any of the others he'd sealed. Things much, much worse than a giant cobra or leshy could have come through here, and this was the perfect environment for most of them.

He had seven seeds left. That would have to be enough.

When he landed, Vesryn looked at him and grimaced. "That bad?" he asked.

"We've made no progress," he snarled. "And we're off course." He swung the spear at a nearby vine with a shout of frustration, only for it to rip itself out of his grasp and continue further, flying through a bush where it sounded like it landed in something soft. Muttering dark curses the entire way, he stalked after it, ripping apart the bush with his talons.

He came up short when he found the spear lodged inside a giant flower. It had five large red petals surrounding a cavity that smelled like rot. "Why?" he snapped, yanking at the spear. "This looks like as much of a threat as the fucking chair you destroyed."

The spear came free with a wet pop. "When we're done with the throne, I should dismantle you and melt you into a piss pot." He carefully flicked black slime off the blade and spikes, then turned towards Vesryn and scowled at his amused smirk.

Before he could say anything, the earth beneath them trembled. A flock of birds squawked nearby as they took flight.

Vesryn braced himself against a tree with a wary glance around. "Why does it feel like you pissed so—" His words cut off with a startled shout as he was ripped off his feet. He hit the ground hard and disappeared before Nox managed two steps.

"Vesryn!" he yelled, following the sound of a body crashing through the forest, but it quickly grew fainter. Whatever grabbed him was impossibly fast, the crack of branches coming from farther and farther away, until the only sound was Nox's harsh breaths.

"No," he gasped, glancing at his hand and relying on the Fate string to guide him. Except a moment later, Vesryn's pained scream pierced the air and then the string flickered out.

No. *No!*

"Vesryn!"

DYING WAS never a pleasant experience, but at least it was usually quick. Vesryn didn't remember much of this one. One moment he'd been watching Nox, the next, something wrapped around his ankle and dragged him across the ground. Before he could get his bearings or cut his ankle free, something sharp stabbed him in the chest.

When he came back to himself, he was somewhere dark and rank, and it felt like ropes were wrapped around his limbs and chest. When he moved, they tightened. He tried only once to wiggle free. The ropes tightened enough to threaten snapping him to pieces.

"Blood and bone," he hissed, forcing his body to go limp. With a flick of his fingers, he summoned a small orb in his palm and immediately wished he hadn't. Thick brown and green vines surrounded him, and he was sure the bits of white he could see stuck in some were bones. When he moved the orb higher, there were only more vines.

"Wonderful. Eaten alive by a plant."

The quickest way out would be to set everything on fire, but he didn't exactly want to choke to death on smoke if it could be avoided. He guided the orb down, and if he squinted he could make out the glint of his sword hanging precariously below him. "You going to make yourself useful?" he asked.

The jewel flickered in a familiar insulting way, and he muttered an insult of his own under his breath. If he couldn't summon his wings, the sword likely didn't have enough power to reach him, but it could have at least tried.

He tried one more time to free his arm, only for it to be twisted behind his back with a quick, sharp yank. Then something wet and faintly green landed on his other arm. He screamed as it burned and smoked with a disturbing sizzling sound, like fat dripping into fire.

Burning his way out suddenly seemed like the less painful option. White flames erupted around his entire body. They caught on the brown vines wrapped around his torso and spread quickly, but the green ones around his limbs smoked, oozing sap that sparked and burned against his flesh.

"Fuck this," he hissed through gritted teeth. He summoned giant orbs of fire and sent them out in every direction. Flames raced along every brown vine, filling the space with light and smoke.

A high-pitched shrieking started as the vines began trembling, and when he dared to look down, he saw a massive pit filled with jagged teeth and black ichor.

"Oh absolutely not," he yelped, clutching the green vine around his wrist a moment before the flames finally ate their way through. The vine snapped, followed by the ones around the rest of his limbs. As he dropped, he managed to snag the hilt of his sword with his toe and quickly flicked it into his hollow.

Another shriek nearly deafened him, and the teeth below him started moving, twisting and turning and somehow getting closer. He may not have to fear death, but the sight of an endless mass of teeth advancing towards him made his heart lurch, and he quickly turned his attention to climbing the vines.

The smoke from the crackling fire thickened around him. "Fuck, fuck, fuck," he hissed in time to his pounding heartbeat. He couldn't see any opening or way out. Nothing but vines, vines, and more vines.

When the smoke started getting too thick to breathe, he tried moving sideways instead of up and slammed into something hard and sturdy. "Please be thin," he begged, pushing off it and slamming back into it with his feet. His grip on the vine slipped, and he inhaled too much smoke and began coughing.

When he finally managed a breath, he retrieved his sword, pushed off the wall again, and jabbed the blade into the side as he swung forward. It sank nearly to the hilt, and he left it there as he swung back, before driving it all the way in with his feet. When it lit up with a blaze of fire, another terrible shriek vibrated the vines around him.

He crashed into the weakened side again and felt it give. Cracks appeared with the promise of sunlight and fresh air. Another two swings and he finally burst free, crashing through thick branches that knocked what little air he'd gotten out of his lungs.

He landed hard on dense roots and mud, finally rolling to a stop with a miserable groan. His sword clattered to a stop by his side with a disparaging flare of light. "Oh fuck off," he choked out, spitting foul mud out of his mouth as he struggled to his hands and knees. His ribs might not be broken, but they were definitely bruised.

An ominous cracking came from around him, and he cursed as some of the roots started to flex and break free of the ground. He snatched his sword, stumbled to his feet, and turned to find a large tree with smoke billowing around it, flames breaking out along its trunk, and somehow looking extremely angry despite not having a face.

It groaned and creaked as it bent forward and swung its branches at him. His sword sliced through most of them, but one swept him off his feet, throwing him back to slam into the trunk of another tree.

His breath wheezed out of him, and he nearly lost his footing as his vision wavered black. More of the tree's roots popped out of the ground, splattering him with mud. Then the sound of something large crashing closer with a loud roar caught his attention.

He turned in time to see Nox break through the line of bushes and trees marking the edge of the clearing. Vesryn's relief was short-lived when a giant brown bear more than twice his height chased after Nox, followed by two more.

"Run!" Nox yelled.

Vesryn swore, pushing away from the tree as he found a surge of strength from panic. "How?" he cried. "How are you pissing off this entire forest?"

Nox let out a wordless, irate yell.

From behind them came a roar and a sharp, pained howl, but Vesryn didn't dare risk looking back.

When the sounds of things chasing them seemed to fade, Vesryn finally slowed enough to look back, then stopped to catch his breath.

Nox stopped beside him, slumping against a tree and sinking to the ground as he gasped for air.

He tentatively put his weapon away when the forest remained quiet, aside from birds and insects and the rush of moving water somewhere nearby.

"You died," Nox said.

Vesryn glanced at him, wincing from the twist of guilt along their bond. "Yeah," he said, leaning back against his own tree as he explained what happened. "And where did the bears come from?"

Nox looked away, tightening his grip on his spear. Which, now that Vesryn was looking at it, was bloody and had tufts of brown fur stuck in the spikes.

"Blood and bone," he swore, but he couldn't help but laugh. It died out quickly when his entire torso reminded him of the thrashing he'd suffered.

In the distance, there was the loud splintering crack of a giant tree crashing to the ground.

"Let's go," Vesryn said, straightening and offering a hand to pull Nox to his feet. He followed his raven when he started walking, assuming he was resuming their course for the mountain, but the river soon came into view. "No," he said, snagging Nox's wrist before they got any closer. "No, no, no. I do not want to see what kind of creatures live near the *water*."

Even as he spoke, he spotted a dark shape moving through the river. "Please no," he whispered, calling his sword to his hand as an enormous beast that might have resembled a cow swam past, completely submerged. Its curved horns were long enough to reach nearly from one bank to the other.

"Right," Nox said faintly. "Let's assume everything here will try to kill us."

Chapter 24

Between the lack of sleep the night before and running from plants, bears, and a giant spotted cat they stumbled over, they were exhausted by the time the light started to fade. Neither of them wanted to risk walking through the night, so they found a small space to make camp.

Nox called on the earth to shape a large dome, and they climbed inside before he sealed them in. A tiny opening on the side and at the top appeared for air and to let the smoke out as they started a fire.

Vesryn slumped against the wall with a groan. "Days or weeks?" he asked, accepting a piece of fruit after Nox coaxed a seed into blossoming.

Nox grimaced and bit into his own fruit. He hoped it was days. The thought of being stuck out here for weeks, continually chased off course, was unbearable. "How long before you can fly?" he asked, and Vesryn groaned again.

He flexed his fingers, a hint of magical lines appearing along his wrists and forearms. The tips of what looked like feathers curled away from his skin, but then the lines faded as the magic winked out. "A couple more days at least."

They only needed to survive until then. Hopefully they could make more progress tomorrow without provoking the wildlife.

When they finished eating, Vesryn set out his bedroll and stretched out. Nox crawled over to join him, throwing an arm and a leg over him. He drifted to sleep easily, lulled by the steady rhythm of Vesryn's heartbeat beneath his cheek.

He woke briefly when he heard something prowling outside, but it moved on when it failed to dig the hole open any further. The next time he woke, it was to something tapping against the wall near the opening.

"Wake up," Ciarán called, startling Nox into sitting upright.

Vesryn grunted in protest. "What's wrong?"

"Ciarán is outside."

Vesryn cracked his eyes open with a frown. "What?"

"Get up," Ciarán called again.

Nox shared a look with Vesryn before sending the earth dome back where it belonged.

Ciarán stood with his sword in hand and a sour look on his face. His sleeves were torn, but he otherwise seemed unharmed. And he was alone. "Did you two even consider that it might be better for all of us to travel together?"

"We might have," Vesryn said, scrubbing his hands over his face, "if we'd known it was a forest intent on killing us."

Ciarán stared at them as if they'd lost their minds. "This is the territory of the Wild Court." He said it like that should have been warning enough, but Nox didn't remember the land being so hostile. Or overgrown.

"What's done is done," Vesryn said, annoyance thrumming along their bond.

Nox was sure it was because of Ciarán's sudden appearance and not the thought of another day risking their lives against wild creatures.

Ciarán huffed and sheathed his weapon.

"Where are your guards?" Nox asked.

"I sent them ahead to ensure the tear is secured."

"And you found us how?" Vesryn demanded, putting away his bedroll before standing.

Ciarán raised an eyebrow, slowly turning his head to glance back the way they'd come the night before. "Your trail wasn't hard to find."

Nox handed Vesryn some fresh fruit and half of the last bit of dried snake meat he'd been rationing. They ate as they walked, and it was readily apparent that Ciarán was able to navigate the forest far better than either of them had managed.

Around high sun, Nox started to believe that maybe they could traverse the forest without another incident. That was also when Vesryn couldn't hold his silence any longer.

"What are your intentions for the throne?"

Ciarán glanced over his shoulder without slowing. "I told you. I'm here to help you against the Summer Court."

Vesryn hissed softly, but Nox pressed a hand to his arm.

Neither of them wanted the throne, but he didn't like the idea of someone trying to steal it from them either. "Do you intend to take the throne for yourself or anyone else?"

Ciarán sighed and stopped as he turned to face Nox. "No. But I am here to ensure *you* don't claim it." He lifted a hand when Vesryn took a threatening step forward. "I hold no animosity for either of you, but the Raven sitting on the Wild Throne? The Harbinger of Calamity? You would destroy this realm from within. But if that is truly what you wish, I won't stop you. So long as you understand the consequences of your actions."

"Then who?" Nox asked. He hadn't even considered his powers might corrupt the very realm.

Ciarán glanced at Vesryn before turning to resume walking. "Anyone but the Raven."

WHEN THEY made camp for the night, Nox flew above the canopy to check their progress and was astonished to find the mountain looming close in the distance, the red glow within its caved-in peak bright in the fading sunlight.

He landed lightly and stared at Ciarán. "How are we so close?" When Ciarán looked up in confusion, he motioned towards the mountain hidden behind the never-ending trees. "We've covered more than half the distance in a single day."

"The paths," Ciarán replied.

It took Nox a moment to realize what he meant. He hadn't used the fae paths since before the humans stole the throne, and he wouldn't have expected them to still be accessible even if he'd remembered their existence. He glanced around them and realized the faint thrum of fae magic he'd been sensing was from the path they were on and not leaking from the tears.

He sat beside Vesryn, not bothering with an earth dome for protection; they'd be safe on the paths.

Ciarán shared his rations. Thick slices of bread that still smelled fresh, soft white cheese with herbs mixed in, and honey-coated nuts. It tasted like home, or what Nox imagined home should be like. The food had obviously been prepared by someone who cared for Ciarán, and the protective and subtle restorative magics that came from those feelings were mixed into every bite. The lingering aches and bruises from his fight with the bears and the fatigue from running slowly faded as he ate.

Before he could become too sentimental over his bread and cheese, Ciarán looked at him expectantly. "We should reach the mountain tomorrow. Do you know what to do to create a new throne?"

Nox winced. "I thought I would figure it out when I get there."

Ciarán shook his head, though Nox was sure the fae looked more amused than anything. "You'll need to go into the cradle of the mountain and summon a powerful storm."

The cradle of the mountain, where the liquid fires from deep in the earth were pooling in the center of a giant rock. With a storm overhead. Wild magic in its most raw and potent aspects, shadowing chaos. It made as much sense as anything else. Calling all that magic together to create the throne would certainly be enough to infuse one of his last ylren seeds. That a seed was needed was the only thing he'd ever been sure of.

The original throne was carved within the trunk of a ylren tree, and it once sat above the largest ley line of the realm. Hopefully, by this time tomorrow, the throne would be restored. The wild and shadow magics would be removed from human control, and chaos' return would be thwarted.

"Get some rest," Ciarán said, settling against a tree with his sword resting beside him.

Nox glanced at Vesryn, who'd been unusually quiet for too long. "Are you all right?"

Vesryn's smile was more a grimace. "Who's claiming the throne?"

Nox shook his head. "Not me." Even if he'd had no love for this realm, he didn't want to see it destroyed.

Vesryn scrubbed a hand over his face, then looked at Ciarán, who returned his gaze with a blank expression.

Nox wasn't sure if he expected Vesryn to offer the throne to the prince or not. It wasn't like they had a better option. He'd rather take it himself than see the Summer Court claim it.

"I don't trust you," Vesryn finally said.

Ciarán's lips twitched into a faint, mocking smile. "That's likely wise. You should never blindly offer trust to a fae."

"If it were your choice, who would you put on the throne?"

Ciarán tilted his head, glancing between them before sighing. "Not a fae."

"So none of us," Nox muttered.

Ciarán raised an eyebrow. "Neither of you are fae. Not truly."

Nox could believe Vesryn wasn't a fae, or an elf, even if he was still using his elf name. But Nox had been born in a fae body, lived as a fae for Ages, before being trapped in the ley lines. Except he was fairly certain if any other fae had been sacrificed in his place, Sorren's plans to steal the magic of the other thrones would have come to fruition. He couldn't imagine any fae was powerful enough to wrest control of the wilds and seal the magic with their essence for three hundred years. Except maybe a ruler of one of the courts.

He glanced at Vesryn and gave up trying to find an answer as they settled in for the night. Whatever happened, they'd figure it out, or Fate would show them the way.

CHAPTER 25

THE MOUNTAIN peak finally came into view above the canopy the next morning, though any resignation or doubts Nox may have had were forgotten when the clangs of swords and yelling reached them.

Ciarán swore and drew his weapon as he quickened his pace, Nox and Vesryn following his lead.

When the forest line came to an abrupt end, they found themselves on the edge of a battlefield. The bright gold of Summer Court soldiers were locked in conflict against the black and silver of the Winter Court. Archers and casters were spread along the edges. Behind the Winter Court lines, Nox could see several fae dressed in greens and reds, likely the Spring and Fall Courts, casting spells or healing the injured.

"Get to the mountain," Ciarán ordered before rushing forward to join the fray.

Nox glanced at Vesryn, hoping he could summon his wings, but the lines that lit up briefly along Vesryn's wrists winked out before making it much farther than they had before.

There was no clear path to the mountain. The shortest way was through the battlefield.

Nox turned to Vesryn, meeting his radiant sunfire gaze and holding it. Now that they were here, he couldn't help but fear Fate would somehow punish him further, but there was no time to dwell on that.

"I'll carry you." Even if they didn't make it all the way across, it would be faster than trying to fight the entire way. Vesryn nodded and offered his left hand, his sword held in his right. Nox gripped Vesryn's forearm with his right and kept his spear in his left. Then he glanced at the field again, found what looked like a lull on the far side, and launched into the air.

His balance was off, and he nearly careened into a group of Summer Court soldiers before righting himself. Then they were flying, with curses shouted up at them from the battlefield. He could already smell the bloodshed, the trampled earth, the tang of clashing metal and spells.

They made it halfway, and his chest tightened with tentative hope. Just a little farther.

Vesryn shouted a warning, but the arrow still took Nox by surprise. It pierced through his left wing and sank into his back. He managed to stay in the air, but then a volley of arrows rose into the sky like a dark wave.

Vesryn cursed and twisted his wrist, dislodging Nox's grip on him. "Go!" he shouted as he fell. "I'll catch up." Then he hit the ground and was lost in the swarm of soldiers.

Nox couldn't turn back. His only goal had to be getting to the mountain. He rose and spun, wrapping himself in the eye of a small cyclone as the arrows reached their zenith and fell towards him. The high winds blew most of the arrows away. A few broke through, but he continued on, gritting his teeth against the sharp pain as they pierced his wings and arms. One sliced across his forehead as it whooshed past. Vesryn could heal him later, so long as he survived and restored the throne.

He released the cyclone as he neared the far end of the battlefield, the winds knocking back most of the soldiers there as he continued for the mountain. There was a clear path up, but it looked like it disappeared into a tunnel, so he flew up the side instead.

The air became unbearably hot near the summit and smelled of brimstone. He landed on a ledge overlooking the roiling molten rocks and coughed, struggling to catch his breath while breathing as shallowly as he could. He dug one of the last ylren seeds from his pocket with one hand and lifted the other as he focused on calling a storm.

He expected it to be more difficult than the small clouds he summoned for their showers, but the air and clouds answered as if they'd been waiting for him. The sky turned green and the wind howled as dark clouds converged, lightning sparking inside them. Rain fell in thick, heavy sheets, and the earth trembled beneath him. Chunks of rock shook free around the mountain and crashed down the sides.

Magic surged through him and filled the area, making his skin and feathers tingle. A high-pitched ringing started on the edge of his hearing and quickly grew louder. He swiped the ylren seed through the blood coating the side of his face and held it out, calling the wilds to him to fill the seed with the power to create a new throne.

Lightning flashed, blinding him as it struck the molten rocks. Once, twice, then again and again. Six times in quick succession.

Thunder cracked like an earthquake, and Nox landed on a knee from the concussive force of magic slamming into him. Then the ringing and pressure faded, the storm clouds dispersing, leaving behind only smoke and wet rocks as evidence of their passing.

Was that it?

When he looked at the ylren seed it didn't seem to be any different. There was no additional power or magic infusing it.

"No," he whispered, throwing the seed to the side with a snarl. He lifted his hand to glower at the Fate string. "What the fuck am I supposed to do?" he yelled. "You forced a bond on me! Forced Vesryn to follow me here. Am I not supposed to restore the throne? Is that what you want? For chaos to overrun us?" he screamed.

The string pulsed around his finger, but he hardly felt it as agony punched through his chest. He collapsed on his hands and knees as he choked for air. Something crawled across his neck, and he instinctively slapped it away, but his hand brushed against the sprout of a ylren tree.

Dull panic filled him as he ripped the top of his tunic open. The pocket he'd kept the last of the seeds in was torn and soaked with his blood, all six remaining seeds burrowing into his chest.

"Nox!" Vesryn screamed from somewhere behind him, but his voice sounded far away.

There was no chance of his phoenix getting to him in time to heal him. Even if he could, Nox realized with subdued horror that "blood and bone" wasn't merely a curse—it was the price of subduing chaos and creating the first throne.

CHAPTER 26

"Nox!" Vesryn raced up the tunnel as fast as his injuries allowed. He'd seared the worst gash on his leg to stop the profuse bleeding, but there was nothing he could do about his twisted ankle or missing finger. He was lucky it hadn't been his sword hand, but he had more important things to worry about.

He'd seen the storm and felt the enormous flow of raw magic like everyone else. It had brought a halt to the fighting as everyone stood in shock and confusion. That was one of the only reasons he'd been able to break free and make it to the mountain. He was sure that much power should have resulted in the throne forming, but something was wrong. He could feel Nox along their bond, but the connection was faint. Muffled and fading.

He reached the end of the tunnel and almost sagged with relief when he spotted Nox on his feet, braced against the wall and coming towards him. Then he saw the blood and arrows sticking out of his limbs.

"What happened?" he asked, reaching Nox in time to catch him as he stumbled and fell. "Where's the throne?"

Nox's laugh turned into a cough that left flecks of blood on his lips. "I am the throne."

"No." That was impossible. He reached for the sprouts, sure he could get them out and heal Nox of whatever damage they'd done, but Nox grasped his wrist, his grip weak.

"Get me to the heart of the ley line."

"Nox."

"Vesryn…. *Lux.*"

"You can't do this." He'd just returned. They'd just found each other again after Ages. That bitch *promised.*

"Please."

"Fuck," Vesryn hissed, picking Nox up and turning, except there was no way he'd make it on foot. The heart of the ley line was in the valley, beneath the ruins. The ylren sprouts were growing far too fast to get there before they took root in the ground. He stumbled down the tunnel, the ache in his chest worse than telling a lie when their bond flickered, the ylren trees stealing Nox's magic and life.

His vision blurred, and his legs gave out as his lungs seized. He couldn't lose Nox. Not like this.

Nox pressed a hand against Vesryn's cheek, and he forced his eyes open to look at him. "I'll find you again," he said, turning his face into Vesryn's shoulder as he coughed. "I promise," he wheezed.

"No. You're not going to die," Vesryn snarled, but the twist of fresh anguish beneath his ribs proved the lie. He curled over Nox's body and screamed. Raw magic raced along his nerves before exploding from his arms and back. The heat of living flames wrapped around him as his white wings manifested, filling the tunnel with the light of a small sun.

Nox hummed weakly against his neck. "Gorgeous."

Vesryn tightened his grip on Nox and staggered to his feet. He took a few stumbling steps before his wings flexed and more magic surged through them. He tipped forward, clutching Nox tight as his wings caught them. And then he was flying.

He'd never imagined his first flight with Nox would be like this. He'd wanted to fly together, both of them whole and free to dance in the skies.

The tunnel sped by in a blur, quickly giving way to open air and the sounds of resumed battle. He ignored them as he rose higher and turned for the valley.

He could see the power of the ley line below them, impossibly bright and stretching as far as he could see. It grew even brighter as he neared the ruins, until he had to force his sight to dim the glow of magic. Even then it was easy to find the heart, located beneath what looked like the remains of a courtyard, the bright, pure silver of ancient energy as tangible as it was blinding.

He landed hard and crashed to his knees in the overgrown foliage, only then giving in to the desperate ache in his lungs and chest as he gasped for air. "Nox," he choked. "Let me heal you. We'll find another way."

Nox's breaths were short, blood-soaked wheezes. "Has to be you," he murmured, his arm twitching as he tried and failed to raise it.

Vesryn grasped his hand and lifted it. He'd never wanted the power of a throne, but no one was taking Nox from him. "I won't let anyone else claim you," he murmured against Nox's wrist.

Nox closed his eyes, his wings flickering and disappearing. He looked small and fragile without them. He let out a final soft, shallow breath and his body stilled. The Fate string that should never have existed between them vanished, and then Nox was gone.

The newly forged connection between them shattered.

Vesryn bent forward and screamed. White flames poured out of him, scorching the earth of the courtyard, burning away everything that had managed to reclaim the ruins. The old, rusted iron and silver and stone walls fractured and buckled under the onslaught of his flames and raw magic as the ley line answered his call.

The ground trembled, and the sound of ominous, deep cracks echoed through the valley as the castle itself crumbled.

By the time his voice gave out and he tasted blood, the entire valley was reduced to dust and ash, and Nox was soaked with his tears.

Everything was gone. All but the roots of the First Ylren Tree, still living deep underground and pushing through the blackened earth. Reaching for Nox.

Vesryn bared his teeth in a snarl. "You can't keep him." He wouldn't let Nox be sealed away. Not again.

There was a quiet pulse of magic as if in acquiescence, but he couldn't trust in anyone to keep their word. Not even the source of magic in this realm.

The seeds sprouting from Nox's chest had nearly covered his entire body, and their roots stretched out along the ground, growing towards the ones pushing out of the earth. When they connected, magic exploded with a blinding flash and deafening burst like a thousand simultaneous thunderclaps.

Vesryn was knocked back with the force of it, his ears ringing as he struggled to sort out which way was up. When he finally made it unsteadily to his knees, a large ylren tree filled the remains of the courtyard. And there, as if carved into the trunk at its base, was a throne.

A sob stuck in his throat as he stumbled forward. His legs gave out in front of the throne and he sank to his knees again. "Fuck you," he whispered, his vision blurring as he forced a shaking hand out to rest on the seat of the throne.

For a moment nothing happened, and then new magic burst open inside him. The lush greens of nature, the reds and browns and blacks of the land, the blues and silvers of the skies. Fire had always belonged to him, but now he could feel the rivers of liquid red flames deep in the earth. The dark, cool spaces where shadows thrived.

Pinpricks of irritation appeared around his head, and when he lifted a hand, he found what felt like a crown of brambles. "You're such an ass," he choked out, slumping forward against the throne.

He wasn't sure how long he stayed there. Long enough for his legs to go numb. For his tears to temporarily run dry. Long enough that he didn't want to go on with the anguish constantly squeezing his chest until he couldn't breathe.

It wasn't until he heard footsteps behind him that he finally lifted his head, and he wasn't surprised to find Ciarán standing there, disheveled and splattered with blood.

"The Summer Court has broken through. Their King intends to take the throne."

Vesryn pushed to his feet with a bitter laugh. "He can try."

He'd lost his sword at some point, likely somewhere in the mountain pass, but it didn't matter. The power of the throne was his, and that sword was as much a part of him as his wings. With a flex of his fingers, his sword appeared in his hand as if summoned from his hollow.

"Get your people out of my territory."

Ciarán tensed but dipped his head in a quick nod.

Vesryn looked back at the tree. It was as large as if it had stood there for hundreds of years, but it was still only a fraction of the size of Ylrendorei's palace. It had stopped growing and expanding for now, but he could feel its roots shifting beneath him, drawing on the power of the ley lines to restore what was lost when the humans cut its predecessor down.

He gave Ciarán several long minutes to get his soldiers clear before he turned and stalked out of the valley. The Summer Court was visible along the edge, their golden armor still shining bright despite the signs of carnage all around them. The Winter Court was a receding wave of dark in the distance. The Summer King was easy to spot, even among the glistening gold. He stood several heads taller than the rest and wore a crown of woven antlers at least half again as high.

Vesryn didn't look away from him as he spread his wings and lifted into the air. Wild magic leapt to his fingers as he raised his sword arm. He let it consume him.

The earth trembled and cracked apart, the skies darkened, and a howling wind filled the entirety of his territory. Past the mountains to the south, to the cold seas far to the north. All the way east across the river, to the edge of the singing forests. All the land above where the ylren roots stretched was his.

He had no need for the Summer Court to be there, and they were certainly not welcome.

Lightning flashed through the darkening clouds, but instead of rain, he called down fire. The skies filled with an endless volley of burning hail. It rained down over the soldiers and their king, a wildfire that blazed through their lines and spread across the land. The trees and green of the forest smoked as they burned.

He felt the tears between the realms and the shape of the magic that had formed them. He ripped open several more across his territory, urging the fleeing animals and creatures to pass through to the fae realm. Everything left behind would burn.

The soldiers broke rank and fled to the nearest tear.

Vesryn made no move to stop them, but he didn't lessen the amount of fire raining down on them either. The king didn't move, protected by a magical shield. Vesryn snarled and drifted towards him.

If the fae king of the Summer Court wanted to die, Vesryn was more than happy to oblige.

He landed on the scorched earth and stared at the fae. "Leave."

"Kneel," the king returned, eyeing Vesryn like a misbehaving child.

Vesryn laughed. "You first."

The fae sneered and drew his sword, which looked like solid gold. When he swung it, a ripple of power stopped the rain of fire around them, as if they were encased in a magical bubble. "You will die here."

Vesryn wondered if anyone but Ciarán and his guard knew what he was. If he had knowledge that would surely destroy his enemy, he doubted he would share it either. He remained where he was as the fae lumbered towards him.

The first swing told him the king might be skilled, but he hadn't seen true battle in a long time. Vesryn certainly could have honed his skills fighting him, but he wasn't interested in a clean fight. The Summer Court was as much to blame for this as Fate and the Wild Court's princess.

Peace, she'd promised, *and the power to keep it.*

Except power wouldn't do anything for him without making his message clear. The throne was his, and anyone who tried to take it would die.

They were the only two left on the battlefield now, and Vesryn couldn't truly die. His only purpose was to guard the throne until he found a way to bring Nox back. He only had to get close enough to strike the final blow.

He let the fae push him onto the defensive. He didn't care to block or deflect more than necessary, hardly feeling the injuries as his flesh sliced open. Nothing could compare to the anguish of losing Nox. He saw when the king's confusion and wariness gave way to arrogance and smug certainty. Vesryn made no attempt to dodge the sword coming for him.

The shock of pain as it sank into and through his chest was almost enough for doubt to creep in, but he wouldn't lose here. He couldn't.

He bared his teeth, tasting blood as he grabbed the fae's wrist and used it to drag himself up the long blade. "I hope your heir comes for revenge so I can kill them too," he snarled, before cutting off the king's head. The sword's flames seared the wounds as it cut through. The look of shock and outrage was still frozen on the king's face when it landed on the ground.

Vesryn coughed and spat blood on the body before shoving it away, gritting his teeth as it pulled the sword with it. He staggered once he was free, somehow staying on his feet and tipping his head back as the magical bubble melted away. Fire still rained from the skies.

As he tipped to the side and the world faded to a black void, he called on the magic to ensure everything was razed to the ground.

VESRYN WOKE sometime later to silence and the lingering smell of smoke. His body was covered in ash but restored from death. Even his lost finger.

The sky was dark as he picked himself up, but he wasn't sure if it was because the sun had set or if it was the storm clouds that looked like they covered the entire realm. The king's body was still there, as scorched as the ground around them. He bent long enough to rip the crown of antlers off the severed head before turning and trudging back to the valley.

Everywhere he looked was blackened earth covered in ash, but the ylren tree was untouched. The clearing around it was restored, green and lush with sweet grasses and dark mosses, the silver flickers of fireflies glittering in the dark.

He lifted the king's crown as he approached, hooking it over a branch before sinking to his knees in front of the throne. He let his wings dissipate as he rested his head in the seat and closed his eyes. He'd need to restore the rest of the land. Fill it with gardens of all the flowers between the realms, like it surely had been before, so Nox could feel at home when he returned. But that was too much to worry about for now.

Despite his body being restored, he still felt the magical exhaustion of using so much power that he wasn't used to, and he didn't want to leave Nox's side. He couldn't see the shape of him inside the tree or throne with so much power from the ley lines around them, but he was there. Vesryn could feel him.

He had enough energy left to close all the tears he'd opened; then he gave up on remaining conscious.

Chapter 27

Days passed, but Vesryn barely moved. The throne was restored, his Fate bond was gone, and he was burdened with the crown of the Wild Throne. What did he need to move for?

Was this how Nox had felt while Vesryn's core and memories had been sealed away in his sword for Ages? They weren't meant to be apart for so long.

At some point, he sensed someone step through the nearby tear that the Summer Court had used, but he stayed where he was, waiting to see if they'd leave. When they didn't, he snarled and forced himself to his feet.

He winced with every step as his legs regained feeling, finally resorting to calling his wings and flying out to meet whoever had come to die. The king's body was gone when he arrived, and a younger fae was standing close to where it had been.

As Vesryn landed, he saw the crown. A smaller, more modest version of the one he'd taken. Prince or princess, he couldn't tell, and he didn't care. "What do you want?"

The fae looked him over curiously. "*You* killed my father?"

Vesryn called his sword to his hand and heard the rush of flames as it ignited. He took a step forward, but the fae hastily threw their hands up and backed away.

"I'm not here to fight!"

Vesryn sneered. "Then swear to me that you and your court will make no move to try to seize the Wild Throne." When the fae opened their mouth, Vesryn pointed his sword at them. "Do not twist your words," he snapped. "Speak plain and true or die."

The fae paled, and Vesryn was surprised by the curl of magic in his words. It felt similar to when Nox had invoked his name. At least the throne came with something useful.

The fae dropped to a knee, swearing no one of the Summer Court would come for the throne.

Satisfied, Vesryn extinguished the flames. "What do you want?"

"A truce," the fae said, standing and looking around. The earth was still scorched, but already grasses and weeds were starting to return.

Vesryn wasn't worried about it. The weather was getting colder without the forest to provide heat and protection against the cold winds off the seas and mountain range. When spring came he might feel more like dealing with the land.

"We could provide you with the seeds needed to restore the wilds."

He narrowed his eyes. If any of those seeds were for more of the trees that had tried to eat him, he wasn't interested. "I'd prefer you leave and not return. I have no interest in dealing with your court."

The fae frowned, though it bordered on a sneer. Before they could protest, Vesryn took another step forward. "Leave."

They yelped and nearly tripped as they scrambled back, glaring at him before stalking through the tear.

Vesryn lifted a hand, intending to seal it completely, but something stopped him. A shift of magic at the edge of his awareness. The tears were needed. That was why Nox had sealed them with ylren trees. But he had no seeds to do the same.

As if in response to his needs, mushrooms with bright red caps covered in white spots grew in a large circle around the tear. There was enough room for one or two fae to stand inside, and he could sense the spells that would prevent anyone from stepping outside the circle without his permission. That would have to do for now.

When he returned to the valley, he found Ciarán crouched in front of the throne.

"Get away from him!" Vesryn yelled, flames igniting around his sword as he rushed forward.

Ciarán stood, turned, and drew his sword in one fluid movement. He blurred into Vesryn's space faster than should have been possible and slammed his palm into Vesryn's chest, the force of it enough to choke the breath from him. "I am not your enemy," he hissed, watching Vesryn through narrowed, furious eyes.

Vesryn bared his teeth, wishing he could run Ciarán through with his sword, but he wouldn't betray his help like that. "What do you want?"

Ciarán sheathed his sword and turned back to the throne. "As I said before, I'm here to help."

He scoffed and dismissed his sword, resisting the urge to drag the fae away from the throne. He hadn't wanted Ciarán anywhere near Nox when he was alive; he certainly didn't want him near now. "Unless you know how to restore him—"

"I do."

Vesryn nearly staggered with the mindless hope that filled him, latching on to Ciarán's arm without realizing he'd even moved. *"How?"*

"A ylren seed. And his blood."

The pain as hope died was worse than losing Nox the first time. A sharp, bitter laugh ripped his throat open as he sank to his knees. "Leave," he gasped.

Ciarán ignored him and crouched in front of Vesryn instead. "There is a way to bring him back. Fate needs you both for what's to come."

Fate again. He was so tired of Fate fucking with everyone's lives. "Tell Fate to go—"

"Do not finish that thought," Ciarán snapped. "I am here to revive the Raven. Are you going to help or not?"

"Yes," he hissed. As if that could ever be in doubt. "But there are no more seeds. They were all used to make the throne."

Ciarán tilted his head back as he studied the ylren tree. "You're certain? He had several in his pocket. More than what would be needed for this."

Vesryn pressed the heels of his palms into his eyes, forcing his breaths to slow. He didn't believe Fate cared enough to return Nox for anything but the end goal, but he wouldn't lose a chance to restore his raven. "The mountain," he said once he'd calmed enough to think again. "If he'd known a ylren tree would become the throne...."

Ciarán nodded and straightened as if he meant to go there himself.

As much as Vesryn didn't want to leave him alone with the throne, he could get there faster by flying. "Do not touch him," he said as he got to his feet. He ignored Ciarán's sigh as he pushed into the air and turned for the mountain.

The red glow had faded, the molten rocks crusted over, with thick cracks of red oozing between them. He landed on the ledge and adjusted his sight as he searched for the glimmer of a ylren seed. He froze when he saw the residual magic from Nox's blood, the tiny droplets on the ground a dark glow against the brilliance of the ley line below.

"Fuck," he breathed, closing his eyes and turning away. He couldn't be distracted now. He had no idea how long a seed could survive here without a direct connection to magic or water, but he doubted it would be much longer than it already had. If there was even one here.

He made his way to the tunnel where he'd found Nox, sure this was another of Fate's games. If Fate was ever foolish enough to show Their face, he'd cut Their head off as easily as the Summer King's.

"Where are you?" he whispered, turning when he reached the spot where he'd found Nox. He was about to go back and search again when another dark splatter of blood caught his eye. He tried to look away, but then he noticed a speck of green.

He dropped to his knees and leaned closer, reaching for the dark glow wrapped around the glimmer of a ylren seed. A tiny sprout was pushing through the cracked shell, the edges brown, and his heart lurched. "No," he hissed. "You are not dying." He settled it in his palm and called for a gentle rain, remembering the small rain clouds Nox had summoned in his hand.

Magic swelled around him, a cool breeze cutting through the stifling heat, and a mist of rain coated the seed.

For a long moment nothing happened, and he feared it wouldn't be enough. That the sprout would die before he ever got it back to the valley. But then he felt it reach for his magic, and he blew out a desperate, shaky laugh. He clutched it close to his chest as he stood. He spotted Nox's spear a short distance away and snatched it as he pushed into the air and raced back to the throne.

Ciarán was waiting for him, a small hole ready near the ylren tree, on the opposite side of the throne, where the roots were spread as if making space specifically for the seed.

He didn't question it. Merely knelt beside the hole and carefully dropped the seed into it. He covered all but the tiny leaf with dirt, then sat back. Watching, waiting for some indication that this was going to work.

"Fae aren't born like elves or humans. Did you know that?" Ciarán asked.

Vesryn tore his gaze away from the sprout to narrow his eyes at Ciarán. "No."

"We're born from the ylren. From a single seed, infused with the magic and wishes of our parents. But memories can be passed as well."

"How?"

Ciarán didn't respond immediately, watching Vesryn as if he should know the answer.

It was a look he knew well from his time in the palace. Duaia had often looked at Callith and Julius like that when they were younger, after they did something particularly foolish.

Julius.

Vesryn's breath hitched as he reached for the ylren blossom wine. His darkest hour had passed, or perhaps he was still caught in the midst of it, but he couldn't imagine anything worse than losing Nox and not being able to bring him back.

Ciarán crouched in front of him with a soft grunt of surprise. "That will work. One sip for each of us."

Vesryn pulled the bottle to his chest with a snarl. "What do you mean us?"

Ciarán raised an eyebrow. "That wine is old. Ages old. Old enough the magic can call to like magic and the memories held within. You have the memories of the Raven's past lives. I have memories of his life as a fae. Do you want him to be whole or not?"

Vesryn swore, cursing Fate and desperately hoping he met Them in the future. He opened the wine and took a sip before handing it to Ciarán, who took his own sip before pouring a tiny drop into the soil covering the seed.

The ley line swelled as magic filled the valley. The grasses and mosses began glowing. First white, and then silver and red and black and all the colors in between, each blade of grass pulsing in its own unique shade. The magic climbed up the roots and the trunk of the ylren tree, into its branches and leaves, the throne nearly vibrating as a high-pitched ringing filled the air.

Then Vesryn began to glow. And Ciarán. And the sprout.

Intense, pleasant heat filled him from head to toe, before dizziness swept over him. A pulling sensation started in his head, memories flooding to the surface as if the magic was trying to pull them out of him. Countless lifetimes. Infinite memories. Endless devotion. Unfailing love. All of his emotions for Nox spilled out of him and seeped into the sprout.

Time became an illusion. Moments could have been days or months or years.

When the brilliant light and pressure of magic finally faded, Vesryn was sprawled on the ground and night had fallen. The moon was bright in the cloudless sky.

He sat up with a groan and saw Ciarán sitting nearby, but his attention caught on the bright strings connecting the two of them to the sprout. They appeared white at first, but the closer he looked the more he saw the shifting of colors, like the magic that had blanketed them. Instead of attaching to their fingers like a Fate string, they seemed to disappear into their chests.

Before he could ask, Ciarán flicked his fingers at his own string. "This proves it worked. The sprout will draw magic and memories from us and the ley lines to restore him."

Vesryn closed his eyes with a shaky breath before turning his attention to the sprout. The brown edges were gone, and it had grown into a thin sapling with a single bulb the size of a large berry. He watched it for a long while, willing it to grow or bloom, but the magic around them was quiet.

"How long?" he whispered.

Ciarán hesitated before answering. "Next spring."

An entire year and a season. It sounded like forever, but it was hardly any time at all.

He sat up and shifted to lean back against the ylren tree, unwilling to have the sprout out of his sight. "What were you promised?"

Ciarán stared at him for a moment before answering. "A chance to control my own life."

Vesryn raised an eyebrow, but Ciarán didn't seem inclined to elaborate. As a prince, Vesryn could understand Ciarán feeling trapped. That was something both Callith and Synne had complained about loudly and often. He reached for the ylren blossom wine, stoppered it, and secured it in his hollow.

"We'll need that again. At the start of each season," Ciarán said.

"Are you saying I'm stuck with you for an entire year?"

Ciarán smirked. "You'd be lonely without me. And you'll need help to restore everything you destroyed."

Vesryn grimaced. He couldn't exactly deny that. At least the valley had been spared his rain of destruction. "Fine," he muttered, slumping against the tree. "Where do we start?"

CHAPTER 28

WINTER PASSED slowly. Snow replaced the ash, though the valley remained protected in a bubble of early spring.

Vesryn used his new wild magic to reshape the valley enough for a creek to run along the edge, fed from the high peaks of the mountain range.

Ciarán gave him seeds from the fae realm, and they planned out how to restore the gardens that once covered the entire territory.

He flew to the remaining original tears created with Nox's release from the ley lines. The one Ciarán had used that opened deep in the heart of the Winter Court, and the one across the river where they'd seen the huge cow beast. He sealed them both with another circle of mushrooms, altering the spells enough to allow Ciarán passage to his home as needed.

WHEN SPRING arrived, so did changes to the valley and his crown. Where before brambles and thorns had wrapped around his head, now he wore a crown of soft pale green vines with white-dusted leaves. Various flowers began blooming through the valley. Sky blue bushes with tufts for leaves. Tall straight stems with feather-like flowers in bright reds and pure whites. Patches of moss from crimson red to sunburst yellows.

Mushrooms littered the roots of the ylren tree. Not the red-and-white ones surrounding the tears, but various shapes and sizes. From lightning-blue strings like beads of jewels, to black caps that looked like they were dripping black slime, to small orange spirals that could have passed as seashells.

He and Ciarán shared a sip of the wine, and the magic filled the valley again. When it faded, the sapling had grown as large as the throne, the bulb as large as his head. Ciarán assured him it would grow larger still over the coming months.

Ciarán brought sturdy hammocks back from the fae realm, and they hung them from the branches near the sapling.

Vesryn spent most of his mornings and evenings in his, whistling or humming or telling Nox of the progress he'd made with the gardens.

Sometimes Ciarán joined him and they shared stories of battles or foolish nobles.

Insects began to appear as more flowers bloomed. Large fat, fuzzy bees and butterflies in every color. Leafhoppers and ants and gossamer spiders. Fish found their way into the creek, with tiny crabs and frogs.

They spent the entire spring shaping the gardens and a new forest beyond the valley, without the elf-eating trees. He allowed some creatures to return. The rabbits and other tiny furred creatures. Songbirds and hawks and owls. Black wolves that filled the nights with their songs.

Ciarán showed him how to set the fae paths to allow faster travel, and Vesryn set a self-contained path around the tears that would trap someone inside, in case anyone managed to break through the mushroom circles.

"You're being unreasonable," Ciarán muttered, but Vesryn ignored him. The Summer Court may have sworn not to seek to take the throne, but he didn't trust them to stay true to their word. Or for others not to try.

He built a small house from some moontrees that were popular in the Winter Court. Similar to the dawntrees in Ylrendorei that shed soft amber light, the moontrees glowed with a soft silvery glow. Their leaves were a rich, deep blue that seemed to cool the shade they provided more than other trees. He planted more of them in the forest, near to the paths, to light the way.

When the house was finished, the wood emitted the same glow at night.

Ciarán helped fill it with comfortable furniture. A table with chairs. Couches and armchairs with deep cushions. Two large beds and chests of polished, deep red wood.

They opened the windows with their clear view of the ylren tree and the sapling, the creek in the distance, and shared a bottle of frostberry wine. True to its name, it was cold and tart but warmed the blood.

"Are you ever going to enlighten me about why you're really here?" Vesryn asked when they'd gone through almost the entire bottle. He expected to be tipsier than he was, but he could have been drinking water for all the effect the wine had on him.

Ciarán narrowed his eyes over his glass.

Vesryn stared back, unbothered. "I can't know? Aren't we essentially creating a baby together?" He laughed, Ciarán's look of revulsion more than making up for the foul taste of calling Nox their child.

"You're a dick," Ciarán muttered, which only made him laugh harder.

It felt like forever since he'd laughed or found a sense of camaraderie. Something like it had started to settle between him and Nox, but it'd still been too new to be comfortable. He refilled their glasses, still snickering as he leaned back in his chair.

Ciarán heaved an exaggerated sigh and glanced out the window. "His father was going to sell him to the highest bidder," he said after a long while. He shifted in his seat, and Vesryn didn't miss that it left him room to quickly move. The angle of his body was familiar after years of taking his turn patrolling Ylrendorei's tavern and barracks. It was the posture of someone expecting a fight.

Ciarán didn't look at him as he added, "I was the highest bidder."

Vesryn expected anger for Ciarán daring to purchase another fae, or maybe jealousy, but he thought he knew the prince well enough by now to know he would have only bid to keep Nox from going somewhere far worse. "And?" he asked.

Ciarán tilted his head and finally looked at Vesryn. "And before I could take him back home, the paths between the realms were sealed. The few who escaped here were speaking tales of horror of the Raven slaughtering every fae."

Vesryn snarled softly. The timing was far too perfect to be anything other than Fate intervening. "And now?" he asked. "You're trying to claim what you're owed?"

Ciarán sat back with a look of surprise. "No. I didn't pay in advance, and I would never dare get between the Phoenix and his Raven," he added dryly. He swirled his wine in his glass before taking a sip. "Essentially, my mother blames me for this mess. Restoring the balance here will serve as suitable recompense, and I will be free to indulge in my own pursuits again."

Vesryn nearly choked on his wine. "You've been confined at home this entire time?"

Ciarán let out a long-suffering sigh. "Not quite so restrictive as that, but yes."

He lifted his glass in tribute. "To freedom."

THUNDERSTORMS HERALDED the beginning of summer.

After they shared wine and the magic filled the valley once again, the sapling grew as large as Vesryn.

The storms raged for weeks, the creek flooding to a small river. He adjusted the banks to keep it from encroaching on their sanctuary any further. Within the soft vines of his crown bloomed small flowers with six petals, in every shade from black to red to white.

He and Ciarán spent long hours inside, drinking wine or playing cards, though he was certain the fae cheated more often than not.

The gardens flourished when the rains stopped and the temperature rose. The droning of locusts and crickets filled the days and nights. The ylren tree more than doubled in size over the summer, ivy winding its way around its trunk and the house. When he flew to the top, he could see nearly to the river in the east and the singing forests beyond, and past the single peak to the cold seas in the north. When he followed the paths to the farthest northeastern edge of the wilds, he could see where his mountain range shifted to the white mountains of the north, on the other side of the frozen seas, where the Frost Throne was supposed to reside.

He wondered if Callith and his bondeds had made it there to meet more dragons, or if they'd returned to the Wound or even Ylrendorei by now. Had they seen a sign to tell them it was time to restore the Wound again? Or did Nox have to return first? Was that what they needed to wait for?

The sooner the plains and rich lands between Ylrendorei and the singing forests were restored, the sooner both lands could begin thriving again.

WITH FALL, the leaves of the moontrees changed from blue to white, and when they fell they continued to glow even as they crumbled, littering the ground like tiny fallen stars. The green vines of his crown paled to nearly yellow and the flowers wilted, leaving behind a tangle of vines with fragile-looking leaves.

They shared the wine again, and the sapling grew more than twice Vesryn's size, the bulb large enough for a full-grown fae to fit inside. The deep green shell took on a darker shade at the edges, where it would break apart for the petals when it bloomed. If he squinted and tilted his head, he could see a vibrant violet through the cracks. When he brushed a hand over one of the large leaves, he could feel the steady thrum of raw magic feeding into it.

"Almost there," he whispered, resting his forehead against the bulb. "Come back to me soon."

WINTER'S FIRST bite covered the gardens in thick, glittering frost. The edges of the valley sparkled and the creek ran cold, pieces of ice floating down from the mountains and catching on the banks.

His crown returned to the bramble form it had initially taken.

This time when they shared the wine, Vesryn was left drained and magically exhausted, as if more than memories had been scraped out of him.

Ciarán looked no better but assured him it was normal, that the last bit of growth and the restoration spells needed more energy than usual to complete their tasks.

They slept for days to recover, and the winter passed as slowly as the first.

Light frosts turned to deep snows that blanketed the gardens in a resounding silence, broken only by the occasional howl of a wolf, their pelts faded to white now, and Vesryn found himself walking the paths often, the scrunch of his footsteps echoing around him as his breath fogged the air. Soon he'd be able to enjoy this with Nox. When Fate was finally done with them. With all of them.

Licks of flames melted the snow around him in response to his quiet seething. He would help Callith if need be, because even wearing a crown he still retained a sense of loyalty to Callith's family. He had no intention of creating his own kingdom. Of having a palace with nobles and loyal subjects of his own.

As far as he was concerned, this entire territory was his own personal sanctuary for him and Nox. And Ciarán if he insisted on visiting.

CHAPTER 29

By the time the snows melted and new shoots of grasses began emerging, Vesryn felt like Rashi after inhaling an entire sweet cream pie. He found it difficult to stay still, constantly checking the sapling and bulb, as afraid to touch it as he was desperate for it to finally bloom.

They shared a sip of wine again, though the resulting magic was far more subdued than usual.

"It may still take days," Ciarán cautioned, and Vesryn told himself he couldn't punch the prince until after Nox returned.

He took to sleeping in his hammock despite the cool nights. He refused to miss the moment the bulb finally bloomed.

He knew the day was drawing close when he woke to find sunset foxgloves blanketing the entire valley and blooming from his crown.

They moved the table and chairs outside to keep a closer eye on the bulb, but they didn't have long to wait. By that afternoon, Vesryn could sense the magic fading.

And then the bulb cracked open.

Bright violet petals unfurled and revealed Nox curled up inside, his wings tucked around him like a blanket.

Vesryn's legs nearly gave out on him as he stumbled forward. "Nox," he gasped, catching himself against the giant petals.

Nox blinked his eyes open, their violet color duller than it should be.

"The wine," Ciarán said.

Vesryn hissed as he retrieved it. There wasn't much left. A swallow for each of them. He took a sip and passed it to the fae, who sipped and then held it out to Nox.

When Nox sat up, he stared at the bottle with a blank expression before looking at Vesryn.

He snatched the bottle from Ciarán, secretly pleased Nox hadn't accepted the wine from the fae. He wasn't sure it mattered to the magic or ritual, but he didn't like the idea of his raven accepting such an important thing from anyone but him.

"Drink," Vesryn said softly, offering the wine to Nox himself.

Nox took the bottle and drank what little was left.

Magic flared around the three of them, and then the strings linking Nox to both of them faded.

Vesryn swayed at the sudden shift in his magic. He hadn't noticed how much the connection had been draining from him until it vanished.

Nox coughed and hunched forward as if he was going to be sick. Vesryn caught him with a hand on his shoulder, keeping him from falling to the ground as his body shook with dry heaves. "What the fuck happened?" Nox rasped, his eyes the vibrant violet they should be when he looked up.

Vesryn laughed, unable to contain the shaky relief and elation at seeing Nox restored, whole and unharmed. "Welcome back."

IT WAS well into the evening by the time they explained the past year over a pot of hot stew and bottle of frostberry wine. Ciarán made it clear their next steps needed to be leaving for Ylrendorei. He didn't have a Fate string to guide him, but he was adamant that was where they needed to go.

Vesryn didn't mind the thought of leaving after being stuck here for a year, but he was loath to leave before Nox had at least a few days to adjust. As far as they could tell, Nox retained his memories up to the moment the seeds had pierced his chest to claim him as the throne, which Vesryn was grateful for. As much as he might have enjoyed pursuing Nox the first time, he needed the warm grip of Nox's fingers around his own and the weight of his head on Vesryn's shoulder.

The wandering fingers of Nox's other hand against Vesryn's thigh wasn't amiss either.

Ciarán eyed them with exasperation. "I think I'll return home for a few days," he said dryly.

Vesryn hummed, not about to dissuade him.

"When I come back, we need to leave."

Vesryn narrowed his eyes. "Go before I find a tree to feed you to."

Ciarán made a rude gesture on his way out, finally leaving him alone with Nox.

He breathed a sigh of relief and pressed his face into Nox's sunset hair. The firelight added a soft shadow to the dim glow of the moontree and the soft crackle of wood. He was more than content to sit and bask in the silence until Ciarán returned, so long as Nox was there with him.

"I think I met Fate while I was dead," Nox said, soft enough Vesryn might have imagined it.

He tightened his grip on Nox's fingers as he failed to completely stifle a snarl. "And?"

Nox blew out a long exhale, lifting his head off Vesryn's shoulder. "I think we need to meet with the elf king and the others. Soon."

"That bad?" he asked, tempted to seal the entire house in a cave and then flood the land enough to cover it. Was this how Alais and Hycis felt, dragged from one crisis to another without a chance to truly rest?

Nox shook his head and pressed closer. "I don't want to think about it."

"All right," Vesryn murmured, completely distracted by Nox climbing into his lap. He tipped his head back, finding Nox's lips with his own and sliding his hands over his raven's thighs. "You know I do have a bed now."

Nox practically jumped out of his lap and headed down the hall.

Vesryn hurried after him, grabbing his wrist when he reached for Ciarán's door. "Not that one," he growled, pulling a smirking raven into his own room.

"Is someone jealous?" Nox taunted, kicking the door shut as he pushed Vesryn to the bed.

Vesryn refused to justify that with an answer. He'd been stuck with Ciarán for an entire year, and if he never learned another habit like how the fae liked to sleep naked, it would still be too soon.

Nox snickered and planted a hand on Vesryn's chest to shove him down.

Vesryn raised an eyebrow as his back hit the bed. "Is someone feisty?"

"Yes," Nox grumbled, tugging Vesryn's boots off and tossing them to the side, where they clattered against the wall.

Vesryn's socks and pants followed, and he was not at all inclined to protest. He pulled his own shirt off and tossed it after the rest of his clothes.

Nox didn't seem interested in teasing. He stripped with the same ruthless efficiency, and then he was on top of Vesryn, all long limbs and bare sable flesh.

Vesryn dug his fingers into Nox's back as his wings draped over the sides of the bed, pressing his knees into Nox's sides and pulling him closer, marveling at the feel of their bodies slotting together. It'd been far too long, both since he'd shared a bed with someone in general, and with Nox in particular.

Nox's mouth was hot on Vesryn's neck, and a wet swipe of his tongue drew a moan from them both.

He tipped his head back and to the side to give Nox full access, sliding one hand through a mess of feathers and reaching for a bottle of oil on the bedside table with the other. He nearly dropped it when Nox bit him hard enough to leave a lasting mark. "Ow."

Nox lifted his head enough to stare down at Vesryn with narrowed eyes. "Ciarán was here the entire year?"

"Yes."

Nox scowled, pressing both hands into the bed on either side of Vesryn's head. "Did you sleep with him?"

"Of course not."

Nox continued glowering for a long moment, as if he couldn't believe that. Ciarán might be handsome enough in a brooding prince way, but he couldn't compare to Nox.

"I'm yours," Vesryn said, leaning up to press a kiss to Nox's nose.

Nox hummed, sliding his thumb across Vesryn's lips before resting his hand across Vesryn's throat. "Mine," he murmured.

He swallowed as heat spiked in his gut. He managed a faint "All yours" and tipped his head back further, his body going lax with surrender.

Nox smirked and plucked the oil bottle with his free hand before leaning down and brushing the tip of his nose along Vesryn's cheek. "To do anything I want with?"

Vesryn's breath hitched. "Yes," he gasped. He'd do anything Nox asked of him, and they both knew it, regardless of what was asked.

Nox sat back with a considering hum, studying him for a long moment before pulling the cork out of the bottle with his teeth. He spat it to the side, and Vesryn was glad when it landed on the bed and not the floor to disappear. Nox put his thumb over the opening before tipping the bottle and drizzling oil over Vesryn's chest and stomach, then slid his other hand from Vesryn's throat to drag his fingers through the mess.

His raven's smirk twitched into something more devious as he continued down, pouring oil over Vesryn's hips and groin before coating both his thighs.

Vesryn hissed as the cool oil hit sensitive areas, shifting beneath Nox as his raven silently laughed at him.

Nox bent forward to set the bottle on the floor and swiped his tongue against Vesryn's nipple.

He arched into it with a gasp, burying a hand in Nox's hair to urge him on. He groaned as he was rewarded with teeth sinking into the sensitive flesh. "Nox," he breathed, catching a brief glimpse of violet eyes before Nox moved to the other nipple and sucked it into his mouth.

Nox lowered himself against Vesryn until their bodies were pressed together, the oil warming between them with the intoxicating scent of dawntree and ylren blossom.

Vesryn shifted between sliding his other hand through soft black feathers and digging into the tight muscles of Nox's back. He closed his eyes as he relished his raven's attention and the marks he left across Vesryn's chest.

When Nox finally sat back, it was to press Vesryn's legs together. He wrapped his arms tight around them before sliding his cock between Vesryn's thighs. His wings fluttered and spread wide behind him, blanketing Vesryn in their shadow.

Even without his magical core, how had he ever forgotten that he and this magnificent creature belonged together? No realm or passing of Ages could separate them. Chaos itself couldn't keep them apart.

He curled his hand in front of his thighs, catching Nox's cock when he thrust forward again and squeezing.

Nox shuddered with a pleading moan and thrust faster, the oil aiding his movements. He dropped a hand from Vesryn's legs and fumbled for a grip on him in return, but most of his attention was caught between Vesryn's thighs when he flexed his muscles. The violet of his eyes nearly glowed in the dark as he neared his limit.

Vesryn couldn't resist forming a small orb of light above them. He slid his hand between his thighs to keep a tight grip on his raven when his pace faltered. His stunning raven. Especially when he was lost in the throes of pleasure.

Nox squeezed his eyes shut, his head tipping back with a guttural moan as he spilled, slicking Vesryn's hand and thighs with spend. He slumped forward, his chest heaving as his entire weight pressed against Vesryn's legs.

The subtle scent of flowers filled the air, and Vesryn didn't need to look to know the floor was covered in clusters of foxglove. He lifted both his hands as he parted his legs, catching Nox as he fell forward and lowering him until he was sprawled over Vesryn's chest. He was still hard and aching, but he didn't mind. Not when Nox was a warm, heavy weight on top of him and they were in bed, with nowhere to be and no pressing crisis to attend to.

Whatever Ciarán thought they needed to do could wait until Vesryn had ample time to properly ravish his raven.

He was content to let Nox rest and recover, lightly stroking his fingers through his raven's hair. Eventually he grew tired of waiting for Nox to wake up and carefully ran his hands along the edges of Nox's wings, coaxing them to tuck in, before nudging him onto his side. The wings flickered to insubstantial shadows as they dipped against and then through the bed.

Vesryn hummed and slid down Nox's body, trailing kisses along the way. When he found his target, he spent a long while kissing there too, before nudging Nox's leg over his shoulder. Then he took Nox into his mouth, swallowing him to the hilt before closing his eyes with a quiet moan. It didn't take long for Nox to swell, or for his raven to instinctively rock into the wet heat of Vesryn's mouth.

He waited until fingers gripped his hair and for Nox to sleepily mumble his name before setting to work. He gripped the firm, supple flesh of Nox's ass with both hands and squeezed.

"Fuck," Nox gasped, his fingers curling tighter in Vesryn's hair.

Vesryn opened his throat with an encouraging hum, and Nox pushed into it with abandon. He tried to roll forward and push Vesryn onto his back, but he held his raven in place, curling his arms over Nox's thighs to hold him still as he lifted his head enough to swirl his tongue around the tip.

Nox's hips pushed against Vesryn's grip as he tried to bury himself in Vesryn's mouth again. "Please."

How could he ignore such a sweet request?

Vesryn took Nox fully into his mouth again and swallowed. When Nox started rocking his hips, Vesryn flexed his tongue, letting his hands explore from Nox's back to his thighs and everywhere in between. Before Nox could find his release, he pulled his mouth away, chuckling when Nox whined in protest. "I'm not finished," he murmured, wiggling out of Nox's grip and coaxing him to his stomach.

He leaned over to find the bottle, then settled between his raven's thighs to pour oil over his ass and his own arousal. Then he set the bottle on the table and kissed his way up Nox's spine, stretching out over his back. He buried his face against his raven's neck, breathing in the rich, spicy scent of him as he began rocking his hips.

The hot, slick grip as he slid against Nox's crevice nearly pushed him over the edge. "Fuck, you feel so good," Vesryn murmured, sliding a hand around to grip Nox and stroke him in time to his own thrusts.

Nox squirmed beneath him with impatient, pleading moans, and Vesryn didn't try to draw it out any longer than either of them needed. He'd waited a year already. Anything more complicated than slaking their lust could wait. A few quick thrusts and strokes and they were both spent.

With a satisfied groan, he rolled off Nox and collapsed beside him. Nox immediately flung an arm and leg over him, his wings tangible once again. Vesryn closed his eyes with a sigh and dragged his fingers from Nox's hair down his spine and back up again. His wings shuddered beneath the touch, the rustle of feathers filling the spaces between their breaths and lulling him to sleep.

They woke long enough to take a shower, and Vesryn noticed the crown on Nox's head, made of dark green vines and bright sunset foxglove. When he glanced down, the same flowers grew, bloomed, and faded to glimmering dust in Nox's footsteps. "You're connected to the throne."

Nox glanced back at him, tilting his head before seeming to notice the crown on his head. He reached for it with a scowl, but Vesryn caught his wrists.

"It's yours as much as it is mine." He pressed his lips to Nox's fingers. "If I'm stuck being a king then you are too." Surely if Nox being connected alongside him was a danger to the realm, the crown wouldn't have formed to begin with.

Nox huffed and dragged him into the shower.

They took far longer than necessary when Nox pinned him against the wall and refused to move until their lips were kiss-swollen and their skin was wrinkled. They ate the bread and fresh pot of stew Ciarán must have left for them, then fell into bed again, their limbs tangled as they traded lazy kisses.

At some point in the evening Nox dragged him outside, where they stood naked under the ylren tree and gazed at the stars. He wasn't sure what his raven was planning, but he could feel the echo of nerves along their bond as the silence settled around them. Finally Nox turned to face Vesryn as he called something from his hollow. A tiny athame settled in his hand, shrouded in powerful spellwork.

"Where did you get that?"

Nox studied it for a moment before glancing up with a frown. "Fate, I think." He didn't explain further, merely pressed the tip beneath his thumb and drew a small line, cupping his hand to catch the spill of blood. Then he turned the athame and offered the hilt to Vesryn.

Vesryn eyed it warily, but he couldn't refuse Nox anything, even if he wanted to deny Fate's hand in something this personal. "What are we doing?" he asked as he cut his own hand.

"I won't be separated from you again," Nox said, the vehemence in his words taking Vesryn by surprise. "You made a bargain once that tore us apart." He ignored Vesryn's flinch and continued. "I won't suffer through that again. This is *my* bargain: Two bound as one. Forever."

He looked from their spilled blood to Nox's determined stare. He knew better than to swear a blood oath lightly, but simply getting through the last year without Nox, even knowing he would return, was not something he was keen on experiencing again. "Forever," he repeated, pressing their hands together.

Magic swirled between and around them, but it wasn't until Nox's dark wings lit up with white light and his own wings burst out of him that he realized what was happening. Blood fused their hands together as their essences twined through their bodies. When the magic faded an eternal moment later, white feathers were scattered throughout Nox's dark wings.

Vesryn didn't need to see his own to know black feathers dotted them; he could feel the dark glow of them. No longer a balance between

Death and Rebirth, they each now shared access to both, and to the Wild Throne.

Surely that much power would be enough to shatter the stability of the realm, but nothing happened. No ominous tremors in the earth or skies cracking open with poisonous lightning.

When he looked at Nox, he saw only a calm, satisfied smile before his raven stepped closer and pressed their lips together in a fierce kiss.

"Fly with me."

Heat and excitement washed through him, and he tried to temper the eagerness in his "Yes" but judging by Nox's hooded look he'd failed.

They took to the sky, and he immediately knew he had a chase on his hands.

Nox flew higher, nearly disappearing into the shadows of the clouds hiding the moon, but even without the tiny glimmers of white feathers, the Phoenix would always be able to find his raven. They twisted and darted through the clouds, flew over the restored forest, dipped low to drag fingers and wingtips through the river. Occasionally Vesryn drew close enough to grasp Nox's ankle, but Nox would manage to twist free with a laugh and speed away.

Eventually Vesryn had his fill of the chase and put more effort into truly catching his raven.

They tumbled through the air when Vesryn finally latched on and refused to let go. A few moments later and he had his arms properly secured around Nox, their chests heaving even as they kissed each other even more breathless.

Sharing pleasure in flight was every bit as complicated and entrancing as he'd thought it would be.

Time ceased to matter, and at some point they made their way back to the house and their bed. Vesryn lost count of how many times they brought each other to the peak of pleasure. He knew it couldn't last, not yet, not until Fate released them. But soon. They'd been promised peace, and he might be tempted to destroy this entire realm if they didn't get it.

They were woken from one of their many dozes by the sound of the main door opening.

"Stop fucking," Ciarán called. "It's time to go."

Vesryn cursed and pulled a pillow over his head.

Nox growled and curled closer. "Can we kill him?"

He laughed, pushing the pillow off his face to run both his hands through Nox's hair. He tugged his raven's head back to steal a quick kiss. "Maybe later."

Nox huffed and rolled out of bed. "Fine. Let's get this over with."

THEY SLIPPED through the shadows, crossing an impossible amount of space with a single step. It was as disorienting as it was nauseating. One moment they were standing in front of the Wild Throne, the next they were in front of the Sun Throne. The slant of light through the windows was no longer late morning but shortly past high sun.

There were exclamations and shouts of surprise, and a flurry of motion before they were surrounded by several guards.

Vesryn shifted to put himself in front of Nox and Ciarán, lifting his hands with his palms up. "Stand down," he ordered.

One of the guards closest to them startled in surprise. "Vesryn?"

"Yes." He looked at the dais where the thrones sat and found Synne standing with a look of shock.

"It's truly you?" she asked.

Vesryn smiled. "It's me."

She hurried down the steps and threw herself into his arms. "I knew you'd come back," she said, her voice muffled against his shoulder. She tipped her head back with a brilliant smile, but her eyes widened when she saw the crown of vines and flowers. "What in darkness happened?"

Ciarán cleared his throat. "I am sure you have plenty of things to discuss, but we don't have time."

Vesryn offered an apologetic wince. "He's right. Has Callith returned?"

Synne frowned at them for a moment before nodding. "He's actually at the docks meeting with the siren queen."

Vesryn didn't get a chance to say anything before Nox stepped through the shadows again, pulling him and Ciarán with him. His stomach protested, and he squeezed his eyes shut as he took a slow breath. He wasn't sure he would ever get used to that, though at least it explained how Aster had appeared in the throne room from nowhere.

When he could see again, they were on the docks. Callith, Haru, and Rashi, all three bearing crowns, were gathered with Julius, Duaia, the siren queen, and a few other sirens. Whatever the problem was had to be dire for them to be at the surface in the middle of the day.

One of the sirens beside the queen made a startled noise, staring at them with wide eyes. "No… it's too late."

Vesryn frowned as he met Callith's frustrated and surprised gaze. "What is?"

Beside him, Nox let out a resigned sigh. "Chaos is coming."

Find out how the story started in
Shadow's Wound
by Saria Bryant!

CHAPTER 1

"YOU'LL BE stabbed and left for dead."

Cal stared out the window of the carriage as Julius' words echoed in his mind. Unfortunately, unraveling a Seer's vision to find who could possibly want him dead wasn't even the most pressing issue he needed to deal with.

His father's death had brought the court and general government processes to a grinding halt. Part of that was his own fault, as he refused to be crowned, but a month seemed like far too little time to pass before he accepted the throne.

He might have brushed Julius' vision aside as a nightmare, but his Sight was never wrong. Still, his experience with visions was that they were confusing at best, and Fate's way of fucking with everyone involved at worst.

The carriage jolted as the cobblestone road gave way to the dirt and gravel of the seedier part of the city. He'd been working on plans to restore the worst areas within the next few years, but even that would have to wait now.

"We're here," Julius said as the carriage rolled to a stop in front of the prison.

Dread and excitement burned hot in his gut as Cal stared at the large iron building. He glanced briefly at his left hand, at the shimmer of a red Fate string coiled around his little finger. It'd been there for as long as he could remember, stretching into the distance, so faint he'd been convinced it was just his imagination. Until several weeks ago, when it started growing brighter and he couldn't deny its existence anymore.

Whoever his Fate was tied to, they'd finally arrived in his kingdom. And now the string was brighter and thicker than ever, pulled taut and leading directly into the prison.

He sighed and climbed out when Julius opened the door. He straightened his tunic and smoothed his hands over the fabric before striding inside. The threshold sparked along his senses, but the original function of the prison was so long forgotten, the lingering magic laid into its boundary was little more than an echo.

One of the guards took a single, imperious step towards them before shock settled on his face. He quickly bowed and fell into step behind Cal. "Your Highness."

Cal left the guard to Julius as he glanced at his hand, following the string deeper inside, past the iron-and-silver-wrought walls that still stood as testament to darker times, when they were needed to protect against the creatures and beasts that ruled the night. Creatures that hadn't been seen in Ages.

He ignored the oppressive weight of metal towering over him, his heart thrumming in his ears as the string brightened and seemed to pull tight enough to snap. He stopped in front of a solid iron door and found it locked. He flicked a glance to the guard. "Open it."

The guard hesitated. "Your Highn—" he started, but Julius didn't let him finish.

Julius stepped forward, grabbed the handle, and with a burst of condensed magic, wrenched the door open so hard the metal gave a sickening screech as it bent and twisted. He preceded Cal inside, but stopped two steps in.

Cal's heartbeat skipped at that hesitation, before the scent of blood, piss, and worse hit his nose. He grimaced and stepped inside, scanning the room. There were instruments strewn on iron tables and hung on the walls that wouldn't have been out of place in a torture chamber. Which, he realized, was exactly what this was. Most had signs of old blood, and all of them were iron or silver or sharp-edged metal.

His gaze landed on the table in the center of the room and the man bent over it, his back a bloody mess, his thin pants torn and soaked through. Two others stood near him. Not guards, they were dressed like human nobles. One held a whip, the other a single long strip of leather with jagged metal pieces woven through it, glinting with malicious spells.

His Fate string stretched out across the room, connecting him to the one strapped to the table.

"Release him," Cal snarled, taking another step into the room.

The man with the whip turned with a sneer that melted into horror. The other man ignored him completely and lifted his weapon for another strike.

Julius surged forward, but Cal was faster, lifting his hand as he gave his magic and rage an outlet. Coils of light wrapped around the man's wrists and throat, and he screamed as the magic burned him enough that he dropped his weapon, the stench of singed hair and skin mixing with the filth.

The other man hastily dropped his whip and scrambled back, hands lifted in surrender.

Cal stalked to the table, intending to release the man tied down, but Julius planted a hand against his chest.

"Don't you dare," Julius hissed, pushing him back a step and giving him a warning glare before going to the table himself.

Cal twitched at being denied, but he'd waited thirty-five years. He could wait a few more moments to get a look at the man Fate had decided belonged to him.

He ordered the new guards, arriving due to the commotion, to arrest the two men, as well as the first guard. Only then, as he turned back to Julius, did he notice his finger. The string was still there, glowing pure and bright and leading to the man now collapsed on the floor beside the table. Except it was thinner than before, because there was now another string, just as pure and bright and stretching to the other side of the room.

His breath stuttered as he moved to follow, faltering to a halt in front of what looked like an upright, rounded iron casket. He reached for the lock, but even when he strained with all his strength, it wouldn't budge.

"Juls," he said, his voice rough as his stomach twisted with a fresh wave of unease.

Julius appeared a moment later, pressing Cal back before studying the casket. He found the seam, gripped it, and heaved. Metal scraped against the floor with an ear-piercing screech. As soon as it was open, a slim form slumped forward.

Cal reached out instinctively, in time to keep the young man from being impaled on the spikes sprouting from the lid.

"Don't—" Julius started, but it was too late.

The magic inherent in the Fate bonds shimmered through him, and a heavy pulling sensation he'd never even realized was there eased away. It was almost enough to distract him from the very soft, furry ears brushing his chin.

"Don't fucking touch him." The words were slurred and rough with pain, but laden with a promise of violence.

Cal turned in time to see the other man he was bound to struggle to his feet, leaning heavily against the table to stay upright.

The man took an unsteady step forward and nearly collapsed again. "Give him back."

Cal ignored Julius' protests and slowly closed the distance to his other bonded. The man in his arms was barely coherent, but he was aware enough to keep his feet and seemed possessed of the same frantic need to be reunited with his partner. Once they were close enough, Cal released his hold and watched as the two clung to each other, like they'd never expected to survive this room.

He had a feeling they hadn't been meant to.

He turned to Julius. "Get a healer. And you," he said, pointing at one of the new guards. "Bring me whoever is in charge here."

Scan the QR code below to order

SARIA has been an avid reader since childhood and a fan fiction writer since middle school. They enjoy traveling and exploring and learning about other cultures and languages.

They are constantly dreaming up new ways to torment their characters and feeding a caffeine addiction.

Their favorite stories are M/M/+ relationships with a healthy dose of angst and drama with an HEA. When not reading or writing, they can usually be found watching anime or playing video games.

Saria can be found on Twitter / Instagram / Tumblr / Bluesky @sariabryant.

SHADOW'S
WOUND
ELEMENTAL THRONES
BOOK 1
SARIA BRYANT

Elemental Thrones: Book One

With the realm teetering on the brink of magical annihilation, Callith Ratearynn, the reluctant heir to the Sun Throne, is thrust into power centuries too soon. With his father dead and corruption tearing the kingdom apart at the seams, Cal must battle rising racial tensions and unravel a dark conspiracy. Justice, a manipulative human official, has stirred hatred between humans and the magical community, using enslavement collars and control over the Black Sun—an elite group of soldiers loyal to the Shadow Throne.

Just as civil war seems inevitable, Cal's Fate string—a magical bond tying him to his soulmate—leads him to a grim prison where he finds Haru, his bonded, broken and tortured. But Fate has more in store. Cal discovers he is bound not to one, but two: Rashi, a fox shifter, and Haru, a fierce dragon warrior. Together, this reluctant triad must face cult attacks, dark rituals, and the creeping Wound, a void threatening to consume their realm.

Cal's new reality is one of impossible choices—between duty and heart, loyalty and passion. As war looms, the only hope lies in Cal's ability to trust in his newfound soulmates and uncover the depths of the corruption before it's too late.

Scan the QR code below to order

◆ SARIA BRYANT ◆

MAGE'S MARINES

UNDERWORLD MAGES
BOOK 1

Underworld Mages: Book One

Max Savino has spent his whole life refusing to conform to the expectations of his father, the head of the Denver mafia—until his defiance crosses the line and his father decides he'd rather have a dead son than a disobedient one. Instead of waking up dead, Max wakes up with a power he only dreamed he could possess.

When his father sells him to a pack of shifters, Max finds himself in a world he doesn't understand, claimed by three wolves and fighting for control over his new magical flames. He'll have to learn to trust these dangerous men and the devotion they're promising him, because now that Max's father knows he's a mage, he wants him back—and he doesn't care who he has to kill to get what he wants. It's time for Max to stop running if he has any hope of protecting his future… and the pack that's somehow become the family he's always wanted.

Scan the QR code below to order

If You
LET ME
TOUCH OF LEATHER ·BOOK 1·
SARIA BRYANT

Touch of Leather: Book One

When Jasper is invited by his cousin to a kink club, he's all too eager for a chance to try something new, especially when Vincent, a gorgeous man in a suit, offers to bring his fantasy to life. After an amazing scene together and his first true taste of kink, Jasper is hooked. What starts as a one-night-a-week exploration quickly turns into a request for more and a contract between them.

Having given up on finding a sub for himself after his last disaster of a relationship, Vincent is surprised to find himself drawn to Jasper. More than the contradiction of shy young man and bratty personality, Jasper seems made specifically to submit to Vincent. Their chemistry is amazing, and Vincent is willing to try again. The only problem is Jasper's self-doubt and near-desperate need to please.

Scan the QR code below to order

FOR **MORE** OF THE **BEST** **GAY** ROMANCE

www.ingramcontent.com/pod-product-compliance
Lightning Source LLC
Chambersburg PA
CBHW070539100726
47907CB00004B/1186